CW00338361

TASTEFULLY TEXAS

TRUE HEARTS OF TEXAS
BOOK ONE

K.S. JONES

WOLFPACK
PUBLISHING
— EST 2013 —

Tastefully Texas
Paperback Edition
Copyright © 2023 K.S. Jones

Wolfpack Publishing
9850 S. Maryland Parkway, Suite A-5 #323
Las Vegas, Nevada 89183

wolfpackpublishing.com

This book is a work of fiction. Any references to historical events, real people or real places are used fictitiously. Other names, characters, places and events are products of the author's imagination, and any resemblance to actual events, places or persons, living or dead, is entirely coincidental.

All rights reserved. No part of this book may be reproduced by any means without the prior written consent of the publisher, other than brief quotes for reviews.

Paperback ISBN 978-1-63977-982-6
eBook ISBN 978-1-63977-981-9
LCCN 2022951621

Dedicated To

Richard Lee Jones

You've always been my reason for coming home.

ACKNOWLEDGMENTS

Special thanks to Mike Bray of Wolfpack Publishing for inspiring this story. And to Jenn Brown, my first reader-extraordinaire, who makes every story better. So many others deserve my sincere appreciation, too, including Michelle Ferrer for her ever-present encouragement and guidance; Kathy and Mike Gear for tolerating my ranching questions; Charlie Scott and Drew Scott for talking me through my chili and chili cook-off crises; Jan Moffitt for teaching me about catering from home so long ago; Carmen Peone for her western woman expertise; Sheri Groom for her gift of the proper Texas vernacular, and also for being the quintessential Texas woman she is; Adam Jones for every helping hand along the way; Mia Harrison for inspiring one of my favorite lines in this book, and to all of my Facebook friends and family who are always willing to join in the fun and answer every question when asked. Each one of you has added flair and flavor to this story.

TASTEFULLY TEXAS

CHAPTER 1

When her cell phone jingled in the breast pocket of her paisley cotton blouse, worn unbuttoned over a Texas Lone Star T-shirt, Mia Ellis set down her luggage, withdrawing the device. She glanced at the caller ID, and with an annoyed mutter, she answered.

"Mom, I don't have time for this. I'm on my way to the airport, and the Uber is waiting."

"Is this Mia Ellis?" The man asking didn't even hesitate at her aggravated tone.

Mia stopped, her mind whirling. "Um, yes. Who is this on my mother's phone?"

"This is Dr. Davis from the Mason-Kimble Medical Center. Your mother's been in an accident, and your name is on her phone, listing you as her daughter."

"What kind of accident? Is she okay? Do I need to come?" The words rattled off her tongue. "Is she..."

"She's stable but heavily medicated right now. She was in a car accident and has a badly broken leg, a patella subluxation, and a slight concussion. She'll need surgery."

"I'm in Houston." Mia wasn't sure why it mattered to say that, but it was the only thing that came out.

"Is there someone else we should call? Maybe someone closer?"

"No. We're the only family we've got. It'll take me about four and a half hours. Please tell her I'm on my way."

Funny that her bags were already packed, her townhouse sublet, cash, bank cards, and rental receipts were in her purse, and her life was in order and perfectly poised for a six-month stay in a chef apprentice program in New York. Now all she needed to do was put every dream she ever had on hold —again.

For how long, she wouldn't know until she got back to her childhood home north of the Pedernales River, which was 298 miles from nowhere, in her opinion.

It was her mother's *gift*. Like second sight. Extrasensory perception. Not that Josie Ellis had clairvoyant abilities—she simply knew the exact moment her daughter was on the verge of escaping her stale, small-town past, and then, one way or another, her getaway was thwarted.

Mia scribbled a note to Vicki, her new tenant:

Not going to NY yet. Took Prius. Will call you later.

Her Sea Glass Pearl Prius was four years old, and its odometer was nearing 70,000 miles. She'd bought it her first year in Houston while working in the cafeteria at the Houston Medical Center. The hospital hadn't exactly been the culinary start she'd wanted, but the job had helped her buy the car and rent an apartment while she earned her culinary arts degree.

The midweek afternoon traffic on I-10 West was the best possible scenario to get out of Houston, so Mia headed for the freeway. The Austin route was shorter and usually quicker, but major road construction on TX-71 meant I-10 through San Antonio would be faster.

It'd been almost five years since Mia had been home. She'd left intending never to return. It wasn't that she hated her hometown of Legacy. There was just nothing left there to inspire her anymore. Most of her high school friends had gone off to college years ago when she did, but then they'd all gotten married, had babies or careers, or both, and according to their social media pages, they were happily living their best lives elsewhere. Her mother was the only tie she had to the town now, and that was a weak link.

The Texas Hill Country—where the American Southwest met the Southeast—was where everyone who didn't live there wanted to be. Everyone except Mia, that is. Its 1,142 miles of pristine streams and twelve major rivers ran from the land like she was trying to do, but a fish on a hook is always reeled back. She had to cut the line or drown. A chef had no hope of a real future in a rural cattle-call town. New York was her chance.

But this was her mother. And this time, it didn't sound like a ploy. She would never be able to live with herself if she left Texas, not knowing her only parent's fate.

The freeway ran far south of Legacy, but the town wasn't where the hospital was located. It was still another thirty miles west. She never even glanced at the freeway exit as she passed.

When Mia pulled into the parking lot of the two-story limestone block hospital, the sun was low on the horizon, marking the skyline in shades of barely blue, white, and variegated gray. Even the sunset was uninspired by the place.

At the admissions and registration desk in the lobby, Mia said, "My mother, Josie Ellis, is here. I'd like to see her, please?"

"Hold on, honey." The woman with blonde bouffant hair was almost hidden behind the large computer screen.

At the delay, Mia offered more. "I don't even know if she's been admitted yet. I've been driving for over four hours to get here."

The receptionist stood. "Yes, I see that she was admitted several hours ago." She leaned across the reception module, pointing toward an overly wide hall marked Medical-Surgical Unit. "She's in room 132, but stop and talk to the nurses before you go in."

"Thanks." Mia started down the hall toward the nurses' station. "Hello," she said to the first nurse she came to at the desk. "My mother, Josie Ellis, is in room 132. Is it okay if I go in and see her?"

After a glance at her computer, the nurse said, "The orthopedic surgeon is with her now." She came from behind the cold, counter-long desk. "I'll take you in."

When they entered, the doctor turned. Even though the barely-mint-colored drapes were wide open, the room only offered muted sunlight. One dimly lit light above the bed made it hard to identify the face belonging to the person beneath it. Mia approached.

At the sight of her mother, bruised but somewhat alert, she gently said, "Hi, Mom."

"Mia, you're supposed to be in New York." Her

voice had a sedated gravel. "They said you were coming, but I didn't think you would." Then she squinted, hardening her focus. "Your hair is different colors. Why did you do that?"

Mia gave her a slight smile. "Of course, I would come. And these are highlights. It's not really different colors. You always hated my plain brown hair, remember?" Then she glanced at the doctor. "I'm her daughter. How is she?"

The gray-haired doctor wore a white lab coat over a lavender dress shirt with a security pass clipped to his starched lapel.

"I'm Dr. Perry." He reached across the bed for a handshake. "Dr. Davis, the ER doctor, referred your mother to me for surgery."

"What kind of surgery?"

Her mother took hold of Mia's hand when it was withdrawn from the doctor. "He says my legs are broken and…" Her tone trailed off into a painkiller-sluggish mumble.

"And she'll need surgery," the surgeon finished. "I've scheduled an open reduction and internal fixation at eleven o'clock tomorrow on her left leg." When a confused squint came from Mia, he explained. "It's a surgical procedure to realign and set bone—in her case, the tibia—but the fibula will have to be rebuilt."

"Rebuilt? What does that mean?" Mia asked.

"A section of bone basically disintegrated on impact in the car accident. I'll use a rod and bone putty to rebuild it for her."

"Why hasn't that been done already?"

"Two reasons," he answered, his tone methodical. "First, her fractures extend into the talocrural joint, complicating things. I've asked Dr. Nickles to assist—

he's the foot and ankle specialist, but he isn't available until tomorrow. And two, Dr. Davis and I agree that we'd like to see her a bit more stabilized."

Mia took hold of the bed railing and squeezed. "So, how long will all of this take?"

"The surgery will be several hours." Then he glanced at his patient. "An anesthesiologist will give you general anesthesia. That will put you into a deep sleep during the surgery so that you won't feel a thing. Does that sound okay to you, Mrs. Ellis?"

Drowsy-eyed, Josie swung him a look. "Miss," she said in dazed protest. "Never married. It might be the only thing my daughter and me have in common. Just ask her."

Mia shrugged when the doctor shifted his reluctant attention to her. "She might be right."

WITH THE HOUSE KEY FROM HER MOTHER'S PURSE, Mia drove the thirty miles back to the shabby little gray house with a yellow front door that was on the wrong side of the tracks. Not that the small town had train tracks, it was just the way her mother had always described their home. Mia took it as meaning they lived in the undesirable part of town, and she couldn't argue about that.

It was almost nine o'clock and dark when Mia pulled into the driveway. They'd never had a garage, so she shut off the engine where she stopped and got out of the car, retrieving her luggage from the trunk before slamming it shut. Dogs throughout the neighborhood barked, and country music blared from an unidentified house somewhere down the road.

She should be in New York right now. Not here at this house. Not here in this town.

Mia used the key and opened the front door—the smell of rotting fruit, dirty dishes, and garbage assailed her nose. She flipped on the overhead light and dropped her bags.

How had she ever lived here?

She walked through the house, turning on lights in flashes of memories.

The same gray leather couch and loveseat her mother had bought in the late 90s still sat precisely where they'd always been, piled with pillows and throw blankets. A recliner, covered by a bedsheet, was in the corner. The flat-screen TV was new. Newer, anyway. It hadn't been there when she'd left home.

In the kitchen, dirty dishes, stacked high in the sink, overflowed onto the brown Formica countertop, and the god-awful brown and tan fleur-de-lis vinyl flooring was still there. Her loafers detected a sticky film of grime.

She could go to a motel. At least there, she'd have clean sheets. The thought turned her toward her childhood bedroom.

The 1,220-square-foot home, built in 1967, had three bedrooms and one bath. Instead of a garage, the original owner had opted for the third bedroom, which her mother had always used as a sewing and crafts room. Mia's room was on the opposite side of the house.

She crossed the living room to the closed door and opened it. Stale, long-imprisoned air tainted the room. Not at all what her bedroom used to smell like with her beloved sweet orange and thyme-scented candles.

Mia flipped the light switch, but the darkened room stayed dark. No matter how many times her irritation flipped the switch, it wouldn't turn on the burnt-out bulb. She pulled her cell phone from her pocket and tapped the flashlight app, using it to make her way across the room to her old baseball-in-a-glove accent lamp.

Clicking on its forty-watt bulb brought an unintended laugh. "I was such a tomboy."

The dimly lit room hadn't been disturbed since she left it more than five years ago. Dust covered the secondhand pinewood desk, lampshade, candle top, and purple notebook. The wood-framed photo of her on horseback had fallen over, so she reset it, blowing off its dust.

Mia pulled the lid off the old orange candle on her desk and sniffed, and then she took the Bic lighter from the drawer and lit the wick. The memories it had saved were good ones.

Her antique iron bed, three generations old, was still as sturdy as it had always been, but the burgundy and white comforter had grown a fusty smell.

"Okay, first things first," she said aloud to the room that knew her so well.

Her mother's bedroom was the last place she wanted to be tonight, but that's where the linen closet and bathroom were located in the house. She had no choice but to open that door.

Clothes, piled high in the only sitting chair in the room, spilled over onto the floor. They looked and smelled clean, just unfolded and wrinkled. The bed was sloppy but made.

Stuffed inside the linen closet, Mia found towels, sheets, pillowcases, and lots of colorful blankets, but what caught her eye was a white and light gray quilt crafted with dark gray hearts. Her mother excelled at sewing and quilting, and other than her job at Gloria's Crafts, it was how she made her living.

Mia moved her luggage into her bedroom and then remade the bed with clean linens and the heart quilt before returning to the kitchen.

She opened the refrigerator, scanning the shelves for some semblance of a dinner, but her focus veered to the sink and its stink. She closed the refrigerator door, pulled off her pink paisley overshirt, and tackled the dishes. What she couldn't fit in the dishwasher, she washed by hand, using the drainboard to let them air-dry. She emptied the garbage, scoured the can, dried it, and then put in a new liner.

When the stickiness on the floor became intolerable, Mia grabbed a box of baking soda off the open pantry shelf and sprinkled it over the floor, then filled the mop bucket with water, white vinegar, and a spoonful of detergent. She scrubbed until her disgust faded, and then she rinsed.

It was nearly three in the morning before she fell into bed, clean and almost content after a long hot shower.

The blackout drapes staved off daylight so well that Mia slept straight through her early morning alarm, only waking when a knock followed the chiming doorbell. Groggy, she reached for her phone, checking the time.

"Nine o'clock!" Mia threw back the sheet and quilt and bounded out of bed. Her mother's surgery was scheduled for eleven, and it was a half-hour drive to the hospital. If she left now, she would barely make it in time to see her mother before they wheeled her back for surgery prep.

Again, there was a knock—louder this time.

Mia hurried to the front door and opened it a crack, the bright morning sunlight squinting her tired eyes. "Yes? What is it?" she asked.

There was a hesitation, then, "Mia?"

That voice. The one that had haunted her dreams for half a decade. Mia opened the door an inch wider, letting her vision focus on the man wearing dark Lucchese boots and a Silverbelly Stetson.

"Jace." His name came out in a whisper. "What are you doing here?" She'd done such a good job trying to forget Jace Farr that she'd forgotten how gorgeous he was.

"I heard Josie was in an accident yesterday. I came by to see if she was home from the hospital yet." He glanced back at the driveway. "I saw the car, but I didn't know it was yours."

"Yeah." Mia opened the door all the way. "Come in."

"Thanks," Jace said, removing his hat, barely mussing his chestnut-colored hair, as he stepped inside the house.

Mia tried to look away, but the man knew how to wear a pair of jeans, and she loved the look of a cowboy in a long-sleeved dress shirt.

"Nice Stetson," she said.

"I still have yours, you know?"

She was wide awake now. "You kept my Stetson?"

"Of course, I kept it." His tone never wavered. "You threw it at me, remember?"

Mia's glare landed squarely on his beautiful, earthy-brown eyes. "If you'll recall, that's because I didn't have a ring to throw."

CHAPTER 2

J ace held his Stetson close to his chest, his fingers stationed in its Cattleman's crease. They'd been teenagers in love once. That's what he needed to remember, not how it had ended.

"How's Josie?"

He tried to stop himself from staring, but Mia had never looked more stunning. Her milk chocolate brown hair, shoulder-length and silky, had honey-brown and blonde highlights, and all she was wearing was a navy two-piece shorts pajama set, which intensified the blue of her eyes and showed off the tan on her long, slender legs. She was barefoot and beautiful.

Mia ran her fingers through her hair, combing stray strands off her forehead and face the way she always had when she was stressed. "She's okay, I guess." Then those blue-gray eyes of hers found the deep brown of his. She took a breath. "She has a badly broken leg, a concussion, and something else. I can't even remember what," she said. "They're doing surgery this morning, so I need to get to the hospital. I'm running really late. How did you know about the accident?"

"Ramirez owns the tow truck company now. He bought it from Bart Haskins two years ago. He called this morning, but all he could tell me was that her car was totaled, and she'd been transported by ambulance to Mason-Kimball."

"Wow, I haven't thought about Ramirez since high school. Did he ever marry Silvia?"

Jace nodded, memories stirring a smile. "Yeah. They've got three kids now."

After a moment, Mia silently walked to the door and opened it. "It was nice of you to check on Mom, Jace. I'll tell her you came by."

He turned, but he didn't make a move toward the door. "Listen, Mia, since you're here and all..."

Mia held up a hand, stopping him. "Jace, don't. I'm on my way to New York. I only came back because of the accident."

"Right," he said, nodding. He made his way outside, stopping on the front stoop to fit his hat on his head. He turned with another glance as she stood in the open doorway. "What's in New York?"

"A job. An apprenticeship, actually, but it pays."

Jace looked down at the ground and its dry summer lawn before raising his eyes to her again. "Well, it's really good to see you."

After a nod, Mia closed the door.

Jace walked to his truck, but he hesitated before he stepped up into it and closed the door, finally starting the engine, but he couldn't bring himself to put the truck into gear and back out of the driveway. He stared at the bright yellow front door until its paint should have peeled. Thirty seconds. A minute. Two.

Maybe five. He waited, wanting her to come back outside and stop him from leaving, but Mia was stubborn, and if she'd missed him in the last five years, he couldn't tell, and she would certainly never admit it to him. She'd always been a willful woman with her own mind, and he had never been able to read her thoughts.

He jammed the truck into reverse and backed out onto the street, glancing in his rearview mirror just once.

At the feed and seed store, Jace walked to the check-out counter. "Mornin', Clint. Is your dad around?"

The clerk sat on a high stool, flipping through *Off Road Magazine* while the store's aging long-haired cat sprawled beside him. Without bothering to look up, the man gave a swipe to his uncombed blond hair and then pointed. "He's out back."

Clint was just one more high school graduate who had never left Legacy.

"Grandma sent me in for seed for the backyard birds, and she says he's the only one who knows the mix she wants. Can you go get him for me?"

He glanced up. "Oh, hey, Jace. Sorry man, I didn't realize it was you." He stood and started around the counter but stopped—his attention landing squarely on Jace. "Did you hear Mia's back in town?"

Jace straightened. "How did you know about that? I just found out twenty minutes ago."

"Tessa rents the house across the street from Josie. She was out walking that rotten little Chihuahua of hers last night and saw Mia taking out the trash." He snickered. "I doubted it until just now, but that look on your face says it all."

Annoyed at the small-town gossip, Jace snapped, "Just find your dad for me, will ya?"

"Sure thing," Clint said, making his way down an aisle, straightening cans of insect spray on his way to the double doors leading out into the yard.

It was no secret that Jace had loved Mia more than life itself or that Mia had loved him. Or that Longhorn High School and the yearbook staff had voted them *The Couple Most Likely to Get Married*. Everyone knew it—the curse of a small town. But none of that mattered anymore, and he wished everyone would just forget about the two of them, even though he had never been able to forget Mia. And now that he'd seen her again, looking like she looked, he would have a hard time slowing down the pounding of his heart.

"Mornin' Jace," Craig Cobb called out, taking long strides across the store's tan concrete floor. "Hannah needing more wild bird seed?"

Jace turned. "Yes, sir." Once upon a time, the Feed and Seed store owner had worked for his grandmother. Craig had been much younger and inexperienced back then, but she had taken a chance and taught him how to ride and be a ranch hand. There had never been a "weaker sex" at the Farr Reaches, and Hannah Farr had proven it every day. She outrode, out-roped, and outworked nearly every man on the ranch in her prime.

Jace reached for a handshake. "Grandma is getting a bit testy with me about always buying the wrong birdseed. She says that you know what she wants. If you just tell me your secret to making her happy, I'll be glad to do it myself for her."

"It's easy, Jace. Come on. I'll show you. She just wants a handpicked mix."

Jace followed the feed store owner back to the seed section.

At the mix and match bins, Craig Cobb pulled an empty twenty-pound sack from its box and counted out the measurements as he dumped full scoops into the bag.

"She wants three scoops of black oil sunflower seed, three scoops of safflower seed," he reached into the bag with his hand and stirred, "and then you got to mix it up. Then you add two scoops of Nyjer and mix again, then two scoops of white millet. Mix it up after every scoop. She likes the peanut bits, too, so I always add a scoop of those." He looked at Jace, who stood with his hands on his hips. "You need to write this down?"

Jace shook his head. "Why couldn't she just tell me that?"

Craig gave an understanding smile. "I think she just forgets. I don't mind." He sealed the bag and handed it to Jace. "She wants to draw the cardinals, doves, wrens, and buntings. I know it's a pain in the butt to mix it yourself, but Hannah likes what she likes, and if the right birds don't come to her feeders, she knows it's the wrong seed. She's always loved those birds." He looked at Jace. "How is she anyway? I haven't seen her in a couple of weeks."

"She's doing okay for an eighty-two-year-old with a failing memory." Jace smiled, but then he turned serious. "I'm having a heck of a time getting her to eat anything, though."

"Yeah." Craig nodded. "That's what I heard." Then, he said, "I asked Dr. Evans about her a few days ago when I had Mary in to see him. We talked about all those years when Mary used to go out and cook and clean for Hannah, but Mary just isn't able to do that kind of thing anymore. Her hands shake so bad she can't even drive now." He put his hand on Jace's shoulder. "I'm sure sorry about Hannah's memory getting worse. You know we'd help if we could."

"Yeah, sure, of course I do." Jace reached for a handshake. "You tell Mary we said hello, will you?"

Craig gave an affectionate slap on Jace's back. "You headed out to the Farr Reaches now, or do you got other stops in town?"

"I'm headed back. Grandma was still asleep when I left this morning," Jace told him.

"Well, hold on then."

Jace followed him to the cashier counter, where Craig opened a box of Shonda's Donuts.

"I bought these for the boys working the lot. We had a full shipment of probiotic powder come in this morning. They're unloading and stacking, and it's a hot day already." Craig grabbed a brown paper lunch bag and inserted a pastry into it. He handed it to Jace. "Maybe Hannah will eat an apple fritter this morning."

He took the bag. "You're a good man. I'll tell Grandma it's from you. Maybe she'll eat it." He closed the bag by folding down the top. "Thanks for your help with the seed. I'll do it myself next time. I appreciate you showing me what she wanted."

"It's always good to see you, Jace. You come back soon."

At his truck—a deep dark blue F-350 bearing the gold Circle FR brand—Jace stopped, back door ajar when he heard his name called. He turned toward the feminine voice.

"Yoo-hoo! Jace!" A woman with unmistakable carrot-red hair came hurrying across the street toward him, waving her hand high in the air.

Jace set the sack of birdseed on the back seat floorboard before closing the door.

"Mrs. Hale," he said to her. "Good morning."

She reached for his hand and squeezed. "Jace, you'll never believe it, but I just heard Mia is back in town!"

His gaze dropped to the ground. "That's what I heard."

"Are you going to see her?" Without missing a beat, she said, "She has to stay in that awful house, you know? That mother of hers was in some sort of accident on her way to Junction yesterday." Mrs. Hale straightened, pulling her neck back and then jutting her chin forward like a strutting Banty rooster. In a pretend whisper, she said, "Probably going over there to buy those trashy books she reads all the time."

Jace turned away, opening his driver's side door. "You still teaching freshman algebra, Mrs. Hale?" he asked.

"Yes, of course," she told him.

He tossed her a look. "You know, that's something I've never found any use for—adding letters to math problems. It just doesn't make any sense. It's kind of like adding manure to cattle feed and expecting the herd to thank me for it." Jace stepped up into his truck and shut the door. From his open window, he said, "But then, I guess everybody's got a little manure in 'em. Some just got more than others. You have a good summer now."

Sixteen miles northwest of Legacy, a galvanized pipe stood cemented into the dry ground near a blooming prickly pear cactus at the turnoff to the Farr Reaches Ranch. At the top, the pipe squared into a frame for a certificate entrapped in Lucite, naming the

property a Texas Century Ranch in honor of its contin-
uous operation for more than one hundred years by the
same family.

Its 5,439 acres of diverse soil, vegetation, and
topography started west of the homestead at the Kimble
County line and spread eastward across the James
River and a dozen other spring-fed creeks, over high
limestone cliffs, and down rolling hills that dug low into
the grassy plains on the eastern half where his herd of
Charolais cattle grazed. His Brangus herd was still
small and grazed in a separate pasture to the north.

Through the years, selective clearing had removed
most of the Ashe juniper off the east side, but an abun-
dance of live oak, post oak, cedar elm, and some shin
oak still stood. Native grasses grew well there, even
during times of drought.

Still, it was a hard region for cattle ranchers. Thin
soil littered with rocks and underlain with limestone or
granite made grazing a challenge. Many of the local
heritage ranches had been sold off in the decades before
because the families couldn't earn enough from the land
to sustain themselves and their operations.

Jace faced the same problem, unbeknownst to
anyone, including his grandmother.

He was a fifth-generation owner, and he, and his
father before him, had already sold off most of the
acreage from the original forty thousand just to stay
afloat. After the last sale, they'd vowed to each other
that they'd never sell the last five thousand acres.
They even shook on the deal, but Jace hadn't worried
about that promise. He'd expected Jacob Farr to live
a good long life like his grandfather and great-grandfather had done, but an accident had ended him,
leaving the ranch in the hands of Jace, his sister,

Cecelia, who lived in Colorado, and Hannah Farr, his grandmother.

The ranch was his responsibility now. Although his grandmother's advice had carried him the first few years, her mild cognitive impairment had stolen parts of her memory and much of her decision-making abilities, and the guidance of his ranch foreman, Travis Hill, was focused where it needed to be which was on the animals and their care not on the finances.

The main house, built of wood, painted white, with white and cream-colored limestone blocks, stood nestled among the live oak trees near the banks of a spring-fed creek. The flow hadn't stopped in 121 years —the entire time the Farr family owned the land.

In the distance, between the James and Llano Rivers, stood the Blue Mountains.

Jace parked in the driveway near the garages and got out. When his Australian shepherd came bounding around the corner of the house, he braced himself against the truck and prepared for an overzealous greeting.

"Hey, Cowboy," he said moments before the red Aussie bounced against his legs, ending up in spins with barks of joy. When the dog calmed, Jace knelt and ruffled his wavy mane. "Did you watch over Grandma for me?" The dog's ears perked. "You know I would have taken you with me if I could, but I needed you here with Grandma. You're the only one I trust."

He gave the dog another ruffle, then he stood and took the birdseed out of the backseat and carried the sack around to the back of the house. He set it down on the limestone block patio near where the bird feeders hung, and then he went inside through the back door.

"Grandma, it's me, Jace," he called out. With the

Aussie on his heels, he headed through the house with the brown paper bag from Craig.

On the main bedroom door, Jace knocked. "Grandma, can I come in?"

When no answer came, he opened the door. The polished cedarwood bed was perfectly made with pillows lined at artistic angles, allowing the morning light to fall on its earthy shades as if autumn had arrived each morning, no matter the season. The room was in order, neat and clean, and the scent of jasmine hung lightly in the air.

Jace closed the door and headed back through the 3,700-square-foot home, checking rooms and areas along the way for his grandmother.

In the kitchen, he found Hannah Farr, standing with her back to him at the brown granite countertop near the sink, scrubbing five cinch-waist hummingbird feeders, then setting each one aside on a tea towel to dry.

"Grandma, I've been looking for you."

She turned, her gaze falling on him with a smile. "I've been right here, Jace. Have you been calling me?" Hannah turned back to her last feeder, rinsing it before setting it aside with the others. "I think my hearing is getting worse. I can barely hear the chatter of the hummingbirds anymore."

The thin, gray-haired eighty-two-year-old stood just five feet, three inches tall, but even at her age, she was an attractive, well-put-together woman. She wore Wrangler jeans, a tan leather belt with a robin's egg-blue crackled turquoise stone, and her button-down long-sleeve shirt was a teal and tan floral print. She had an air about her that said the world around her was in control.

Jace leaned and kissed her cheek, then set the brown paper bag on the counter beside her.

"I got the birdseed. I had Craig show me exactly what you wanted so I wouldn't mess it up again." When she laughed, he got serious. "Craig sent you an apple fritter. He wants you to eat it, Grandma. We're all worried about you not eating."

Hannah glared at him. "Jace, are you out telling people my business?"

"It's not your *business*, Grandma. It's your health, and I worry about you."

She turned away, grabbing a pitcher full of home-made nectar. "I'm as healthy now as I ever was." She poured a feeder full of sugar water, screwed on the base, and then handed it to Jace. "Hang that outside on the far hook for me, will you?" She started filling another.

"I will if you'll eat the fritter."

She set the pitcher down and turned around again, facing him full-on. "Listen to me." Her angry tone was always hard. "Your job is to run this ranch. Not coddle me. You got a herd out in the north pasture that those hands are neglecting. I watch the direction they ride every morning, and I know how long it's been. I've been paying attention. Now, stop worrying about me and start worrying about them. You're a rancher, not a babysitter."

Jace nodded. Just when he thought she was slipping farther away, she'd bounce back with a verbal backhand. But she was right. She was always right.

"Okay, Grandma." He carried the feeder to the back porch, then hung it, watching the waiting hummingbirds descend.

CHAPTER 3

The surgery waiting room would never pass the HGTV test, being utterly devoid of any décor other than drab seating and wall art. It was painted in quiet tan tones accentuated by alternating gray and cream-colored chairs, but that didn't matter because Mia wasn't interested in sitting. She was mad at herself for arriving late and missing her mother.

She took a few deep, cleansing breaths and tried to focus on other things.

Hospitals prized noncommittal colors meant to calm the emotions and lessen the fears of those left waiting, usually hanging French-inspired or abstract art against those ambivalent colors so as not to offend any sector, but in the heart of Texas, it was the Old West that ruled the walls.

Mia stood, staring blankly at an oversized painting of a far West Texas prairie with a lone cowboy driving a half dozen longhorn strays across a creek. His posture in the saddle, his worn cowboy hat and dusty boots, and his hard focus on the herd said he belonged there on that land. He *was* that land. She knew the look because Jace had it, too.

But it wasn't the same for her. Not anymore. Leaving Texas was a hope and a dream that every Texan who wasn't deeply rooted considered—if there were such people in the Lone Star State—but for the past five years, it felt like Mia was the only one trying to cross the border *out* of Texas. No matter how desperate she was to uproot herself, she just couldn't pull free.

Granted, her move to New York was only delayed by a day, but she still resented having to cancel her flight, putting her future on hold. Texas had almost moved into her rearview mirror, and she was antsy about finding out when her next chance might be.

"Miss Ellis?"

"Yes." Mia turned. The nurse hadn't even entered the room—she just stood in the opened doorway.

"Dr. Perry asked me to let you know the surgery went well. He'll be in to talk to you in about ten minutes."

"Thank you," Mia said.

Surgery went well. Mia took that as a green light. When the nurse disappeared down the hall, she pulled her cell phone out of her leather bag and called the airlines.

"Hi, I need to rebook a flight from Houston to New York."

Her new flight wasn't ideal, but staying another few days was tolerable. She'd need a day to drive her Prius back to Houston and leave it with her new tenant, Vicki, for safekeeping in the garage, as agreed, and she wanted to be sure her mother had a ride home from the hospital.

A feeling of having control over her life again was returning.

"Miss Ellis, good afternoon," Dr. Perry said, entering the waiting room.

Anxious to hear the news, Mia said, "So the nurse said things went well?"

"Very well, yes. Your mother will need a lot of physical therapy after she's released, which should be another day or two." He handed Mia a business card. "Riverstone Rehabilitation will coordinate the sessions directly with you. I work with them all the time, so they already have my instructions."

Mia held the card, noticing the San Antonio address. "How will she get to her rehab appointments if they're over an hour away? Mom lives in Legacy."

Dr. Perry nodded. "Riverstone has rehab therapists in several locations. The therapist they have in Legacy is one of their best. You're lucky."

"Oh, good. So, they'll just come to her house?"

"Yes, three times a week for the first four weeks. But that's all her insurance will allow. After that, she'll need another eight weeks of in-facility rehab at their Legacy office."

Mia's brows scrunched together. "How will she get there? Will she be able to drive by then?"

"No," Dr. Perry said. "She'll need help. A transport, or someone to drive her. Someone to get her into and out of the vehicle from her wheelchair."

"Wheelchair?" Mia stepped back, a wave of nausea hitting her. "How long?" She hadn't thought further than the surgery. She assumed her mother would be on crutches. Difficult but doable.

"Rehab is six to eight months, but her full recovery will be about twelve months. Her left leg is certainly our long-term concern, but the patella subluxation in her right knee will hinder her mobility for the first few weeks. She'll need rehab on both of her legs. The success of today's surgery depends highly on her commitment to a physiotherapy program."

"No." Mia backed away until a chair met the back of her knees. She sat, focused on the doctor. "I'm going to New York. I delayed my move to come here after her accident. My flight is rebooked for Monday evening."

"Miss Ellis." Dr. Perry spoke in a decidedly colder tone. "Your mother will need help around the clock for at least the first few months. She will be almost completely non-weight-bearing for the first few weeks." The gray-haired doctor glanced at the door behind him. "I'll send in social services to discuss your options. Are there any other questions?"

Her response was some semblance of a thank you, mostly spoken as the doctor retreated from the room.

After the cost of her plane ticket and the deposit paid to hold her new sight unseen 350-square-foot furnished studio apartment on the Upper West Side, Mia barely had enough money to support herself until her first paycheck. That was supposed to come on the first of next month. There was no way she could afford to hire around-the-clock help for her mother, so unless Josie Ellis had recently won the lottery or found a rich relative, her bank account had never had more than fifty dollars after paying her monthly living expenses. That's how it had always been, and Mia had no reason to believe it had changed.

At her mother's bedside, Mia said, "Hi, Mom." When the sound of her voice failed to rouse her mother from a sedated state, she brushed her short blonde hair away from her eyelashes, studying the face. "Mom?"

She took hold of the hand that had aged since its last holding. Softly, she spoke again, "Mom, can you hear me?"

Josie opened her eyes, squinting to focus. "Mia?"

"I'm here, Mom."

"I thought you were in New York."

"No, remember, I saw you after your accident yesterday?"

"Accident..." she mumbled. "I had an accident?"

Mia scooted closer. "You were in a car accident, Mom. Don't you remember?"

Josie fully opened her eyes and focused on Mia. "Oh, yes. A little red car flew through the intersection. It crashed right into me."

"That's right. They said the driver ran a red light."

Josie glanced down the bed, her gaze scanning the length of her elevated and cast left leg. "How long will I have to be on crutches?"

"No crutches. You'll be in a wheelchair for a while," Mia told her. "You can't put weight on your left leg, and the doctor says your right kneecap was sort of dislocated in the accident. He called it a patella subluxation. You can't put any weight on that leg either for a few days. After that, you'll only have minimal use of it while you start rehab. You probably won't be able to use crutches for at least a week."

"How am I supposed to work if I can't walk?"

Mia shook her head. "I have no idea."

Visiting hours still had another three hours to go, but when her mother fell back to sleep, Mia gave her forehead a good-night kiss and then drove the thirty miles back to Legacy.

Regret, anger, and a lot of self-doubt about deciding to come home whirled through her mind. Her chance to be a professional chef was slipping right through her fingers, just like every other important thing in her life had always done.

Tomorrow she would call the culinary program. Whether they would hold her spot open for a few more weeks until she could get there was a question she had never thought to ask.

THE ARMADILLO DINER ON THE OUTSKIRTS OF TOWN had so many cars and trucks in its parking lot that Mia almost hadn't noticed its newly paved surface—a vast improvement over its previous hard caliche lot. But the diner itself hadn't changed much at all. It was still the same 1980s feedlot farm building, renovated twenty years ago into a Tex-Mex restaurant, except now it was painted barn red instead of white. The hip-high vertical branch railing that lined the walkway entrance still looked as rickety as it always had, like it might collapse at any minute.

Mia parked and walked across the lot, never looking up. At the door, recall sent her hand to where the handle had always been, but a grab at empty air pulled her focus up from the walk.

"Jace." She hadn't expected him. "What are you doing here?"

"I live here, remember?" Jace smiled at her, holding the door open with one hand while drawing his Stetson to his chest with the other. "Can I buy you dinner?"

"Yes." The acceptance had slipped out. She hadn't intended to see Jace again, but Legacy was a small town. Spending more than twenty-four hours here meant you would likely run into just about everyone at least once. "Thank you," she said.

Tejano art blazed across the corrugated tin sidewall inside the diner with a painted scene of four vaqueros working a Texas ranch circa 1830.

Jace led Mia to a corner table in the back. *Their table.* The chrome-plated steel dinette with four chairs still had Mia's name scratched into the top. A nameplate of sorts. Jace's teenage way of permanently saving her place at the table.

Mia sat after Jace pulled a chair out for her, then he set his cowboy hat on an empty seat and took the chair beside her for himself. Just the way he had always done.

"Menu?" He handed her the double-sided, laminated menu. "Not much has changed."

"That's the problem," Mia said, accepting it from him. "Nothing around here ever changes." She glanced at the meal selections.

"Change isn't always good, you know?"

Mia set down the menu. "Why, Jace? Why isn't change good?" Her tone was angry, but she had no regrets about it. "You're acting like nothing is different between us." She leaned closer, laser-focused on him. "But *everything* has changed. *I've* changed. My whole life has changed in the five years we've been apart. It's still changing, and I have no idea how to stop the slide."

With her heart revving, she picked up her menu again, scanning the selections without acknowledging the look Jace had on his face. Neither of them noticed the waitress approaching.

"Well, if it ain't Mia Ellis!" The blonde server stopped with her hands planted on her hips before giving Jace a playful slap on the shoulder. "You dog! How'd you get her to come home?"

A flush heated Mia's cheeks. "Hi, Cindy. You're still working here?"

The waitress laughed, jabbing a thumb back over her shoulder to the kitchen. "Didn't you hear? Me and Trace got married the year after high school. Probably a month after you left. He's been managing this place ever since, and he's not about to let his best server work someplace else. Are you back to stay?"

"No." Mia shook her head. "God, no. I'm on my way to New York." To justify her reason, she said, "I'm a chef now."

Cindy nodded, her gaze toggling between Mia and Jace. "I heard, but I thought you were doing that in Houston."

"I was..." Mia sat straighter. "But now I'm on my way to New York to be an apprentice to some of the best chefs in the nation." She glanced at Jace, then back to the waitress. "As soon as Mom is back on her feet again."

"Oh, that's right," Cindy said. "A car accident, huh? How's she doing?"

"Okay. I think she'll be okay."

"Good. Real glad to hear it." Cindy picked up the menu unused by Jace, then asked Mia, "What do you want tonight, darlin'?"

Mia took a last look at the selections. "I'll have the jalapeño chicken enchilada platter with a glass of sweet tea, please?"

"Sure thing." Cindy scribbled on her order pad. "What can I get for you, Jace?"

"I'll have a double burger, fries, and a Coke. And

ask Bobby to add a couple of pieces of bacon to that burger for me, will you?"

"You know I will."

"I swear, Jace," Mia said. "If you had a headache, you'd wrap bacon around the aspirin."

He laughed. "I like bacon."

"Yes, I remember." Mia sat back, arms crossed, trying to hide the smile Jace had always been able to coax from her. He had a way of touching her that no other man had ever been able to do. "Unfortunately, I remember everything."

CHAPTER 4

The woman who had broken his heart sat beside him, eating enchiladas as if the nightly news had just proclaimed them a cure for every ailment. Yet here he was, so nervous about being near her again that he couldn't eat, pushing French fries around on his plate, trying to decide how to tell her he still loved her.

"So, how's Josie after surgery?"

Mia glanced up from her food. She wiped the corners of her mouth on a napkin. "Surgery went well." Her gaze stayed glued to him. "But I may have to stay for a while."

"Why? Does she need more surgeries?"

"No." Mia shook her head. "But Mom won't be able to walk for a couple of weeks. And she can't drive. I can't afford to hire round-the-clock care for her."

When a glisten formed in her eyes, Jace reached for her hand. He held it gently. "I'm not going to say I'm unhappy about you having to stay for a while, but I hate that it's because of Josie. I know being a cook is a big deal to you."

Mia leaned back in her chair, withdrawing her hand from his. "I'm not a *cook*, Jace. I'm a chef."

"What's the difference?" He was annoyed she'd pulled her hand away over something so insignificant.

"There's a big difference. Anyone can cook, but not everyone can be a chef."

"No, *everyone* can't cook. I can't cook. I mean, I can make oatmeal. I can scramble an egg. Hey, I can even toast bread, but that's not cooking."

A genuine laugh came from Mia. The same laugh she'd had when they were together and happy. "You're right. *You* can't cook. You might be the exception."

Jace wanted to keep listening to the sweet sound of her voice—to hear her talk about the life she'd been living without him.

"So, you've got me curious now. Really, what is the difference between a chef and a cook?"

Mia scooted her chair closer to the table, leaning in. "A chef understands complex flavor profiles and knows how to properly pair those to create dishes from them, whereas a cook follows an established recipe that someone else created. A chef also understands all the different cooking techniques," she explained. "The institute taught me so many things, like how to craft my own recipes, making most things from scratch, and then taught me to build complete menus around them. A chef has a whole different vision and a higher level of responsibility, too. When a cook goes home, they're done for the day, but a chef is still creating menus, choosing foods, handling the scheduling, managing costs—the whole business side of a kitchen."

Her face lit with an energy that came straight from

her heart. There was life in her eyes. The familiar Mia still existed, buried deeper maybe, but definitely still there.

"Do you have a specialty like making cakes, or pies, or something?" Jace asked her.

Mia hesitated at first, then said, "Actually, I've spent the last few months in a pasture-to-plate program, which connects chefs to those producing beef, like the King Ranch, but when I go to New York, I'll be an apprentice in the gourmet chef program."

His interest spiked, scooting him closer. "Pasture-to-plate, huh? I'd like to talk to you more about that sometime."

She sat back, taking the last bite of her enchilada. "Ranching and cows always get your attention. Does your interest ever wander anywhere else?"

"I'm a cattle rancher, Mia. It's what I do and what my daddy and granddaddy did, too. Five generations, remember? Where else should my interest be?" Before she could answer, he said, "There's no land in New York."

She laughed. "Of course, there's land in New York."

"Not like Texas. I'll bet a chunk of money that you can't find more than a hundred acres to buy up there, and if you do, it'll have limits on what you can do with the land."

"I'm not going up there to buy land, Jace. I'm going so that I can become a gourmet chef. They have amazing restaurants and resorts in New York that are hiring all the time."

He didn't want to talk about her leaving again. Jace sat back, pushing his uneaten dinner to the side. "Why do you want to work for somebody else anyway?"

Mia followed suit, pushing her platter away, too,

but her plate had been cleaned down to the last jalapeño. "What else am I supposed to do? I didn't get a five-generation opportunity laid in my lap." She gave a waving swish to the air. "You've always had the ranch with its thousands of acres, big enough to support the Farr family lineage for generations. You and your sister have nothing to worry about for the rest of your lives. But it's not the same for me, Jace."

The vision of his desk at the Farr Reaches, piled high with unpaid bills, popped into his head. She had no idea the pressure he was under.

"Okay, you two," Cindy said, arriving tableside. "You want dessert? We've got pecan pie, bread pudding, or churros."

Mia glanced up at the waitress. "Are they still using that premade churro mix, or have they finally started making their own?"

"It's a mix, but it's good."

"What about the pie?"

"It comes frozen."

Jace laughed, his focus on Mia. "And it still has the same pie crust you've always hated."

Mia shook her head. "I'll pass, Cindy. No dessert for me, but thank you."

After the waitress removed Mia's dinner platter, she reached for Jace's plate. "Jace, you didn't eat a bite. Want me to box it up for you?"

"Yeah, that would be great. I'll need an order to go for Grandma, too." He checked the time. "What's fast? I should have had her dinner home thirty minutes ago."

"She likes the cheese enchiladas with refried beans. That's fast."

Jace nodded. "Sounds good."

When the waitress left, Jace turned back to Mia.

"I'll bet if you stayed here and opened a restaurant, you'd make a killing."

Serious, Mia said, "There's nothing here for me, Jace."

"Josie is here," he said. "And I'm here."

"And both of you are the reasons why I left."

POTS OF RED GERANIUMS BRIGHTENED THE WHITE, spindle-railing front porch of the ranch-style home on the Farr Reaches Ranch.

Hannah Farr was in her rocking chair when Jace drove in, dust boiling up off the old dirt road. Her gaze never turned away from the truck as Jace got out and then braced himself against the side for Cowboy's greeting.

Hannah called to him. "Jace, you shouldn't let Cowboy jump on you like that. He's smart enough to learn."

On the porch, Jace leaned to kiss his grandmother's cheek, and then he sat in the rocking chair beside her. He put the Styrofoam container he'd brought from the Armadillo Diner on the side table between them.

"I brought you cheese enchiladas and refried beans home from the diner."

Hannah glanced at the container. "That was nice, but I just finished a piece of buttered toast."

"Grandma, you need to eat more than toast for dinner."

"It's getting hot out. I'm never very hungry when warm weather hits." She turned to him. "Can you believe summer is just almost here?"

"It snuck up on us this year, didn't it?" The setting

sun painted yellow, orange, and pink ribbons across the evening sky. Jace let his gaze sweep over the land. "We sure could use some rain."

The grazable ground needed water badly. His remaining cows, calves, and heifers needed the highest nutrition he could provide, and feeding hay year-round wasn't an option.

"What took you so long in town this afternoon? Is everything all right?"

No, everything wasn't all right, but he would never be able to admit to her that the ranch was losing money too fast. The Farr Reaches was a cow-calf operation, but he'd been forced to sell some of his calves and a quarter of his pregnant heifers to cover ranch costs in the fall. And although Cattlemen's Bank hadn't actually turned him down today, they'd looked over his profit-and-loss statement, evaluated the number of animals and acres he had to feed them, and asked how he planned to use the money to increase his net profit. He hadn't been able to tell them.

The bank president, Don Goss, had been a family friend for decades, but business was business, and Jace knew that. Goss had sent Jace away with a pat on the back, requesting he come back with a new proposal before they would consider his request for a second loan. What would the ranch do with the money that would impact their future earnings?

"Mia is back in town," Jace blurted to his grandmother. "We had dinner."

Hannah quieted; her brows scrunched in thought before she turned to him. "Wasn't she your old high school girlfriend?"

"Yeah," Jace admitted. "Mia Ellis. One and the same."

"I think I liked her, didn't I? Where has she been since high school?"

"Houston. She just finished the culinary program at the Art Institute." He stood. "But she's not staying. She's on her way to New York in a few days."

"Well, bring her by before she leaves, will you?"

"If I see her again, I'll be sure to ask." He picked up the container of food. "I'll put this in the fridge for you, just in case you get hungry later, okay?"

With Cowboy on his heels, Jace headed to the ranch office inside the house.

Signaling the Aussie to lie down on his fleece bed near the champagne-colored cowhide armchair, Jace closed his office door. He sat at the old oak executive desk that probably hadn't moved an inch off its spot in twenty years except for the day he'd had a flooring company rip out the old carpet and tile the room instead. His father had only been dead three months at the time, but his grandmother had said the room needed to reflect his spirit now. The next generation was depending on him to lead them into a new future, and things needed to be his way, but there had been little he wanted to change.

Jace clicked on the lamp. Everywhere he looked, signs of his father, grandfather, and his great-grandfather surrounded him. *As it should be*, he thought. He stared at the library wall unit opposite his desk. The lower half had twelve solid wood cabinets where decades of ranch ledgers were stored. He could pull one out, open it to any page, and read exactly what was happening on this ranch in any given month for the last one hundred and twenty years. "You can't manage what you can't measure," his grandfather had told him. His heritage was in this room. Sometimes the weight of it all was heavier than he had ever imagined.

The Farr family had retained title to the ranch for more than a century through hard work and determination, and previous generations had survived drought, low prices, and high costs, but he'd been dealt a tougher economic hand than a rancher deserved. The pandemic had ravaged his opportunities in what had promised to be his first good year as a descendant landowner, and he hadn't been able to pull out of the nosedive.

He had made changes when he needed to adjust to the conditions, like crossbreeding the Charolais and Brangus cattle during winter so calving would occur the following fall. Heifers were bred so they would calve at near two years old, and calves were worked at four months old, receiving treatments that would qualify them for premium prices at auction sales. The standard ranch rules had always worked to keep the ranch afloat, but times were still changing, and he was struggling to find his way out of the mud this time.

Jace opened a desk drawer, took out a tan leather ledger marked *Production Records* and opened it. Breeding history, pregnancy checks, and calving were counted and up-to-date. Again, he scanned the numbers, looking for an invisible answer.

The Farr Reaches Ranch had always taken pride in producing quality commercial cattle that could perform in the pasture, on the rail, or in the show ring. They'd strived to make each generation better than the last. His biggest job was always to improve the herd. But the buyers just weren't there this year. The big ranches had lured most away with prime fat cow weights that he couldn't achieve without more corn, but his feed payment was already six months overdue.

When a knock came on his office door, Cowboy was up with a bark.

"Hey, Jace, you got a minute?" The ranch foreman, Travis Hill, pushed the door ajar just enough for Jace to see him.

"Yeah, Trav," Jace said, standing. "Come on in."

"Hey, sorry to bother you after sunset, boss, but I need to talk to you."

Travis was thirty-five years older than Jace, but he'd been with the Farr Reaches for more than forty-one years, so his loyalty and respect for the family were undeniable.

"It's no bother, Trav." Jace motioned to a chair. "Have a seat and tell me what's on your mind."

Travis sat in the barrel-shaped brown leather chair opposite the desk after Jace retook his seat. He held his cowboy hat in his hands.

"The new kid we hired last month quit this evening. He said it was too much work for too little pay."

Jace sat back in his chair with a sigh. "You said he wouldn't last. You were right. I should have listened to you."

"Well, it's not like we have a whole lot of cowboys applying for the job. It was worth the gamble, I guess." Travis straightened, stretching his back and pushing himself taller in the chair. "There's more, though. Daisy quit today, too."

Danny Bloom had been with the ranch for almost six years, earning the nickname Daisy because he never failed to quit on a day he saw a snake. He was terrified of the reptiles and was sure they were a bad omen.

"Another rattler?" Jace asked.

"No, sir, not today," Travis said. "Danny claimed he'd had a dream and saw the Farr Reaches flood away in a once-in-a-century storm. He said we were all going down with it. He was more serious than I ever saw him with a snake." Travis sat back. "He packed his gear and left for West Texas this evening."

Jace leaned forward, his elbows on the desk. "So, we lost two men today?"

"Yes, sir," Travis told him. "I thought you should know right away."

Jace stood and reached for a handshake. "Thank you, Trav. I'll drive into town tomorrow and put the word out that we need another hand."

Travis stood and shook. "Boss, is everything okay?" He shifted. "There's talk of some money trouble, and the bunkhouse is nervous about it."

Jace gave an easy laugh to ward off worry. "There's always money trouble on a ranch, Trav. You know that."

Travis laughed. "Yes, sir."

After his foreman left the office, Jace closed the door.

Ranching was his way of life, but it was also a business. If he didn't find a solution soon, he would lose them both.

CHAPTER 5

It was sunny and warm when Ames Medical Transport brought Josie Ellis home. Mia had the air conditioning cranked so that the house would be cool and comfortable for her mother, and the place was spic-and-span spotless. Bedsheets were freshly laundered, the beds made, and the refrigerator was filled with good but easy food.

Mia held the front door open for the transport driver while he wheeled her mother inside.

"You cleaned the house," Josie said, her tone almost annoyed. "I hope you didn't organize, or I'll never find anything."

Mia pointed toward the main bedroom and then said to the driver, "Mom's room is that way. Do you mind helping me get her into bed before you leave?"

"Not at all," the man said.

"Bed?" Josie twisted in her wheelchair to glare at Mia. "I've been in bed long enough. Why can't I just sit out here and watch TV with you?"

The driver stopped with a glance back at Mia. "Living room or bedroom?"

"Bedroom," Mia directed him.

At the bedside, he locked the wheelchair, then took off the removable arm and set it aside.

"Just let Mia do it," Josie told him. "The hospital taught her how."

"Mom," Mia said. "Since he's here, let's just let him help, okay?"

Josie was right. The hospital had taught Mia how to transfer her mother from one place to another, which was necessary considering she had two non-weight-bearing legs, but the transfer looked easier than it was. Mia was strong but was still thirty pounds lighter than her mother.

The driver moved into position for the transfer, locking his inner thighs at Josie's knees. Together, they rocked to a count of three, and he lifted with a pivot and set her down on the bed.

Mia unlocked the wheelchair and rolled it back to a spot out of their way. Josie's mobility would improve in a few days, and Mia wanted the chair within her mother's reach whenever that happened.

"Thank you," Mia told the man.

With a grumble, Josie said, "You've got to start doing it yourself, Mia. You can't depend on someone else all the time. Now help me get my legs onto the bed. And I need that bed pillow so I can see the TV."

"Is there anything else, ma'am?" the transport driver asked Mia.

"No, I really appreciate your help."

Mia walked him to the door while Josie shouted, "Mia, ask him if he's single! Maybe you can cook him one of those dinners you learned how to make in that school."

"I'm sorry," Mia told him, a flush heating her cheeks. "You know how mothers are."

"Yes, ma'am," he replied politely, leaving more quickly than he'd come.

"Mia?" Josie called. "I need help with my legs. I can't lift them onto the bed. Are you coming back?"

"Yes, Mom. I'm on my way."

Mia had already cleaned out the drawer of her mother's nightstand, putting medications, her personal items, and a notepad and pens inside. On the top, beside the lamp, she set the remote control, her mother's phone charger, and three new summer romance novels.

With Josie comfortably situated, Mia pulled the bedsheet over her mother's legs.

"Do you need anything else?" Mia asked.

"Yes." Josie pointed to the window in her room. "Close those curtains so I can see the TV better, and I'm hungry." She clicked on the television. "I left half a can of refried beans in the refrigerator. Can you warm it up in the microwave and bring it to me with some corn chips?"

"No." Mia stared at her mother. "You've been gone five days, Mom, and that can of beans looked like it had been opened a week before I got here. I threw out all the old food, and those refried beans were the first to go. The fridge is cleaned and restocked with good, healthy food now."

Brows scrunched, Josie leveled a glare. "I wanted those beans, Mia."

After a glance at the clock on the wall, Mia said, "I

can make cheese quesadillas to hold you over until dinner. How does that sound?"

"Oh, I like quesadillas!" Josie smiled, then pleasantly asked, "What are you making for dinner?"

"I don't know, Mom." Her tone snowballed into annoyance, but Mia tried to conceal it. After all, it was her mother's first day home from the hospital, and she'd complained about the food she had been fed every day of her stay. "How does pork tenderloin with cream sauce and garlic mashed sweet potatoes sound to you?"

Josie pulled the quilt to her waist. "Can't you just cook something normal?" She looked at her daughter. "And turn the air conditioner up to eighty-five. We're not made of money, you know?"

Mia turned and walked out of the room. Her shoulders were tense. Her throat tightened. At the thermostat, she unclenched her fists and shook out the stress. She inhaled a good deep breath and then slowly exhaled before adjusting the temperature. Her mother needed her. There was no one else. But the urge to flee was soaring fast.

MIA WALKED INTO THE OUTREACH AND SOCIAL services building at Cenizo Plaza, signed in on the sheet attached to the clipboard, then took a seat in the hard plastic and chrome environment. She scanned the room filled with unfamiliar faces. Almost all were women accompanied by children or the elderly.

Mia pushed herself into a corner chair and focused on her phone, ignoring a call from her mother. She scrolled through her emails in search of the promised update from the director of the culinary program. It had been three days since she'd put in her request for a delayed admission to the six-month program, and every day without a decision was more torturous than the last.

"Miss Ellis?" A woman called into the waiting room from an opened but unmarked door. When Mia stood, she said, "Mrs. Goode can see you now."

Halfway through Mia's explanation of her mother's situation to the social worker, Mrs. Goode stopped her.

"Miss Ellis, if insurance is covering the cost of your mother's in-home rehab three times a week, and transportation has been arranged for her travel to and from her medical visits for the next month, and she doesn't require any medications to be administered by a professional, and you're home with her full-time, I'm not sure I understand how we can help. Unless, of course, you're saying that you're not willing or able to be her in-home support person."

Panic rose Mia to her feet. "I'm moving to New York. I'm already packed."

"I see," Mrs. Goode said, her gaze dropping to the notepad. She scribbled—her silence lingering longer than the pen. "We can certainly start the eligibility process for home healthcare assistance, but the service will require your mother's approval and signature and an evaluation from her physician." She put down her pen and stood. "In fairness, Miss Ellis, you should know that even if the application is approved, there will be about a five-week wait. We just don't have enough staff to go around right now. Families are urged to provide as much care as possible. We encourage people to consider us supplemental help, not total care."

A tinge of anger bubbled to the surface. "What if I weren't here? What would happen to my mother then?"

Mrs. Goode didn't bat an eye. "If her insurance approved, she would probably go into a nursing home for several weeks."

Mia left the building frustrated. She hadn't planned for this, but then, does anyone?

Texas had lowered its defenses against the glaring afternoon heat. There wasn't a cloud in the sky or a single tree in the paved parking lot to offer a speck of shade.

Head down, Mia crossed the fading lines on the blacktop, following her midday shadow to the Prius, and then unlocked the door and got inside. She started the engine but then sat silent, staring through the windshield that needed cleaning, with the air conditioner fan turned on high. She closed her eyes, welcoming the blast of cool air blowing into her face and lightly blowing her honey-highlighted brown hair. She didn't move from the parking lot full of cars.

When an email alert chimed, Mia grabbed her phone and read:

Dear Ms. Ellis,

Due to your extenuating circumstances, your request has been approved for a delayed admission. You've been reassigned to our January apprenticeship program. No other delay requests will be considered.

Six months! She had requested a four-week deferred admission into the current program. A half-year delay was a setback she hadn't expected. She'd sublet her Houston townhouse for the next six months to an incoming culinary student, and her deposit had already been forfeited on her studio apartment in New York. She'd been scrimping, trying to save money in hopes of finding another studio once her delayed admission was approved, but a six-month postponement meant everything was on hold.

Her life was swirling down the drain again.

The town of Legacy was a trap. For her, it was anyway. Mia had been caught in its snare since birth. Once, in a lucky moment, she'd escaped—as far away as Houston for a few years—but just when she thought she was completely free, she was snatched up and dragged back.

She looked at the stores, offices, and other buildings at the town's main intersection.

Upstairs over the Keller Insurance office was the apartment where she'd once practiced piano, and next door, at The Shady Porch Inn, she'd attended recital parties. On the other corner was the Pink Brick Pancake House, where she'd waitressed one summer, and across the street at Well Remembered Antiques was where her friend Diana Duren had worked.

But it wasn't until her gaze found the Roadrunner Theater with its big red marquee—the place she'd had her first kiss—that her crushed heart felt a tingle from the life she'd left behind.

She had loved Legacy once—no, that wasn't true—she'd once loved *Jace*. He was the reason she'd loved Legacy.

Swiping tears away, Mia shifted the Prius into drive and then pulled out onto the street, her eyes on the road, not the buildings, and drove home, trying to push aside the memories that no longer belonged in her heart.

"Mom, I'm home," she called out after entering the too-warm house.

"Mia?" Josie called back.

"Yes, Mom, it's me," she said, leaning in from the doorway to her mother's room. "I'm starting dinner. Do you need anything?"

"You were gone a long time. What if I needed you? What would I do then?"

"Did you need me?"

"I might have—you never know. Things happen, Mia. What if the house had caught fire? I can't walk, you know? You shouldn't go too far."

Mia pointed to the nightstand. "Your phone is right there. If the house is on fire, you need to call 911 for the fire department, not me, okay?"

The kitchen was Mia's comfort zone, so she retreated to it quickly. Now that it was clean, organized, and restocked, she had reasons to stay in it. She tuned the small portable radio on the window ledge to a country music station and then listened while she prepped a whole chicken, finally sliding it into the oven for roasting.

On her last shopping trip, she had purchased a dozen aluminum foil pans with lids, which she planned to use for frozen meals. She was making King Ranch chicken casserole tonight, one of her mother's favorites, and there would be enough for another two pans. Easy freezer-to-oven meals that could be ready in an hour. Tomorrow night, Mia planned to make lasagna and would add another two meals to the freezer.

In assembly-line fashion, she made one casserole dish for tonight's dinner and two more in aluminum pans for the freezer. With a marker, she wrote on the lids: *King Ranch at 350 degrees for 1 hour 20 minutes*, but

before carrying the two extras to the freezer, the doorbell rang.

Mia grabbed a kitchen cloth and wiped her hands
on the way to the door, the television in her mother's
bedroom blaring. She opened the front door, suddenly
wishing for a storm door.

CHAPTER 6

It was foolish to be nervous, but Jace couldn't shake the feeling. He was disappointed when a smile hadn't greeted him. Deliberately not giving himself more time to think, he said, "Hey, Mia."

After a hesitant moment, she said, "Hey." Then she pulled open the door. "Come in."

Jace removed his hat before stepping inside, unable to stop his gaze from swimming the fine, thin line of her. She had always been slender and still was, but her twenty-five-year-old self was more of a woman now than when she'd left him five years ago. Her white V-neck T-shirt clung to her curves, spurring his thumping heart, and her tight-fitting stonewashed jeans, tapered down to her bare Lone Star-tattooed ankles, revealed an inch or so of tanned skin before sinking into a pair of navy canvas slip-ons.

Although his gaze settled on her beautiful blue-gray eyes—the ones that had never failed to mesmerize him—his hand still motioned to her flat canvas shoes. "Your boots would look really good with those jeans."

He took a step closer. "The heels gave you perfect kissing height, too."

Mia stepped back. "I threw out those boots five years ago, Jace. Along with everything else I loved."

"Well, I didn't," he said.

"Didn't what?"

"Throw out everything I loved."

Mia glanced at his Silverbelly Stetson, held close over his heart. "Right. You upgraded." She closed the door behind him, shutting out the late day heat blazing in. "I assume you came to see Mom?"

Without a nod, Jace said, "I'd like to say hello, yeah, but it's you I came by to see. I want to ask you about something." When she stiffened, he clarified. "About cooking."

Mia laughed. "You want to ask me about *cooking*? Really, Jace. Cooking?"

"I'm serious, Mia." He hung his hat on the free-standing brass coat rack, discolored by age, that stood empty by the door, hoping he would be allowed to stay for a while. "I have a couple of questions that I know you can answer for me."

Mia stared at him in silence, softening at his length-ening quiet.

"Okay," she finally said. "But I'm busy in the kitchen, so you'll have to talk to me while I work."

Jace followed Mia to the open kitchen. "What smells so good?"

"King Ranch chicken. Mom's favorite casserole. She asked for it."

Jace inhaled, filling his lungs with the scented air and rousing a growl from his stomach. Mia glanced at him, her focus dropping to his midsection, then down onto his Texas Longhorn belt buckle.

"When did you start loving longhorns? I didn't think you'd ever give up wearing that old trophy buckle."

He smiled, remembering how she used to complain about it. "I gave up rodeoing a long time ago." Then he pointed to the sealed square aluminum pans on the counter. "Don't tell me a trained chef is buying premade food."

Mia looked at the stack of casserole pans still on the counter. "Of course not. I made extra King Ranch casserole for the freezer."

"Man, I wish I could do stuff like that for Grandma." Serious, he looked at Mia. "I can't hardly get her to eat anything."

"Ask Mary to make this casserole for her." Her voice softened. "Hannah loved *arroz con pollo*, too. For a cattle rancher, she sure loved chicken."

"Mary doesn't cook at the ranch anymore. She hasn't for maybe three years now." Jace leaned with his back against the Formica counter. "She was diagnosed with a medical condition that Craig says makes her shake so bad she can't even drive anymore."

Mia's hand went to her heart. "I'm sorry to hear that. Mary was always such a nice lady to me. And she loved your grandma."

"Yeah, and not having Mary around to take care of things changed the whole dynamic of the ranch for Grandma. She even stopped serving lunch to the bunkhouse. She doesn't go riding anymore either. She hasn't been on Hardtack in probably two years. She just doesn't have much interest in things these days other than her birds. There are a lot of things she just doesn't remember loving."

"I'm sorry, Jace. I didn't realize."

"It's okay. I just get worried about her." Jace pushed his thumbs into the front pockets of his jeans. "Getting older is harder than I thought. Craig's having a tough time managing things for Mary, too. He's still running the store full-time, so Mary is home alone a lot. Clint just isn't stepping up to the plate for his dad, if you know what I mean. He barely shows up to work."

"I'm surprised he's still there. I thought he would be long gone by now," Mia said.

"He would be, except the Feed and Seed is probably the only paycheck he'll ever get."

Mia nodded. "I'll stop by and see Craig next time I go shopping."

"He'd like that." Then Jace pointed to the freezer pans again. "Do you think maybe I can buy one of those casseroles from you for Grandma? I'd be curious to see if she'll eat it."

Mia's brows arched. "I'd be glad to send one home with you." She picked a pan up off the counter and handed it to him. "Cooking instructions are on the top."

Jace took the pan but then set it down on the counter before reaching into his back pocket for his wallet. "How much do I owe you?"

"Oh, no, Jace." Mia held up a hand. "I can't take your money. I'm glad to help Hannah. I hope she likes it."

Jace opened his wallet anyway, pulled out a twenty-dollar bill, and handed it to Mia. "You can't be cooking free for people. You're a professional chef. I can't take this if you don't let me pay you for it." He held his offering hand steady until Mia reached for the cash.

"Thank you." She slipped the folded twenty into her back pocket. "I'm a little short on cash right now. This helps."

From the main bedroom, Josie called, "Mia? Are you still here?"

Mia glanced at Jace, calling back, "Yes, Mom, I'm here. Do you need me?"

"Yes, I need you!" She was irritated.

Not intending to, Jace laughed, which made Mia laugh. "Can I come with you and say hi to Josie?"

"Please." Mia started for her mother's bedroom with Jace following. She went straight to the remote and turned down the volume.

"I've been in the kitchen cooking and talking to Jace, but the television was so loud, you probably couldn't hear the doorbell when it rang."

"Hey," Jace said, approaching from behind Mia. He leaned and kissed Josie's forehead. "How are you feeling?"

"Jace, it's good to see you." Josie had hold of his hand and was squeezing. "Mia said you came by the house while I was in the hospital."

"I was worried about you. I needed to be sure you hadn't up and died on me."

Both chuckled as Mia stood looking at the two of them.

"You were probably just worried about me because I haven't finished the quilt for Hannah's birthday yet," Josie teased him.

Jace patted her hand. "How's it coming along? Do you think it will be ready for Grandma's birthday on July 4th?"

Josie let go of his hand and then gave a swish to the air. "Don't worry about that quilt. It's almost done. I won't let you down. It's going to make a real nice gift."

"I know it will," Jace told her.

"Can you stay for dinner?"

Jace glanced at Mia, but when his gaze caught silence, he said, "Not tonight, Josie, but I do have some things I'd like to talk over with Mia. Do you think I can have her for another ten or fifteen minutes?"

Josie turned with a glare for Mia. "What are you doing in here? You have a guest."

"Mom," Mia said gently, straightening the bed quilt. "You called me. Did you need me?"

"I just wanted to know when dinner would be ready. I'm hungry, and you know I like to eat right at six o'clock. Will it be ready at six o'clock?"

"Yes, it'll be ready at six o'clock. It needs to cook for twenty more minutes," Mia told her. "But then it needs to cool after coming out of the oven. I'll make a salad to go with it, too." Mia fluffed the scattered bed pillows and then repositioned them against the head-board. "Does that sound okay to you?"

"Yes, go, go." Josie looked up at Jace even though she was speaking to Mia. "Don't keep Jace waiting." But then, anxiously patting the quilt, she said, "Wait, what did you do with my remote?"

"Here it is." Jace handed it to her from the nightstand.

Josie reached for his hand again and squeezed it. "You're a good boy, Jace. You've always been a good boy."

Mia took Jace by the shoulders and turned him toward the door. "I'll be back with your dinner, Mom, as soon as it's ready." She guided Jace out of the room, then closed her mother's door.

In the privacy of the living room, Jace stopped and turned around. The energy of Mia's touch had over-taken him. He took her in an embrace and kissed her.

Mia was pushing against his chest in an instant, but she hadn't pulled her kiss away.

He tightened his arms around her and stepped forward, taking Mia to the pale-yellow wall. At the touch of it against her back, she raised her arms, encircling his neck—the place they felt so natural. Jace eased his hold, moving his hands to her waist and then lowered his lips to her neck. The scent of her was intoxicating.

He whispered, "I've missed you so much."

At the sound of his voice, Mia tensed. "Jace." She pushed him back—reality hard set in her eyes. "I can't do this." She moved out of his arms, stepping from between him and the wall. "*We* can't do this again."

She was beautiful with her brown highlighted hair and her heart-stopping blue-gray eyes that had a story all their own. "You never should have left, Mia."

"But I did leave," she whispered, still only a foot from her mother's closed bedroom door. "C'mon," she said, starting toward the kitchen.

Jace followed her, stopping when she turned. The kitchen seemed to shrink in size with the two of them in it.

Softly, she said, "You had no right to kiss me." Her gaze lingered on him.

"You kissed me back."

Mia pushed her splayed fingers like a comb through the hair, grabbing a handful at the crown of her head. Looking down, she said, "I know I did. I don't know why I did that."

"Maybe it was because you've missed me, too." Jace reached for her, gently pulling her to him. "I never wanted you to leave."

CHAPTER 7

Jace was her weakness. That's why she'd left Legacy five years ago. And why she shouldn't be here now.

Mia wasn't ready to have this talk. She glanced at the clock on the wall above the oven. "I should make the salad," she told him.

"I can help." He held open the refrigerator door while Mia took out a bottle of ranch-style dressing and a head of romaine lettuce.

She laid the lettuce on a cutting board and then reached for the bowl on the counter that held fresh tomatoes, cucumbers, and bell peppers, but then she stopped and took a breath.

"You came here for a reason tonight, Jace. What was it?" It was hard to control the sound of her emotions.

"Right," Jace said. "I did." He leaned a bit to see her eyes, which she diverted from him, her gaze directed to the cutting board. She made it obvious that she didn't want to look at him. "I've been thinking about making a change at the ranch."

Mia grabbed the cucumber and a peeler, busying herself with the salad. "What kind of change?" Jace was a dreamer. Nothing much ever changed at the Farr Reaches, and she doubted it would now.

"I haven't mentioned this to Grandma yet, but I've been talking to some of the smaller ranches like us in the state about their direct-to-consumer operations."

Mia stopped peeling and looked at him, her interest piqued. "Pasture-to-plate?"

"Yeah," he said with a nod. "I think it might be the direction to go for the future of the ranch."

Mia put down the cucumber and focused her full attention on Jace. "It could be an amazing opportunity for a ranch like the Farr Reaches. When I was in Houston, we had a tribal member from South Dakota in the program. Her cousin invited us to tour their pasture-to-plate operation. Five of us drove up together on a private trip and spent two days with them. They were more profitable selling direct to the consumer than they had ever been, but they were still able to keep the consumer prices low. It was important to them that their beef be affordable to the community."

"I knew you'd understand. That's why I wanted to talk to you." When Jace stepped closer, she instinctively took a step back. "Mia, you're the only one I've ever been able to talk to about things that count."

"And it counts now?"

"Yeah," he said seriously. "It counts."

His expression was different. For the first time since coming home, Mia realized his face had changed. Hardened. More mature, yes, but it seemed more than that. Why hadn't she noticed it before now?

"What's going on, Jace?"

He lowered his gaze, eyes focused on his boots. "Cattle ranching gets harder every year, and I'm having a tough time getting a grip on the finances." He raised his head until his eyes met hers. "If the ranch fails, it will fail on my watch, and I can't let that happen. The Farr Reaches has been our home and livelihood for over a hundred years, and I don't want to go down in our family history as the one who lost it all."

The thing about Jace—the thing everyone except him knew—was that he was a truly good man right down to the soles of his beloved Lucchese boots. He was hardworking, honest, loyal, and committed. Was there anyone who knew him who didn't love and believe in him?

A tug to her heart sent her to him. She laid a hand on his forearm. "Jace, you're also the youngest member of the Farr family ever to run the ranch. Your dad was forty-one when he took over. You were only nineteen when he died."

Jace smirked. "Yeah, it only took me six years to push it to the brink of bankruptcy. That's probably a record."

THE FARR REACHES HAD A SUCCESSION PLAN. IT'D been in place for generations, but the plan went to hell when Jacob Farr died too young.

Managerial capability took time, effort, and mentoring. Jace had the people skills and work ethic essential to the ranch, but ranching was complex and required focused instruction on production, finance, and marketing. Other than what he'd been taught about ranching as a young man, Jace had less than a year under his father's tutelage after high school before inheriting the ranch. The role of manager should have grown slowly —not arrive all at once.

His sister, Cecelia, was set to be the other half of the team, but less than six months after their father's death, she married a Colorado attorney who had his own family succession plan to follow.

"What does Hannah say?" Mia wanted to know the matriarch's thoughts.

"Oh, I can't tell Grandma." He shook his head. "It would kill her to know I can't keep the ranch afloat. She's eighty-two and has mild cognitive impairment, and I'm worried about her physical health, too." Again, he shook his head. "She's helped me all she can. It's my fight now."

Jace was stubbornly proud. It was hard for him to admit to anyone that he was failing.

"What do you need me to do?" Mia asked.

Her words caused Jace to draw a deep breath, exhaling it as a lungful of relief. "I've asked Cattlemen's Bank for another loan, but Don wants a full proposal— an overall plan and vision with a description of my business goals—before he takes it to the board. He wants it spelled out as to what I'll do with the money and how it will change the outcome of the ranch. I figured since you're stuck here for a few days, maybe you could help me write the proposal for a direct-to-consumer operation."

"More like a few months."

"What do you mean?"

"The New York culinary program won't have another place for me for six months." She shrugged, blinking back the glisten in her eyes. "I don't have anywhere else to go."

Jace pulled her to him, not in intimacy but in compassion.

Mia melted into him. "I lost my studio unit in New York, and my Houston townhouse has been sublet for six months. Mom needs help for a while, and there's no one but me to do it, so I might as well stay here until the apprenticeship program opens again."

Jace shifted her back a step, holding her at arm's length—a gleam in his brown eyes.

"It's fate, Mia. You were meant to come home. This is a good thing."

"How is everything I just told you a good thing? I have no income. No means of support whatsoever for six months." She glanced around her mother's home. "And I have to live *here*."

"It's good because you need to be reminded of who you were when you were here. Who *we* were. I was afraid you'd never come back."

"Jace…" Mia shook her head. "I don't want to pick up where we left off. This doesn't mean we're back together. It just means that I'm stuck here."

"But stuck in Texas. Not New York," he clarified with a grin. "What's that old saying? You can take the girl out of Texas, but you can't take Texas out of the girl. You're meant to be here, Mia."

"Well, I don't know about that," she said. "But I have time to help you with the proposal. Besides, it'll keep my head in the game." Then landing a glare on him, she added, "Until I can get to New York. I'm still going."

"Got it," Jace said.

"So, when do we start?"

The smile that refused to leave his face was beginning to hurt his cheeks.

"Tomorrow?" he suggested.

Mia hadn't even asked him to explain why the ranch was failing. She had taken him at his word and trusted him to disclose only what was needed without pushing him into uncomfortable territory. The woman had a way of righting his world. She was a strength he never had alone. His life was better with her in it. It always had been.

"Okay, tomorrow it is," Mia agreed. "Mom has in-home therapy at ten o'clock. We'll be able to work uninterrupted for an hour. Bring your notes."

When the timer went off on the oven, Mia pulled out the casserole, setting it on a cooling rack. Her glance told Jace his time was up. "I need to finish the salad."

"Yeah, right," he said. Jace picked up the aluminum pan off the countertop. "I need to get this home to Grandma anyway." He glanced at the instructions written on the lid. "So, an hour and twenty minutes in the oven?"

"Oh, no!" Mia grabbed the marker, scribbled through the time she'd written on the lid, and then wrote the number thirty. "Those instructions were for a frozen casserole, but I didn't have time to freeze this one. It only needs thirty minutes in the oven. Let it cool before serving."

HANNAH FARR HAD CLEANED HER PLATE FOR THE first time in weeks. "Who did you say sent this casserole home with you?"

"It was Mia," Jace explained a second time. "Do you remember Mia? I dated her in high school."

Not only had his grandmother eaten dinner, but they'd also sat together at the dining table to do it. It had been a family tradition to join together for their evening meal, but when Hannah had stopped eating anything more than a cracker or toast, Jace had seen no use in sitting at the big table alone. He'd taken to eating Tex-Mex at the Armadillo Diner in town, or he'd made himself a sandwich at home and eaten it outside.

After dinner, Jace went to the horse barn and saddled Ghost, a blue dun so smoky gray that it was hard to spot her on the rise.

With his back to the orange sherbet-colored sunset, he rode the stretch of creek-fed hills, stopping beneath the far-spreading limbs of an old red oak overlooking a lowland where his herd of Charolais grazed.

Every plant and animal went about its life, growing, living, reproducing, and surviving, constantly changing, somehow content and peaceful in its existence.

The rugged hillocks settled Jace, giving him perspective on his cattle-concentrated roots. His entire life had been spent working the Farr Reaches and he loved everything about the ranch, including Ghost. He'd rarely admitted it to anyone, but up until the last few years, they had spent countless hours together riding through green valleys bisected by spring-fed creeks, over logs, and through the brush, stopping when no one else was around to hunt for arrowheads hiding in the soil. His collection from childhood had grown through the years, and one day, after mounting them in display cases, he intended to give them to his children, or his nephews if he had none of his own. He could almost name the place and the day each had been found. They were part of the history of this land.

The Farr Reaches was raising the most profitable range cow possible for their terrain, and if any breed could meet the demands of an ever-changing beef market, Jace had faith that it was his creamy-white Charolais. If he could create a profitable pasture-to-plate program, he could successfully maintain a productive herd and keep the ranch from going under.

On the nearly level pastureland below, Travis and Ray sat their horses. They'd spent the day moving weaned calves from one pasture to another, and it looked like their day was almost done.

They never noticed Jace on Ghost until Cade, the newest and youngest ranch hand, rode the Gator UTV roaring up and over the hill headed for the herd. At the sound, Travis turned in his saddle, saw Jace, and raised a hand. He started toward him in a slow trot.

The relationship between a cowboy and his horse was special. It was built on long, hard daily work routines and a level of mutual understanding and trust, but in the last twenty years, many a ranch horse had been replaced with utility-terrain vehicles. Jace felt strongly that cattle should only be moved, sorted, and worked from the back of a horse, so why Cade was headed toward the herd like a bat out of hell on the UTV was a question he wanted answered.

"Hey, boss," Travis greeted Jace. "We got the calves moved, but our count is off. We might have a few strays back down in that tangle of mesquite."

Mesquite was one of the toughest species of brush that grew on the Farr Reaches.

Jace pointed. "That UTV won't do much good. You'll have to go in on horseback to push them out."

"I know it, sir," Travis told him. "But the fence is down, and I want those strays back with the herd before fixing it tonight. We need that UTV for its lights."

"Well, that vehicle isn't a toy. You need to tell that to Cade."

"Yes, sir." Travis adjusted his hat before saying, "He's just a kid, sir. He'll learn." He looked skyward. "It's getting dark."

A turn in the saddle brought the fading light on the horizon into view for Jace. He looked back at Travis. "True enough. I guess we're burning daylight. Let's go find those strays."

CHAPTER 8

It was ten o'clock on the dot when Mia heard Jace's truck pull into the driveway. She had the door open, waiting when he stepped onto the concrete porch.

"Morning," Jace said with a smile. After stepping inside, he took off his hat and hung it on the rack. "How's Josie this morning?"

"Complaining already," she said. "Cruz just got here a few minutes ago. He's in the room with Mom. They just started today's session."

"Cruz Delgado?"

"No." Mia pulled a business card from a trinket plate on a lamp table. "Cruz Trujillo. From Riverside Rehab." She handed Jace the card. "Do you know him?"

Jace shook his head, handing the card back. "That place just opened up about a year ago. Nice building. I think most of their employees came from San Antonio. They're good, I hear."

"Mom's surgeon said the same thing. I'll be glad

when she's finally up, using crutches." Mia motioned to the kitchen. "Do you want to work at the dining table?"

Mia's laptop was already set up and open at a seat, so Jace set his on the opposite side of the table.

"Before we start, I want to thank you for the casserole last night." He laid a dark leather satchel on the table. "Grandma ate the whole serving I put on her plate, and she loved it." He gave a touch to his heart and smiled. "You're a really great cook."

"I'm glad she liked it. Thanks for letting me know."

Jace pulled a half dozen manila file folders out of the satchel before seating himself. "I really appreciate your help with this."

He handed a new spiral notebook to Mia, keeping one for himself before opening a folder with loose papers inside. He pulled out a sheet, laid it on the table, then slid it across, facing her. He pointed to the rows of handwritten calculations. "Initial estimates are that a cow that sells at auction for $950 can bring in about $2,600 in the box, so my goal is to sell more beef in the box than on the hoof."

Mia studied the computations. "You've got to have reasonable processing costs to keep this profit margin. Do you have any quotes yet?"

Jace took out another folder and presented it to Mia. "You remember Blake, don't you? He was a couple of years ahead of us in school."

"Blake Dowd? Sure. His folks used to own Dowd and Out Meat Processing."

"Yeah," Jace said. "They still do. I sat down with Blake last week and worked out those numbers." He pointed to the new folder. "They're giving me a good deal."

Mia glanced at the numbers. "How much is he charging to store the meat for you?"

"He's not. Everybody I talked to said they bought their own freezers, set them up, and then got their Meat Safety Assurance certification. They're storing and selling the processed beef from their ranches, delivering the orders themselves. Dowd's has the Grant of Inspection, so we don't need one."

"Do you already have the freezers?"

"No, that's part of what the loan will be used for." He opened another folder and pulled out a cost sheet on the different sizes of freezers but then handed her two eight-by-ten-inch photos. "The storage building on the north side of the house has full electricity and air conditioning. Two walls have good sturdy shelving units installed, and it has two generators. It's not being used for anything right now, so I'm planning to use it for the freezer storage."

"How much meat are you planning to start with?"

"Two thousand pounds." He adjusted in his chair. "Selling it will be the real test."

Mia leaned forward, her focus intent. "Jace, this is a really good idea."

He smiled at the compliment. "You think it will work then?"

"Oh, yeah." Mia scribbled a note on the pad. "The biggest challenge will be creating a marketing plan to get your beef to the consumers. Do you have any thoughts on that?"

He sat back in his chair. "Restaurants," he offered after a moment of thought. "Maybe Alamo's Grocery. And maybe Central Supermarket, too."

"Well, if you want the consumer business, you'll be a direct competitor to the grocers, so scratch Alamo's and Central Supermarket off the list. You're not looking for third-party vendors. Restaurants are a good side idea, though. But your main goal is to focus on getting beef direct to the home consumer—beef from your pastures to their tables. Pasture-to-plate. Your customers are the local families."

"Right." Jace made notes, then asked, "How do I do that? How do I tell people I want them to buy beef from me instead of the grocery stores? Newspaper advertising is the only thing I know."

"Word of mouth. And the Internet. Do you have a website? Do you have a name for the business yet?"

Jace shrugged. "Just Farr Reaches, I guess."

"No, it needs to be more than just the name of the ranch to distinguish the two. You want the new name to say, 'You can buy beef directly from me.' Most people never think of buying beef from the rancher himself." Mia got up, poured two glasses of her home-brewed sweet tea, and then handed one to Jace before retaking her seat. "You need a strong and memorable name."

"You mean something like 'Steak on a Stick'?"

"Good Lord, Jace." Mia laughed. "Sounds like you're selling it off a wagon at the State Fair. Do you have any creativity at all?"

He laughed when she did, his smile lingering. "I've been known to be creative, maybe just not in naming new businesses." Then he said, "What about 'Beef on a Budget'?"

"And that makes it sound like you're selling low-quality beef."

"Well, I'm not. Our beef is the best around. What we have is generational quality."

"I completely agree." Mia took a pen and started jotting down name suggestions, calling them out as she wrote. "Plate Worthy Beef. Hill Country Beef. Legacy Beef. Best Beef." Failing to spur a response, Mia kept pen to paper and continued to call out other names. "Amazing Beef. Smokin' Beef. Fat Cow Beef." Finally, she put her pen down and glared at Jace. In a harder tone, she ground out the words, "Farr Ranches Quality Beef."

Jace came up out of his seat. "Why don't we just call it that? That's what it is—it's quality beef from the ranch."

"Well, at least it got a rise out of you." Mia leaned across. "But I'd love to see the credit go to you for creating this new business. What if you put your name on it, too?" She raised both hands and then used her fingers to frame an imaginary headline. "'Jace Farr' and then right under your name, it would say, 'Farr Reaches Quality Beef' instead of just using the ranch name in the title."

"I don't need my name on it, Mia," he said. "All I need is for people to know it's our beef and to trust us for our quality. The ranch name does that well enough."

"Okay, then." Mia stood. "Farr Reaches Quality Beef, it is."

"I love it," Jace said. He walked around the table, pulling Mia into his arms and kissing her. "And I love you."

A throat-clearing "excuse me" came from Cruz, who stood a short distance away. "I don't mean to interrupt."

Mia stepped back from Jace, wiping at the flush on her cheeks. "Cruz." Her fluster added a stammer to her voice. "I'm…Is everything okay?"

"We're finished for the day," Cruz said. "But your mom wants you to come and listen to the instructions I have for her about using her crutches." Since Mia was looking at Jace and not at him, Cruz made sure she was listening by giving a touch to her shoulder. "But the crutches are only ten steps or less, like getting to the bathroom or from the couch to the kitchen. Her knee is still too unstable for anything more."

"Sure." Mia acknowledged him with a look, pushing her loose hair back over the crown of her head. "Got it."

When Cruz turned and left the kitchen and dining area, Mia followed.

HE HADN'T MEANT TO SAY IT. I LOVE YOU WAS probably the one thing he shouldn't have said. When Mia returned, he expected to be thrown out of the house and told that she never wanted to see him again.

Jace wandered through the living room, listening to the voices from Josie's bedroom. Mia sounded calm, collected, and interested, taking direction and asking questions. She didn't sound like a woman who had just been gut-punched by an unexpected confession of love.

The door to Mia's bedroom stood wide open. Jace was drawn to the room by the scent of an orange candle. Pictures tacked to the cork bulletin board on her wall were the same as they'd been five years earlier. It was a look back in time he hadn't expected today. He stood studying the photographs, remembering. Mia hadn't taken any of the photos with her when she'd moved to Houston. But at least she hadn't thrown them out.

From the bedroom, Jace saw Cruz with his rehab bag, leaving the house. Mia was behind him, thanking him. When she closed the front door, Jace came out into the living room with her.

"There you are," she said. "I thought maybe you'd left."

"Should I?" he asked, a soft surrender in his voice.

Mia went to the couch and sat, the morning sun blazing through the sheer yellow curtains on the front windows. She motioned Jace to the loveseat squared next to her. "We need to talk."

Jace felt a chastising on the horizon.

"Look, Mia," he said without sitting. "When I said 'I love you,' I didn't mean it the way you think." He wanted to look away because he didn't want her to see the lie in his eyes, but he just couldn't pull his gaze off her. She was beautiful in her peach-colored pull-on shorts and white tank top, sitting with her long, tanned legs curled up under her.

Mia focused on him, sending him to the loveseat like she'd asked.

After sitting, Jace reached across the arm of the gray leather sofa and took her hand in his, holding it softly.

"I'm always going to love you," he said. "You're a part of me, and you always will be. There's nothing you can do about that, but I'm sorry I said it. I didn't mean it that way."

"Why didn't you ever come after me?"

The question caught him off guard. "What?"

"When I left. You just let me go. You never called. Not in five years, Jace. You never came after me or asked me to come back." Mia straightened her legs, setting both feet on the floor, and then she pulled away her hand. "After our argument that day—the day I threw my hat at you—I came home and packed, but even then, I couldn't bring myself to leave you. I waited a whole week before I left for Houston."

At the glisten in her eyes, Jace pushed himself to the edge of the loveseat, his boots nudging her canvas slip-ons.

"Mia, you told me you were through with me. You said I was ruining your life. It wasn't my idea to break up. You wanted to cook," then he corrected himself, "to become a chef, I mean. You said that was all you ever wanted."

"Well, it wasn't all that I wanted. I wanted you, too." Mia looked at him, almost emotionless. "I wanted *us*."

"Then why did you leave?"

"Jace, after your father died, you were so wrapped up in the ranch there was no room for me. I was always in the way." She glanced down at her hands, now curled into knots on her lap. "When I told you that I was leaving—that I was going to culinary school in Houston—you just let me go without even a word of goodbye." Mia looked at him again. "That's when I knew you would never love me like I'd loved you. What we'd had was just a high school thing, and high school was long over by then. I needed to get on with my life."

Jace reached for her hand. "Mia, if my silence made you leave, I'm sorry. That was the biggest mistake of my life. I was trying to give you what I thought you wanted."

"What I wanted was a ring."

Jace shook his head. "I couldn't ask you to marry me."

She sprang to her feet. "Why the hell not?"

Jace stood. "Mia, you wanted out of this house so bad that you weren't thinking about a future with me or even a future as a professional chef—you were looking for an escape. And the dreams you had weren't things I could give you. You wanted to go to cooking school and have your own restaurant. You wanted bigger things, and the training you said you needed couldn't be had in Legacy. You said I was holding you back and ruining your life." He moved his hands up, propping them on the rim of his tooled leather belt. "You hated it here, remember? But I'd hoped you'd miss me enough to come home someday. All I ever wanted was for you to love me and the ranch and have dreams about us."

Mia took a step back, lowering her gaze to the floor. She nodded before raising resolute eyes to him.

"I had those dreams, too, Jace, but you turned them loose, just like you did me. You gave me no choice but to go chase them."

By afternoon, insisting that Mia walk alongside to steady her, Josie used her crutches to get from the bedroom to the living room, situating herself in the recliner.

Mia turned the television to her mother's nightly game show and handed her the remote control.

"I'll be in the kitchen making dinner. Do you need anything else?"

"A glass of sweet tea would hit the spot." Josie glanced up at her daughter. "If you're not too busy for me."

Her mother's tone wasn't sweet and understanding —it was contentious. "I'm not too busy," Mia said.

After taking the glass of tea to her mother, Mia returned to the kitchen, already missing the music she'd been able to listen to on the country music radio station yesterday. At Josie's next appointment, she needed to remember to ask the doctor to check her mother's hearing. The TV blared no matter which room she was in.

Buying boxed, no-bake lasagna noodles went against every cooking rule she'd ever been taught, but Mia had none of her kitchen appliances, tools, or accessories. And the truth of it was, this kitchen wasn't even equipped with a stock pot, let alone a rolling pin. Frankly, homemade pasta would be unappreciated anyway. Store-bought would work fine. The joy of cooking didn't exist in this house.

If she'd had the cash, Mia would have bought ripe tomatoes from the farmer's market for the pasta sauce she wanted to make, but her finances were already starting to dwindle, so instead, she opted for big cans of crushed tomatoes, generic, from the grocery store. She'd also purchased fresh garlic, carrots, onions, and parsley, plus ground beef and sweet Italian sausage, so the only thing the meat sauce would be missing was the almost irreplaceable taste of fresh, garden-grown tomatoes.

One day, she wanted a garden of her own with tomatoes, herbs, squash, cucumbers, a variety of peppers, and mesclun greens. If the world knew how good homegrown lettuce truly was, they might never buy it from a store again.

Mia took a baking dish out of the cabinet for tonight's lasagna but then also readied three more aluminum pans for extra meals for the freezer, setting them aside.

When the cooking pot was full of her homemade pasta sauce, she turned the burner down to a simmer and then went back into the living room, sitting on the loveseat across the small room from her mother.

"Mom, we need to talk. Can you mute the TV for a few minutes?"

"What is it, Mia?" She pointed to the television. "They're almost to the bonus round."

"We need to talk about money."

Josie turned off the television. "What about money?"

"Well, first, and most importantly, we don't have any. Unless you have a savings account that I don't know about."

"I thought you had lots of money." Josie struggled to straighten herself in the chair. "You've been working for five years, Mia."

"And paying for culinary school, the townhouse, a car, monthly bills...I have bills just like you, and culinary school isn't free, you know? I've been barely scraping by."

"What about that New York job?"

"It was an apprenticeship, Mom. It only paid a little." It would be harsh, but she needed to say it anyway. "And I had to give up that opportunity to stay here and help you. The program won't open again for another six months."

"So, you don't have any money?"

Her mother stared at Mia in wait of an answer.

Somewhere, deep in her foolish heart, she had hoped her mother would understand the sacrifice she had made. But Josie Ellis didn't operate that way. Nothing had changed.

For a moment—while staring back at Josie in some kind of mother-daughter standoff—Mia thought about her father. Not that she'd ever known him. All Josie had ever told her was that he was a handsome brown-haired cowboy with blue eyes—a one-night stand. Josie had never known whether his name was Merle or maybe it was Merle Haggard singing on the radio. It didn't really matter because, within the hour, Josie was pregnant, and he was gone.

"The little money I have is earmarked for New York. It's in savings, and I don't have any other income right now. Do you have another check coming from Gloria's Crafts?"

"Only about three days' worth." Josie pointed at her. "You should go pick that up from Gloria. I called her the day after my accident, you know?"

"No, I didn't know. What did she say?"

"She said I needed to let her know when I was coming back, and if I wasn't coming back, I needed to tell her so she could hire somebody else. I said I was coming back. What did she think? That I was going to retire at forty-five? She knows I need the money."

Mia stood. "Okay then. I'll go see Gloria tomorrow." She started for the kitchen. "And then I'll figure out a way to make money until you can go back to work."

CHAPTER 9

Mia prepped the pans with no-bake noodles, spread her ricotta cheese mixture over them, and then spooned the meat sauce on top of the mixture. She layered it all again, ending by sprinkling mozzarella and Parmigiano-Reggiano cheeses over the top.

Just like she'd done with the casseroles the day before, she slid one into the oven for tonight's dinner, sealed the remaining three, and put them into the freezer.

The lasagna needed an hour in the oven and twenty minutes after to cool. Too long to sit watching a blaring TV show that she had no interest in, but there was little else left to do. She'd already organized and cleaned the entire kitchen, washing everything, including the spice bottles and cans in the pantry. She had cleaned the refrigerator, microwave, and toaster, defrosted the small chest-type freezer, and she'd scrubbed the brown fleur-de-lis vinyl flooring until the thirty-year-old linoleum had a bleached-out ash-gray and tan design, still yellowed in spots. She'd even cleaned the window above the sink and hand-washed its ruffled, butter-colored sheers.

All she could do now was wait for the oven timer to signal her.

Mia pulled the weekly issue of the *Blue Topaz Times* out from under a stack of unopened bills and took it to the kitchen table with her. She sat and opened it to the classifieds. Legacy had never had a newspaper of its own, or a radio or television station for that matter, so the nearby town of Topaz was their closest link to the available jobs and news happening in the rest of the county.

It had been a while since she'd had to look for employment, and her stomach knotted at the thought.

The help wanted section was just one column long, and only a few listings were for jobs in Legacy: dog groomer, housecleaner, RV mechanic, part-time evening dishwasher, summer school bus driver, custodian, registered nurse for youth camp, and childcare worker. There was not a single work-from-home job where she could make an income while caring for her mother. Worse yet, the only positions she was qualified for were as a dishwasher or housecleaner. How sad was that? She had dual AA degrees in economics and marketing and an AAS degree in culinary arts, yet she wasn't qualified for any of the jobs advertised in the newspaper. Further proof that she didn't belong in Legacy.

Her best option was the part-time evening dishwasher position. Maybe the hours would allow her to work while her mother slept; otherwise, who would fix her mother's meals, clean her house, shop for her, and take her back and forth to medical appointments?

She would call tomorrow and find out who it was that was hiring.

It was midnight, and Jace was still working in his office while Cowboy slept beside his desk. He'd run the numbers over and over again, detailed the specifics of the proposal, only setting the marketing plan aside.

Tiredness set in, giving a blur to his eyesight, telling him to shut the problem down for the night.

"Come on, Cowboy. Let's take a walk outside before heading to bed."

Jace followed the Aussie halfway to the barn before he stopped to look up into the bright moonlit sky. Crickets and cicadas filled the otherwise quiet night, reminding him summer was already here, whether or not the calendar officially agreed.

He glanced at the tin-roofed barn. Evenings, when his mind was worn out from thinking of ways to save the ranch, were when his thoughts drifted the most. Even though the ranch had sold its last milk cow half a decade ago, the smell of Grandma's best Holstein was still right here, just as strong a memory as was the chill of cold air on an early January morning. He could almost feel the rope-rough callouses of his grandmother's hands on his, showing him how to milk. Those memories—the moments from when he was young and learning things that seemed so big at the time—imprinted the importance of this ranch on him. Not just to the family, but to a way of life that he couldn't let die.

Hannah Farr had always been his greatest teacher and biggest ally. Although she couldn't ride the range or manage the ranch anymore, he suspected that on her good days, when memories resurfaced, she still rode Hardtack in her thoughts, herded cattle, and strung wire when needed. The slip of her cognitive abilities was something he never imagined he'd see. Her memory, and problems with her thinking and judgment, were affecting her daily life. A decline into dementia had been mentioned, but she wasn't there yet, and might never be. Some days she seemed strong as ever. He worried, though, whether he was wrong about keeping their financial troubles secret. She was still the family matriarch, and in her lucid moments, she was perceptive—he knew by her eyes that she understood more than she revealed.

"Cowboy! Let's go," he called to the red Aussie who was dutifully trotting the fence line between the yard and the pasture, waiting for Jace to give up the night.

His six o'clock alarm alerted him to a slowly rising sun, its light weaving through the limbs of the old oaks outside and then peeking through his windows.

Jace rose. A few hours of sleep had been better than none. He reached for the bedside light and clicked it on, helping daylight to awaken his spirit. Swinging into a sitting position on the edge of the bed, his bare feet landed on the hardwood floor. As his eyes adjusted, his gaze dropped to a swath of dust topping the base-boards. With intent, he sent a glance around the room, spotting more dust on the window ledges, curtain tops, photo frames, and on the black screen of his mounted television. Daylight's rising also exposed a haze on the windows, which had once been clear. He hadn't even noticed the changes in the upkeep of the house. He'd taken his grandmother's daily cleaning chores for granted these last few years.

He dressed and then left the house through the

double glass doors in his bedroom, just as he did every morning.

At the barn, he saddled Ghost, filled the gallon water bucket outside for Cowboy, and then put a cup of dry food into a stainless steel dish and set it down.

"Stay," Jace told the dog. "And when Grandma comes out to feed you this morning, don't rat me out and tell her that you already ate, okay?"

Lately, his morning check of the herd with Travis resulted in long horseback discussions of cattle and grain prices. When the same talk started again, Jace pointed back over his shoulder.

"Let's get the south pasture ready today. I want those summer-born calves on irrigated pastureland." He glanced at his foreman, who nodded without question. "I'm hoping we might be changing things up a bit soon. We might want to get a head start." He gave a subtle shift in the saddle. "I've got some paperwork that needs finishing up this morning, and then I want to make a stop in town."

"Town, huh?" Travis smiled at him with a raised brow like a man in the know. "I heard your girl's back."

Jace landed him a hard glare. "I don't have a girl, Trav. You know that."

Travis lowered his head but didn't back down. "Talk has it that the girl you were head over heels about in high school came back home." He focused on Jace. "You know, if you start putting a family together now, you could have some dedicated hands in fifteen years, and then maybe I could retire and travel with Ameree."

"And then the legacy in Legacy can live on, is that it?"

"Well, something like that, yeah."

Jace chuckled even though he'd meant to stay serious. "Cowboys never retire, but I'll tell you the truth, Trav, if I ever wanted to marry anyone, it would have been Mia, but she tossed me out years ago. Probably with good reason."

Travis turned toward the herd. "That doesn't mean it's over."

"Yeah," Jace reined Ghost toward home. "I think that's exactly what it means."

MIA PARKED IN THE LOT FOR GLORIA'S CRAFTS AND sat for a minute, staring at the old strip mall. She'd avoided the place like the plague in high school, even though the Dairy Queen was on the corner.

Josie Ellis had been a different kind of mom. Other mothers wore better clothes, had their hair styled and their fingernails manicured, and they never shamed their daughters, at least not in public. But at first sight of Mia having fun with her friends, Josie would shove open the door of the craft shop, march across the parking lot in a blouse and skirt that never matched, wearing iridescent knee-high socks and clunky "stand on your feet all day" shoes and chastise Mia for doing something she found offensive. Automatically, Mia shook those memories from her head.

When the lights came on inside the store, Mia exited her car and headed for the door. At her entrance, the overhead bell tinkled.

"Coming!" Gloria was tying on her merchant apron as she walked toward the front of the store, but when recognition hit her, she stopped. "Mia, you're back? Josie didn't mention it."

"Hi, Gloria," Mia said, her fingers curling in worry.

"I'd like to talk to you about Mom and her accident if you have a few minutes."

"All right," Gloria said. "Come on back to the office with me. I have a paycheck for Josie anyway."

That was a good sign. At least she wouldn't have to come right out and ask for it.

The office was cluttered with stacks of mail and opened invoices, all haphazardly piled together on one side of the desk, and on the floor were opened boxes filled with merchandise.

One metal chair with a black plastic seat and back set opposite Gloria's desk chair. When she sat, so did Mia.

Gloria handed her a sealed envelope. "It's just three days' pay."

"Thank you." Mia slid it into her leather bag. "It all helps right now. Do you know if Mom has any sick days coming or whether her insurance includes anything like disability pay?"

"Josie uses every sick day whether she's sick or not. She doesn't have any left. But every one of my employees has short-term disability insurance."

Mia leaned in. "Can you help us get that?"

"Yeah, I can help. But it takes thirty days and only lasts for a few months, you know? It's not full pay either."

"Do you know how much it is?"

"Sixty-six percent of her regular earnings."

Mia leaned back, expelling a relieved sigh. "That will help a lot."

Gloria had a hard-set stare. "If she's going to be gone long, I'll have to hire someone."

"Mom wants her job back. She needs to work."

With a shrug, Gloria said, "I can't legally fire her

anyway." At the sound of a customer, she stood. "Not that I'd want to. She's a good worker, and she's honest. She's been here longer than anyone else." She scanned Mia. "You want the job while she's out?"

When Mia hesitated too long, Gloria started out of the office, calling "Coming!" to the unseen customer.

Mia followed her. "I would," she said, even though she would never work where her mother worked. "But I need a night job or something I can do from home so that I can be there during the day to take care of Mom. For a few months anyway," she clarified, "then I'm leaving for New York."

Gloria turned. "New York? Why in the world would you go to New York?"

"I'm studying to be a chef." It sounded like an apology.

"Yeah, I know about the cooking thing, but New York? I didn't know about that." When Gloria saw that the customer was actually an early arriving employee, she waved a hand. "Mornin' Peggy. Open the registers, will you?" She turned back to Mia. "Well, if you change your mind, let me know right away. I'll have to put an ad in the paper today."

At home, Mia handed the paycheck to her mother, who tore open the envelope, studied the check, and then tossed it onto the quilt covering her legs.

"That won't even pay the light bill," Josie said. "Did you ask for my Christmas bonus?"

"Mom, it's June. I couldn't ask for your Christmas bonus."

"Why not?" Josie tossed the quilt back. "Get me my crutches, will you?"

Mia reached for the crutches, leaning them against the bed, then helped her mother to stand.

After glaring at her daughter, Josie started for the bathroom—her one usable leg still making her wince with every step from the knee injury. "You've got to get more guts, Mia. Learn to ask for what you want."

When the bathroom door closed, Mia sat down on the bed, calling out, "You have short-term disability insurance." Maybe some good news would break the tension. "Gloria will help us with that, but there's a thirty-day waiting period."

From the bathroom, Josie called back, "That's not a full check, Mia. You need to get a job."

Mia stood. "I know, Mom." She made her mother's bed. "I'll make some calls. I need to buy more groceries, though. I didn't know I'd be staying so long. Do you need anything from the store?"

"Refried beans and corn chips!" Josie shouted back. "Get two cans."

Mia walked to the living room, squinting at the bright morning sunlight blazing through the windows. This was her life. Hands clenched into fists, a stomach in knots, and a headache banded around her skull.

Where had her New York dreams gone?

CHAPTER 10

Cobb's Feed and Seed hadn't changed one iota in five years. The tan metal building set back off the main road just north of town. It had a front porch that ran the width of the building, which held shelving units filled with garden plants, house plants, and hanging baskets, most flowering. The sunny side was stocked with an array of colorful metal yard art and various wind chimes, barely moving in the morning breeze.

Mia wandered outside among the greenery, welcoming the coolness that emanated from the plants. She checked the price tags on five-gallon pots of patio tomatoes but walked on when she saw that they were simply not affordable for her right now. She stopped again when she found shelves crowded with four-inch pots of herbs. The plants were strong and healthy. She picked up one each of oregano, basil, and parsley and carried them inside to the cash register.

The owner stood head down, busy behind the counter.

"Craig," Mia said to him. "It's good to see you." She set down the three little pots.

At the sight of her, Craig opened his arms wide, grinning, and started around the counter. "Come over here and give me a hug, girl!"

"I just had to come by and see you," Mia said in their embrace. When the hug ended, she asked, "How's Mary?"

"Well," Craig said, his focus falling to the floor. "Don't ever let anyone tell you that this getting older stuff is easy because it's for the birds." He looked up at Mia. "But Mary is doing okay. How's your mom after the accident?"

"She's using crutches. That's a good thing," Mia said. "But we still need the wheelchair sometimes."

In his fifties, Craig was still fully fit, physically and mentally. Emotionally, Mia sensed a struggle in the man who had often been a strong male influence in a distant sort of way.

Mia reached out and touched his arm. "Jace told me that after you put in a full day's work here at the store, you still go home and cook dinner for you and Mary."

"Yeah," he said with a nod. "But sometimes I'll pick food up from the diner or just open a can of soup. Mary's not picky."

"I'm a pretty good cook now, you know?" Her affection came with a smile. "I've been putting make-ahead dinners in the freezer for Mom. King Ranch casseroles and lasagna, but I'm running out of freezer room. I'd love to bring one for you and Mary to try."

Craig smiled. "Mary would like that." He put his arm around Mia and patted her on the shoulder. "Sure is good to have you back."

At the supermarket, Mia picked up another five aluminum pans with freezer lids, more salad items, and the ingredients she needed to make Texas Beef Pie. She shopped for the other things on her list, too, but then on the spur of the moment, she put a bouquet of daisies into her cart, a completely unnecessary item that she knew was a waste of hard-earned money. She loved flowers, and with as much time as she was spending in the kitchen lately, a floral arrangement felt like a worthwhile luxury.

When she got home, Josie was in the recliner, watching television in the living room.

"Did you remember the corn chips?" her mother called without turning to see Mia.

"Yes, I remembered the corn chips and the refried beans." Mia carried the grocery bags into the kitchen and set them on the brown Formica countertop.

"Can you just bring me that bag of chips?" Josie shouted over the blaring television.

Mia walked into the living room, took the remote, and lowered the volume. "We need to get your hearing checked, Mom. The TV is way too loud."

"There's nothing wrong with my hearing. I just like the movie theater experience. What's wrong with that?" She leaned and reached out her hand. "Give me the remote."

"No," Mia said, holding it behind her back. "If there's nothing wrong with your hearing, then you need to retrain your brain to listen." She leaned closer. "The volume is making me lose my mind."

Josie eased back. "Okay, Mia," she said. "You should just relax. You're too tense. Will you bring me the corn chips?"

Mia reached and gently pressed her fingers into the

ankle on her mother's right leg. "It's still puffy. Cruz said he thinks you're eating too much salt, and it's causing your ankles to swell. That might be why the cast on your left leg and ankle feels too tight." She focused a look on her mother. "I'm going to make you a salad for lunch, and then I'll make us a Texas Beef Pie for dinner."

"A salad!" Josie nearly shrieked. "I don't want a salad for lunch. And can't you make me chicken fried steak tonight? It's still one of my favorites."

Mia muted the television entirely and then knelt beside the recliner, her hand cradling her mother's hand. "Mom, I might have to work in the evenings, so I might not be here to make your dinner every night. You need good, healthy meals to help you heal and get well. That means you can't eat refried beans and corn chips every day. I've made freezer meals, so all you'll need to do is put a pan in the oven and cook it. I'll clean up whenever I get home. When I make the beef pie tonight, I'll be able to make another two in the freezer. I can make chicken fried steak tomorrow night for you, okay?"

Unexpectedly, Josie reached out and cupped Mia's chin in her hand and then smiled.

"You're a good girl, Mia. I mean it. I know sometimes I don't sound like I appreciate you, but I do." Then she held out her hand. "Now give me the remote, and then you go on and make us a salad for lunch, and I'll eat it."

Mia stood, handed her the remote control, and when Josie turned and pointed it at the TV, unmuting the sound, she went to the kitchen and put the groceries away.

Afterward, Mia opened the classifieds again and

reread the job listings, settling on the part-time dish-washer position. She pulled her cell phone out of her purse and dialed the number.

The deep voice of a man answered. "Boomer's Bar and Grill."

She had no recollection of the place or the voice. "Hi, I'm calling about the dishwasher job you're advertising."

"Yeah," the man said, a lighter lilt to his voice. "Who's this?"

Nerves ran through her. "My name is Mia Ellis. Are you still hiring?" A dishwasher with a degree in the culinary arts—the very thought of it pushed her eyes closed while she waited for his answer.

"Yeah," he said again. "You want to come out so we can talk about it?"

"An interview today?"

"I needed somebody yesterday."

Ranch Road North seemed too rural a place for a bar and grill, but maybe she would go unnoticed there, bringing in a paycheck until this nightmare was over.

In the five years since she'd been gone, exotic animal ranches had popped up along the road, each sporting high fences and gated entrances. Inside the perimeter fencing were beautiful white-faced gemsbok, tan in color with a blackish stripe from ear to chin, and blackbucks with their twisted spiral horns. The rolling terrain was a mix of oak and brush ridges that gave way to flatlands filled with native grasses. At the higher elevation, off in the distance, she spotted a new blue-roofed building that surely had to be a hunting lodge. It seemed that even the rural road had been improved since she last drove it.

Mia pulled into the pothole-ridden parking lot of

what she'd once known as Vista View Café, now called
Boomer's Bar and Grill. She had forgotten all about the
old café that had been a favorite diner for ranchers and
truckers hauling hay or cattle, as well as a scenic stop
for tourists searching for an overlook for a view of the
savanna-like terrain below. She parked, grabbed her
leather bag off the seat, and got out of her Prius.

She pulled open one of the front double doors and
stepped into the quiet, air-conditioned building, its
gray-painted concrete floor reflecting the late morning
rays of the sun.

In the middle of the dining area was a pool table, set
and racked, and along the back wall were arcade
machines, most equipped with mounted weapons for
big game hunting. No more than a dozen tables were
scattered about the room in no particular order. The
scent of freshly brewed coffee battled the odor of
bleach.

Mia stepped up to the counter, standing below a
wooden sign that read, *No Whining.*

"Hello?" she called.

From an adjacent doorway at the end of the long,
saloon-type bar came a fiftyish man, redheaded, tall,
burly, and full of belly, wearing a white canvas bib
apron. He was wiping his hands dry on a bar towel.

As he walked toward her, he asked, "You Mia?"

"Yes." She reached for a handshake. "Are you
Boomer?"

He laughed. "Naw. Boomer's my dog. I'm Steve.
The owner. We talked on the phone."

After answering his four or five questions, Steve
said, "Come on. Let me show you around."

He hadn't asked for a résumé or references, so Mia

decided it wasn't important to tell him she was a professional chef. She followed him as he led her to the triple sinks and a single workstation, explaining that her job included bussing the tables, but he explained that most of the patrons came in for beer or spirits rather than food. Each shift was five hours, four nights a week, Thursday, Friday, Saturday, and Sunday. They settled on Sunday as her first night, although he'd been disappointed that tonight or tomorrow hadn't been an option.

Mia walked out holding a business card for Boomer's Bar and Grill, Steve Miller, owner, with his personal cell phone number handwritten on the back, in case she changed her mind after hours.

ALTHOUGH IT STILL LACKED A MARKETING PLAN, JACE printed a copy of his proposal and drove to Mia's house. She would tell him where he missed the mark and how to fix it. Everything needed to be perfect. He wasn't going to get another chance from Cattlemen's Bank.

Standing at her door, knocking like he'd done a thousand times as a teenager, made him feel like he was a kid asking for a date. He hoped Mia didn't still see him that way.

When the door pulled open, Jace removed his Stetson without taking his eyes off Mia. The woman had no idea that even the sun sought out her radiance. "You look great," was all he could say.

She waved him inside. "I just came from a job interview." She closed the door behind him. "What are you doing here?"

From the recliner, Josie waved her arm. "It's just like old times!" she said. "Come give me a hug, Jace."

Jace went to Josie and leaned down for a hug. "How are you today, Josie? It's good to see you up and out of that bed."

"I'm getting better, I think." She twisted in the chair to see Mia. "Don't you think I'm getting better?"

"Yes," Mia answered. "You're doing very well on your crutches." Then to Jace, Mia said, "Let's go in the kitchen."

Jace hung his hat on the coat rack as they passed, and then he pulled out a chair for Mia at the table.

"So, you applied for a job? Where at?" he asked her.

"Boomer's Bar and Grill on Ranch Road." She waited.

"You cooking there?"

Mia shook her head. "Washing dishes."

Jace laid his papers on the table. His hands went to his hips. "Washing dishes?"

"It's just part-time. Thursday, Friday, and weekends. Mom's disability won't start for thirty days, so I'm using my savings to buy food and pay the utilities right now. At least she has the house paid off. Otherwise, we'd be in a worse bind."

"Maybe you could work for Trace at the Armadillo, cooking with Bobby."

"No." Mia shook her head again. "Everyone in town goes there. They'd all know that I failed if they saw me cooking at the diner."

"Mia," Jace said, moving closer. "You haven't failed. It's just a delay, and that's not your fault."

"I know," she said quietly. "But I still *feel* like a failure. At least Boomer's is sort of out of town, and his customers are mostly truckers and hunters from those exotic game ranches that popped up since I left. I won't constantly need to explain myself. None of those people know me, so they don't expect anything from me."

"You don't have to hide from anyone, Mia. Everyone is glad you're back, even if it is just for a few months. Especially me."

Mia redirected her focus to the table. In a change of subject, she pointed. "Your proposal for the bank?"

"Yeah." Jace picked up the papers and then handed them to her. "Do you think you can take a look at what I've got and tell me what I'm missing?" When she sat, he did too, his hands folded together on the tabletop. "I think it's all I need, except for a marketing plan. I don't even know how to write up one of those."

In silence, Mia read the three pages. When she finished, she straightened the papers, but instead of handing them back, she laid them out on the table, turning them so they faced Jace.

"This is all really good, but the formatting is off. It doesn't have a professional look."

"Does that matter?" he asked.

"Yes. But I think I can fix that for you. Can you email this to me?"

"Sure." Jace stood, pulled his cell phone out of his pocket, and then sat again. "What's your email address?"

Mia laughed. "No wonder I never got any emails from you."

He glanced up at her. "You were waiting for me to email you?"

"Email. Call. Write a letter. Drive down to Houston…"

Jace sat back in his chair, looking into the beautiful

blue-gray askance in her eyes. "Man, I'm sorry, Mia. I swear, I thought you never wanted to see me or hear from me again."

Mia pulled the papers back from him, and at the top, she wrote her email address and then slid them back across the table. "Send it to me and let me work on it. I'll also write up a basic marketing plan, and if you like it, I'll help you add it to the proposal."

"Do you have time for that?"

"I don't start work until Sunday night, and I've already got dinner in the oven for tonight. I promised Mom chicken fried steak tomorrow, so that will be a quick meal." She looked at Jace. "Want to come for dinner tomorrow?"

"Yes," he answered without hesitating.

"Okay." Mia stood. "Six o'clock." She walked to the small chest-type freezer in the laundry room next to the kitchen and opened it. "While I'm working on your proposal, can you deliver a casserole to Craig for me? It's almost five o'clock. He should be able to take it right home and put it in the oven."

"Sure." Jace got up and walked to the freezer, looking in. At the sight of almost a dozen perfectly stacked pans, he asked, "Can I buy another one, too?"

"Are you serious?" Mia asked.

"Yeah," Jace said. "The casserole you sent home with me the other night is the only real food Grandma has eaten all week."

Mia's brows arched in interest. "Does Texas Beef Pie sound okay? I just made them, so they're not frozen yet."

"Grandma loves beef pie." He glanced at Mia. "Does it have that same crust you used to make?" He had loved her pies.

"Better." Mia smiled.

Jace tossed a twenty-dollar bill on the table and said, "Sold." He took the casserole from her offering hands. "I feel like we have our own personal chef."

Though she tried to hide it, the hint of a smile came. Mia wrote cooking instructions on the lids of the aluminum pans—one for Jace and one for Craig—and then she signed each pan,

Tastefully Texas, Mia.

CHAPTER 11

fter their Texas Beef Pie, which Hannah had eaten well, Jace went to his office to email the proposal to Mia. He attached the three-page document but then sat staring at the blank screen, the cursor blinking, for way too long. It was just a bank proposal. The same one he had already shown to her earlier in the day. All he had to do was write "thanks" and hit send, but he didn't.

Mia,

How did things between us go so wrong? It was always you and me together through everything, remember? Yesterday, when I said I didn't mean "I love you" the way it sounded, I lied.

Jace

He hit send, logged out on the computer, and walked the house until he found Hannah outside in her favorite rocking chair on the front porch with Cowboy at her feet.

"Grandma, you seem to be feeling pretty good tonight. Are you?" Jace seated himself in the rocker next to hers, glancing to see if she was paying attention.

She reached across the hardwood arm of the chair and took hold of his hand. Gently, she gave it a loving squeeze. "I'm perfectly fine, Jace. I was just thinking about how much time you've been spending in town lately. Is it because of a girl?"

Jace laughed and used his other hand to pat hers. "Nothing gets by you, does it, Grandma?"

Hannah smiled, shifting her attention to the ribbons of pink and orange that swept across the horizon as the setting sun lowered. "Well, I'm not as sharp as I used to be, but I try." With a hold still on his hand, she glanced back at him. In a kind but understated tone, she asked, "Do you want to tell me what it is that you're hiding from me?"

"Hiding from you?" Jace tried to laugh, but it only came out as half a puff.

"You've been up late every night for weeks, then awake at dawn, riding Ghost toward the west pasture. And you've been in town an awful lot. I've been hoping it's because you've been spending time with a young lady, but burning the midnight oil in your office tells me it has more to do with the ranch than it does with a woman."

He leaned forward in the rocker, the weight of his burdens sending his hands together in a clasp, his elbows resting on spread knees.

"I didn't want to worry you," he admitted to his grandmother. "And I wanted to solve the problem on my own."

Hannah leaned forward, too, searching for his earthy-brown eyes. "Look at me, Jace." When he glanced her way, she said, "No one on this ranch has ever had to solve a problem on their own. Now, you need to tell me what is it that has you so worried."

Jace sat back, inhaling a breath so deep it could have filled the whole Gulf of Mexico.

"We're losing money ranching the old way. It's not working for us in today's world."

Hannah reached for his forearm and gave it a gentle touch. "Money is the enemy, Jace. Don't ever forget that. It's the thing that will constantly fight you for this land." Hannah sat back, pushing her chair into a gentle rock. "But things *are* different. You're right about that. This is your ranch now, Grandson. You can make changes and do the things you think need doing, but don't ever forget that this land isn't just a way to make a living today. It's every tomorrow you'll ever know. You've got to hold onto it no matter the sacrifices so that the future generations will never lose their way in this world."

The clarity of her mental state at this moment gave him hope. She was lucid. Supportive. Clear thinking. He could show her the draft of his proposal to the bank. Lay it out on the table for her and listen to her thoughts and ideas. Up until a year ago, she'd been as sharp as a tack. It was good to see the rebound.

Jace stood, taking in the horizon to settle his thoughts before turning to her. "I've got a rough plan sketched out, Grandma. Would you mind taking a look at it for me?"

Hannah's gaze was on the sunset. She rocked, her focus on the distant Blue Mountains. "What kind of sketch do you have?"

"It's an idea. I want to take the plan to Don Goss at

the bank and see if I can get a loan to take this ranch in a new direction. I'd sure like to have your approval."

Her eyes were blank as she studied him, silent.

"You want to go in and look at it?" he asked her.

"Look at what?"

"The rough draft, Grandma." When her brows tensed to focus her eyes on him, Jace said, "For a new plan for the ranch."

Hannah stood. "Remind me, what was it we were talking about again?"

Her clarity hadn't lasted long.

Jace put his arm around her. "Come on, Grandma. Let's get you to bed for the night."

Cowboy followed them through the house and lay down outside Hannah's closed door. When Jace called him, his ears perked, but he didn't budge.

"Okay, Cowboy," he relented. "I know. It's your job to watch over Grandma. You just come and get me if you need me."

Then Jace went to his office, turned on the desk light, and pulled out the proposal for another look.

IN THE PRIVACY OF HER CHILDHOOD BEDROOM, MIA sat at the desk, reading and rereading the lines in the email from Jace. The man who had broken her heart into a million tiny pieces and cast them to the wind now had things to say. She had needed his words five years ago, not now.

She would never deny that Jace was a good man. Perhaps the best she'd ever known, but his life was on the Texas ranch that had stolen him from her, and hers was in New York.

Circumstances hadn't changed.

Mia downloaded the bank proposal and set to work creating a professional format for the document. Jace had so many things right—good, valid ideas for a pasture-to-plate operation. A new direction for the ranch that she felt sure would work.

The last page of the proposal was the marketing plan she'd created, which included social media, a website with ordering capabilities, a plan for local restaurants, organizations, and event organizers, but most importantly, it included a campaign to educate individual buyers that they had a choice between buying beef from a grocery store or mail order meat purveyor, or buying local from the Farr Reaches Ranch.

When she was finished, Mia sat back and tried to see the proposal as a bank in business would see it, flaws and all, but she couldn't spot any uncorrected errors. The format was almost elegant, which she hoped would prove to the bank that Jace was taking a serious, professional stance on this new venture, and the plan was impressive. She saved the proposal on her laptop and then opened a new document titled *Things to Do*. Finding a website designer was number one on the list.

Mia attached both documents to a new email, and by midnight, she emailed them to him.

JACE RODE GHOST TOWARD THE SOUTH PASTURE with the morning sun on the rise.

Being a conservationist was second nature to him. His grandfather, John, had taught him to identify plants and grasses on the open range whenever they would ride out to check cattle or fix fences together. He hadn't known it then, but he was learning to manage the rangeland by letting the height and condition of each species of grass tell him when to rotate his cattle out of one pasture or rest a field for longer than usual. To manage his range, he had to listen to the land.

The south pasture was the only one with side-roll irrigation—his father's idea, which he had intended to carry through to another pasture, but he had died before implementing the next phase of the plan.

When Jace arrived, Travis had their few remaining ranch hands checking the system.

"Hey, Trav, looks good."

Travis turned to him in the saddle. "I'd rather be branding today. We've got a head count coming up, and I don't want to be moving cattle while we do it."

"I know. I hate to irrigate at all, but this drought is killin' us." He motioned with a side nod toward the pasture. "We raise cattle but can't do it without grass."

"Yeah, sometimes I feel more like a grass manager than a cattle manager."

Jace grinned at Travis and his wit. "True enough."

It was almost noon before Jace returned to the house. Hannah was outside tending to her hummingbird feeders when he approached.

"Mornin', Grandma," he called to her. When Cowboy bounced against him, he knelt and scratched behind the dog's ears. With his eyes steady on the Aussie, he said to his grandmother, "I hope I've got some work to do in my office. I'm waiting for an email." Jace stood and walked closer. "Do you want me to fix lunch for us?"

"Oh, Jace, I'm not hungry." But then she stopped

working on the feeders and turned to him. "Was it last night that we had that beef pie?"

"Yes, it was. And you cleaned your plate." He smiled.

"Do we have leftovers?"

"Half a pie. Want me to put it in the oven and warm it up?"

Hannah slowly nodded. "Yes. Will you do that?"

Glad to see her hungry, he said, "I'll do it right now."

After Jace put the leftovers in the oven and set the timer, he headed for his office, anxious to see if Mia had emailed. Spotting her name on a new message pushed him into the seat of his chair. He clicked open on the email to find two attached documents.

He checked again. No message accompanied the attachments.

It was his fault that he'd lost her five years ago, and it was his fault that she was slipping away again. But just like before, it was either Mia or the ranch, and he couldn't walk away from the Farr Reaches. It was in his soul and in his blood. It was his heritage. He didn't exist without the land beneath his feet, yet he wasn't really alive without Mia.

Jace printed out the documents, setting the proposal aside. He scanned the *Things to Do* list on the second attachment. *Build a website*. Emma Hayes's daughter, Melody, had designed a website for her mother's insurance agency recently. Maybe she would be willing to create one for him, too. He took out his phone and dialed the insurance office.

"Hi Emma, this is Jace Farr," he said when she answered. "I was wondering if Melody might be interested in designing a webpage for me."

Melody Hayes had been four years behind Jace in school. She'd left for college right after her senior graduation, so he'd never known her well, but he recalled she was a sweet and polite kid who'd had a strong single mom raise her.

By two o'clock, a Race Red Mustang Fastback drove slow down the long driveway, dust barely roiling. It stopped directly behind his truck. From the porch, he watched a young woman with long, dark golden-brown hair and blue tortoise glasses step out of the car. She looked little like the girl he remembered.

Dressed in indigo jeans and a turquoise ruffle-shoulder top, her long strides brought her to Jace, her reach clasping his offered hand.

"Jace?" she asked. Then without waiting, she said, "My God, you look just the same, except more handsome than I remember."

Her words brought a smile. "You've grown up," he said. "A lot." His gaze dropped to her white leather boots with turquoise and coral embroidery, jeans tucked inside, and drew upward to her patient smile and waiting brown eyes. "You're not that little kid I remember anymore."

"Nope. Haven't been for a while now."

Jace invited Melody inside, leading the way to his office. He motioned her to a chair on the opposite side of his desk, and then he sat after she did.

Melody glanced around the room, stopping her inspection when she caught sight of the red Aussie who stood in the doorway, docked tail wagging. She scooted off the seat of the chair onto the wood floor into a kneel, calling, "Hey boy!"

Cowboy sauntered toward her, his butt wagging more than his tail, and sat for her to pet him. Paying no attention to Jace, she said, "You're such a pretty boy." She scratched behind his ears and then ran her hands down his silky fur, head to haunches. "What's your name?"

The dog licked her face, his light panting curling into a seeming smile.

"That's Cowboy," Jace offered. "He likes you."

"I like him, too." She held the dog's face and kissed him on his forehead.

Jace stood and walked to where the denim and fleece bed was on the floor, and then he called to Cowboy. "Come here and lay down, boy. We've got work to do." When the Aussie obeyed, Jace returned to his desk, finding Melody reseated in her chair.

Jace explained his new business plan for the next hour, answered questions, and quizzed her on ordering and payment capabilities. She knew more than he expected. He ended by asking, "So, how did you learn to do all of this stuff?"

"I went to Texas State in San Marcos. I graduated a few weeks ago with a degree in digital media innovation. Now all I have to do is find a job." Melody swished a wave at Jace and his computer. "Not like this. I mean a real job. My interest is in sports media. I just wanted to come home for a while." She leaned back in her chair and crossed her lanky legs. "Now I'm glad I did."

CHAPTER 12

Mia hadn't expected Craig Cobb to set up a regular weeknight dinner order, but he had. So had Jace. So had Bette Mills, who ran the dog grooming salon at the feed store. "Whatever you're cooking for yourself and Josie is fine," they'd all said. They had insisted that Mia charge them whatever her costs were plus a solid profit.

Heavy rains drenched the drought on Sunday when Mia reported for her first day of work at Boomer's Bar and Grill. The moment she entered through the front door, all eyes turned to her—male eyes, all of them. She scanned the unfamiliar faces as she walked through the tavern to the back room, where she ran into Steve, the owner. He glanced at the clock hanging above the stainless steel three-compartment sink.

"This is a good sign," he said to her.

"What is?" Mia asked, pulling off her hooded shell jacket.

"That you showed up." He smiled. "Ten minutes early."

Mia hung her jacket on a wall hook and then glanced back at the tables filled with loud customers. "I thought you said Sunday was your slowest night. There's not an empty chair out there."

"It usually is, but this rain drove all the hunters indoors. Truckers, too. If the weatherman could ever predict the weather around here, I could be better prepared."

Steve handed Mia a white apron, which she tied around her waist.

"I've been setting the drink glasses on the drain-board for you, hoping you'd show up. I'm getting low on mugs, so if you could wash those first, it would be a big help. Oh, and when they dry, put them in the cooler for chilling, will you?"

Mia filled the sinks, the first with hot soapy water for washing, the second compartment with rinse water, and the third for sanitizing. When she had the clean glasses set to dry, she went to the dining room with an empty tray and began to clean tables, wiping them down as she went.

The dining area needed a good sweeping. Paper napkins had been crumpled and dropped, and mud was drying in clumps, caking the front entry, but there were too many dishes for her to worry about the floor.

Other than a few "Hello darlin'" greetings delivered in a fake Texas drawl, the men were mainly preoccupied with an NBA Finals game on the big-screen television.

With a large round tray full of empty, or partially empty, glasses and mugs, Mia carried it to the back room and set it down for unloading.

Across the kitchen, smoke rose from the fryer station, curling across a grease-stained ceiling. Steve stood, holding a basket full of chicken wings, shook out the oil, and then dumped them into an oversized bowl. He poured half a bottle of hot wing sauce into the bowl and then tossed the wings, coating them, before putting a dozen wings into each of six individual paper-lined serving baskets. He grabbed the tray she'd used for dirty dishes and set the baskets on it, then carried the tray into the dining area.

Mia washed, rinsed, and sanitized until the smoky smell of overcooked meat caught her nose. She turned to find a billow of dark smoke coming from the steel griddle.

Four thin, flat, charred-black burgers were left on the stainless steel surface. She hurried to the station and used the spatula to flip the patties into the trash. The odor of smoke, old grease, and burned meat permeated the back room.

Using the wood-handled spatula, Mia scraped the grill clean, pushing the old oil and meat tidbits into the waste tray, and then she went to the walk-in freezer for more meat.

When Steve returned to the back room, shouting, "The hamburgers!" they were already in serving baskets and perfect.

"There's no ticket for these," Mia handed him two plates, "so I hope they weren't supposed to be cheese-burgers."

His eyes widened. "You know how to cook?"

"Yes," Mia answered.

"Well, hell's bells! I'm working this whole place by myself tonight, except for you. You just got promoted!"

By the end of the night, Mia was washing dishes, cleaning tables, cooking meals, and serving food.

It wasn't at all what she had in mind.

~

FEELING TOTALLY OUT OF PLACE IN THIS NEW
business world he had entered, Jace walked into the
bank for his ten o'clock appointment with Don Goss,
wearing black jeans, a white long-sleeved shirt, and a
black leather braided bolo with a silver arrowhead
embedded with a black onyx stone. His good luck tie.

"Mornin', Don," Jace said as they shook hands.

The bank president pointed to the file Jace held in
his hand. "Looks like you're serious about this loan."
He motioned Jace to a seat and then took his own.

"Sure am," Jace told him, seating himself in the red
leather chair opposite the president. He opened the
folder, pulled out three printed pages paperclipped
together, and then handed them across the lacquered
desk to Don. "This is the proposal you asked for last
week. I'm happy to answer any questions."

Don Goss took the papers, slowly, methodically,
flipping through, page by page. He was silent until he
finished.

His glance lifted, settling on Jace. "This is remark-
able. No one around here is doing a pasture-to-plate
operation."

"I know it, Don, but even if there was some competition, I think the Farr Reaches is better equipped to
handle it than most. I'm young and not afraid of hard
work. You know that. And our beef is of high quality.
Most ranchers are stuck in a rut, thinking they've got to
stick with ranching the way it used to be, but I think we
can do better, and I'd like the chance to try."

The president glanced through the pages again.
"How do you plan to bring in customers in the
beginning?"

Jace opened his folder again and pulled out the page Mia created for him. He handed over the marketing plan. "This is a start. I have Emma Hayes's daughter, Melody, building a website for me with ordering capabilities. It should be ready in about a week, she said. She's already secured the name Farr Reaches Quality Beef for the website. That's what I plan to call the new business."

Don Goss read through the document, then nodded before setting the page down on the other proposal pages. "I like it, Jace. I couldn't have guessed that this is what you wanted to do with the money, but I'm impressed." He stood and reached for Jace's hand. "Let me present this to the board next week, and I'll get back to you."

For the first time in his life, Jace felt the respect his father and grandfather had once been afforded. When he walked out of the bank, his head was held higher, and his hopes were soaring.

As soon as he got into the truck, he dialed Melody with the news.

MIA HAD THE KITCHEN IN HER MOTHER'S HOME IN complete disarray, making containers of chicken enchiladas with chile verde sauce, then preparing more containers with an accompanying garden salad. She also made a cilantro dressing, dividing it between six, four-ounce portion cups, then setting two aside per salad.

When the six meals were complete, she put all the containers into the refrigerator and then made the same meal for herself and Josie in a glass baking pan. She snapped a storage lid onto the dish and slid it into the refrigerator.

"Mom," Mia called as she took the living room remote control and turned down the volume.

Josie pointed to the television. "Turn it up, Mia. It's the bonus round!"

"Mom, listen," Mia said. "I need to deliver the meals I promised. I'll be gone for at least an hour."

"What about my dinner? Don't I get to eat, too?"

"Of course, you do," Mia told her. "I'll be home in plenty of time to put our dinner in the oven and have it ready by six o'clock."

"Can you bring me the bag of corn chips before you go?"

"No," Mia told her mother. "You'll ruin your dinner, but more importantly, we need to cut down on your salt intake. Doctor's orders, remember?"

"Fine," Josie said, reaching for the remote in Mia's hand. "Go, so I can watch and see who wins the game show tonight." She held the remote, pressing the volume button until the television blared again.

Reusing plastic grocery bags, Mia stacked one pan of enchiladas and one salad container, along with two cilantro dressing containers, into each sack, then to an old camping ice chest with freezer packs, she added all three meals for delivery.

At Cobb's Feed and Seed, she carried in the two deliveries for Craig and Bette.

"Can't tell you how much I appreciate this, Mia," Craig told her. "Sure makes my life easier." He took the plastic bag and set it inside the drink cooler at the end of the front counter. "Bette's in the middle of bathing an Old English sheepdog, but she left this check for you." He handed it to her.

Mia tucked the money into her purse. "I hope you and Mary enjoy the enchiladas."

"You know we will. After all this extra cooking you did for us today, are you still willing to deliver Monday through Thursday for a while?"

"Yes, of course," Mia said. She felt good about helping Craig and his wife, and the extra money greatly benefited her dwindling finances. "I like to cook. Let me know how it tastes."

Residual clouds from the day before still hung in the late afternoon sky as Mia drove to the outskirts of town, rote memory directing her toward the farm-to-market road that would take her to the turnoff for the Farr Reaches Ranch. It'd been such a long time since she'd been there that the thought of driving the last leg —an unpaved road—sent a flutter of nerves through her.

The Armadillo Diner had a full parking lot, and it was only Monday night, but the one thing Texans never disputed loving was food, especially Tex-Mex, so she shouldn't have been surprised. Actually, she wasn't surprised until she saw the dark blue F-350 pickup emblazoned with the branding logo belonging to the Farr Reaches Ranch. She slowed her Prius, then decided to turn in.

Had Jace forgotten about the meal she had promised to deliver? She glanced at the time on her phone. She was early, not late. Maybe it wasn't Jace driving the Farr Reaches truck at all, but the ranch was too far outside of town to make the trip if he was here instead of there.

Mia parked and got out.

Speakers outside the diner shared the live music being played inside. Memories hit Mia as she strode across the parking lot toward the entrance. It wasn't just the backseat of a truck that came to mind, but it was the moment, so long ago, under the spell of a country love song, when she had realized she would never be able to live without Jace. She'd been a teenager. So had he. But she had never loved anyone more than she had loved him that night.

She tried to shake the memories, but Jace had never been easy to forget.

Mia walked through the diner like an invisible woman without anyone noticing her. She scanned the faces—some she recognized, but most she did not. She glanced at the table in the corner that still bore her name and spotted Jace. She started for him but stopped when she realized he wasn't alone at the table. The woman with him was drop-dead gorgeous, and she was leaning into him, a flirtatious grasp on his hand, just like Mia had done so long ago. She knew the feeling, and in that instant, it came back to her two-fold.

Maybe it was an inkling, but at that moment, Jace looked up. When he saw Mia, he stood.

Jace had every right to be there with a woman, Mia knew. Even a beautiful young woman who hadn't yet realized his focus was not on her.

Just days ago, his words had seemed so sincere. So had the truths they'd shared. The kisses, too, so unexpected.

Before her daze was broken, Jace was at her side.

"Mia," he said. "I was going to call you tonight."

"It's okay," Mia muttered. An all-too-familiar shattering shook her. *She had no claim on him! Hadn't had for over five years.* Composed, she said, "I have the meal you ordered. For Hannah. You and Hannah, I mean." She turned. "It's in the car."

Mia left the diner and headed for her Sea Glass Pearl Prius with Jace in tow.

"Mia, the girl I'm with is Melody Hayes. I hired her to build the website you suggested."

But Mia kept walking without comment. At the car, she unlocked the doors and then reached into the ice chest on the back seat, taking out the grocery bag with the ordered meal inside. Feeling inadequate and out of place, she handed it to Jace.

In further defense of himself, he said, "She's just explaining how the website works."

Mia felt the glare rise in her eyes, and she hated it, but the flame was already lit. "And she's doing it over margaritas and beer while holding your hand?"

"Yes," he said, then, "no."

Mia closed the back car door and opened the front. She got inside and started the engine.

"You don't owe me an explanation, Jace. You really don't." Mia tried to close the car door, but Jace held it open.

He asked only one question. "When will I see you again?"

CHAPTER 13

On her mother's orders, the air conditioner was set to eighty-five degrees until noon, so sweat was already trickling down between Mia's shoulder blades under her white tank top.

The kitchen was not the ideal place to be, especially in late June, making homemade bread the old-fashioned way, using muscles and bare hands. Mia's beloved Cuisinart was back in Houston, which might be a good thing. The physical labor of kneading the dough and punching it down felt cathartic.

It was Josie's rehab day at home, so the house was mostly quiet. Cruz insisted that she turn the television off so as not to distract her from their sessions. The only sound was that of muffled voices under the click, then the hum of the air conditioner.

Mia reached for the kitchen radio, intending to turn it down low onto her favorite country station, but she stopped when she realized that one good country song would send her thoughts reeling back to Jace and last night.

That was a place she didn't need to go.

She left the bread dough to rise in six mini loaf pans while she prepared a pot roast with baby carrots and a batch of mashed potatoes. When the pot roast was done, she removed it from the oven, readjusted the temperature, and then slid the mini loaf pans inside.

By early afternoon, she had the meals divided into aluminum pans and bagged, ready for delivery.

With Josie asleep in the recliner, Mia jotted a note and set it beneath the remote control, then quietly carried the bagged meals to her car and loaded them into the ice chest.

Clint was behind the counter at the Feed and Seed when Mia arrived with their two meal deliveries. He'd never been one of her favorite people, but avoiding him would not be possible. She waited patiently behind a rancher buying yellow salt blocks.

When the rancher left, Mia stepped up to the counter.

"Hey, Mia." Clint greeted her with a smile, his eyes dropping to the neckline of her tank top. "Heard you were back."

Holding up the bags, she said, "I have meals for Craig and Bette. Do you want me to put them in the cooler?"

"Hang on," he said, coming around the counter. "Just wait here. Dad wanted to talk to you." He jogged down an aisle and out the back doors to the yard. In a few minutes, he came back inside with his father.

"You're early today!" Craig said as he approached. "What do you have for us?"

"Pot roast, baby carrots, mashed potatoes, and a mini loaf of bread."

"Homemade bread?" When Mia nodded, Craig

said, "Mm-mmm." He took the bags and set them inside the cooler, then he reached into a drawer beneath the cash register and pulled out an envelope with her name written on it. "It would be easier if I could pay the week in advance so that you wouldn't have to wait on me each time. Can I do that?"

"Yes, of course." The money was a big help to her grocery and gas bills.

"Bette is paying for the week, too. Her check is included." Then Craig said, "I was telling a few people about this little deal, and a lot of them are interested in having you make meals for them, too. Are you looking for more customers?"

More customers? She had a hard enough time cooking three extra meals in her mother's small kitchen. As much as she needed the money, she simply didn't have a proper place to prepare, cook, and sell food from home.

"I'm sorry, Craig, I can't," she said. "But if you know of a catering event with a kitchen, I already have all the required licenses, and I sure could use the money."

"Would you be interested in working an event?" Craig asked. "I'm friends with the lady who won this year's Junior Livestock Show Fundraiser bid, and I know she's desperate for an event chef."

"Yes, I'm very interested." That was the kind of job that could replenish her savings.

"Good! It's not for another two months, but she's hiring now." Craig grinned. "I've already bragged to her about you and your cooking, so I know she'll want to talk to you."

Mia hadn't heard about anyone catering events in Legacy. "Is she local?"

Craig laughed. "No. We might have grown a little since you left, but not that much. We don't have any caterers here unless you want to call picking up pans of enchiladas from the Armadillo Diner catering." He took a notepad, wrote *Rocky at Hill Country Banquets* along with a phone number, and handed Mia the paper. "She's from Junction and gets most of the catering jobs around here. Just give her a call and be sure to tell her that I referred you."

"Thank you, Craig." She held up the paper, tightening her hold on it. "This is exactly what I need."

When Mia got back to her car, she called Hill Country Banquets and set an appointment to meet.

Mia had not prearranged a delivery time with Jace, and after seeing him last night, she was hoping he wouldn't be home when she arrived at the Farr Reaches. She had embarrassed herself, acting like a jealous schoolgirl over him being with Melody Hayes. She was a twenty-five-year-old woman, single of her own accord, more or less, and she had no right to lay claim to Jace. It was almost four o'clock. Surely, he would be out checking the herd before nightfall.

It was sixteen miles to the ranch turnoff, which no longer had a wide swath of mowed grass, making it harder to spot now. The two-lane bordering the ranch was paved, but the road leading into the Farr Reaches was not. Mia slowed, searching for the turn. The Texas Century Ranch sign was the marker she needed.

The turnoff was overgrown with old prickly pear and native grasses, looking wild and unkempt as if the place had been forgotten. When in high school, keeping the turn groomed had been Jace's job. Hannah had been insistent about maintaining their ranch road, not just to keep the snakes down but to keep integrity up.

Weeds, she'd said, told an unspoken story. If the land looked good, it was good. The reverse was true as well.

Mia drove the dirt road slowly so as not to stir up dust, then parked behind Jace's truck in the driveway. She got out of her car, retrieving the plastic bag from the ice chest.

At the front door, she rang the bell, then waited. No sounds came from inside. If everyone was out with the herd, how would she leave the food that needed refrigeration?

She rang the doorbell again but still got no answer, sending her around to the back of the house, that door being closer to the kitchen where she might find Hannah. As soon as Mia turned the corner, she saw the grandmother, preoccupied with refilling birdseed feeders.

"Hello," Mia said. Hannah turned, her face blank. "Hannah, do you remember me? I'm Mia."

Hannah set the seed feeder down and walked toward Mia. "No, I'm sorry, I don't. What was your name again?"

"Mia Ellis." When met with a silent stare, Mia clarified. "I'm a friend of Jace's." She held up the bag with food. "I'm delivering the dinner he ordered."

"Well, how nice." Hannah took the bag from her and then set it down on the limestone patio floor. "I'll be sure to tell Jace that you stopped by."

"No," Mia said, picking up the bag. "It's food. It needs to go in the refrigerator."

"Oh," Hannah laughed. "Of course, it does. Won't you come in?" She opened the back door, leading Mia inside. "Cowboy would usually bark to tell me someone was here, but Jace took him to the barn with him a while ago. They'll be back soon." Hannah took the bag from Mia and put it inside the refrigerator, then reached for a pitcher of tea. "Can I pour you a glass?"

"No, thank you," Mia told her. "I really should be going."

But before she could turn to leave, Jace pulled open the back door and walked in with Cowboy.

"There you are," Hannah said to him.

"Mia?" The heel of his hand went to his forehead. "The food. Did you bring dinner all the way out here? I should have called you. I could have come into town to get it."

"Speaking of that," Mia said. "It is a long drive out here."

"You want me to pay extra?" Jace reached into his back pocket and pulled out his wallet.

"No." She held up her hand to stop him. "It's just that with my new job and all, I think I've probably taken on too much."

"You're not going to cook anymore?"

Even though Mia had declined, Hannah handed her a glass of iced tea. "Are you the girl who cooks?"

"Yes," Mia said to her, then to Jace, she said, "I'm still cooking. It's just expensive and time-consuming to deliver way out here."

"So, let me pay more." He took out an extra twenty-dollar bill and handed it to her.

Mia hated to accept money from Jace, but she'd gone into the hole making this meal for them. "Thank you," she said, tucking the bills into the pocket of her blue jeans. Now she just needed to find a way to distance herself from this man who lit a constant fire inside her.

"I'm not going to cook for you anymore," she blurted.

"Why not?" he asked.

Hannah handed a glass of tea to Jace and then took one for herself. "I'll take Cowboy outside, and we'll finish the feeders so you two can talk." At the door, she turned with a look. "It sounds like you have some things to work out."

Things to work out. That was an understatement. Mia set her glass down on the kitchen counter. "I should go." She started for the door.

"Mia, don't…" Jace took hold of her arm firmly enough to stop her from leaving. "Somehow, I'm messing up all over again. Please don't go." He hesitated. "I wanted to tell you that I went to the bank."

Mia stopped. She didn't want a repeat of bad decisions. They weren't kids anymore, and their relationship was no longer personal. It was business. Quitting now would be unjustified.

"Okay," she said. "But just for a minute. Mom expects dinner on the table at six."

"Come to the office with me." He led the way through the house.

It had been a long time since she'd been here in this home, but not a lot had changed. It seemed that time stood still within these walls. All except for the office, which hadn't belonged to Jace for more than a month when Mia left Legacy. It was now tiled in Adobe Saltillo and had plantation shutters instead of drapes.

He pulled out a barrel-shaped brown leather chair on the other side of his desk for Mia. When she sat, he went to his own chair, scooting it close to the desk. He was quiet while he logged onto his laptop and then turned it so Mia could see the screen.

"This is my new website." Jace pointed to the link at the top. "Just like you suggested, Farr Reaches QB dot com." He scrolled. "Melody isn't finished with it yet, but I want to know your thoughts. It looks good so far, don't you think?"

Mia leaned in for a closer look. "There's too much dark brown." She swirled her finger over a section. "If she could make this dark wood background a green pasture instead, maybe with some wildflowers or bluebonnets, it would look good. I like the font she chose."

Jace sat back. "Where would I find a green pasture the last week of June in Texas, especially this year? The drought is killing us. Sunday's rain was the first we've had in months."

"It doesn't need to be a personal photograph, Jace. It doesn't even need to be a picture of this ranch. Stock photos are available online." Mia pulled the laptop closer and typed in an address, entering her password on the website's log-in. After a few more clicks, she turned the screen to face Jace. "This picture looks almost exactly like one of your pastures, in a good year anyway."

Jace looked closer, scrutinizing the stock photo. "Yeah, it does. And it's okay if we use these pictures?"

"She'll have to buy the photos to get the license to use them for your website, but they're not expensive. If she knows how to design websites, she'll know all about this, Jace. It's the basics. Just ask her."

Jace turned his focus to Mia. "I wish you could talk to her about this stuff. I sound like an idiot when I try to explain what I want."

Mia tapped a red spiral notebook on his desk. "Just make notes ahead of time before you meet with her again. You'll do fine. You don't need me." She stood and started for the door. Jace followed.

In the big, open living room were two plastic

storage bins, both lids off, on the floor near the coffee table. Scattered around were photos of all sizes. When Mia spotted an eight-by-ten-inch glossy of her and Jace at their senior prom, she went to it and picked it up. Entranced by it for a moment, she turned to Jace. "Why do you have these out?"

Jace came closer to look at the photo. "My God, you were beautiful that night, Mia." Then his gaze fell on her, standing just one boot-step away. "You still are."

The last time she'd held his gaze, a kiss that shouldn't have happened did, so she looked away, laying the photograph back on the coffee table, but curiosity sent her hand sorting through the others. "What are you planning to do with all of these?"

Jace gave the array of photographs a glance. "Truth is, I've been trying to help Grandma remember. Whenever she's having a few good hours, I'll bring her in here, and we'll sit down, me with a pen, and talk about these old pictures. They never seemed all that important until one day, I realized that the person who knows all of these folks won't be around forever, and I want my two nephews to know their past. To know this ranch and who built it. I don't want to be the one who stopped the line."

Without more than a moment of thought, they both sat on the leather sofa and picked up photographs, analyzing each one.

"I know who lots of these people are, their names at least, but I'm not sure of the dates or the places, so when Grandma remembers, I try to write the information on the back. Except for when we get to the great-greats, and then I'm pretty lost." Jace picked up an old, heavily creased black-and-white photo and handed it to Mia. He pointed to a man wearing Levi's and a work shirt, brushing a quarter horse. "I can usually spot family resemblances, which sometimes helps her remember. Like this guy looks a lot like my grandpa. When I mentioned it to Grandma, she remembered that this was my great-grandfather when he was about my age." He took another and flipped it over. "Sometimes it's easy because names and dates are already written on the back, but lots are still blank." He sorted through a few more photographs. "Mostly, I just wait 'til Grandma's having a good day, and then I show her the photos and ask who they are." He cast Mia a smile. "Sometimes all I get is, 'Why, my goodness,' before she drifts off again, and then I know I've waited too long."

Mia had known Jace's older sister, but their four-year age difference made a friendship hard. "So, Cecelia has kids?"

"Yeah." Jace laughed, a shine in his eyes. "She's got two boys, Jaxon and Joshua. Two and four. I haven't seen them in a year. She doesn't come back to Texas very often. I'm having a hard time helping Grandma remember the boys, and I'd sure hate for them to forget her. Things just slip away before you know it, Mia."

A compassionate hand found its way to Jace. "You'll have kids someday, too, you know? And they'll grow up right here on this ranch, just like you did."

"Well, I don't know about that," he said. "I can barely manage myself. And I'm not doing very good with the ranch. I doubt I could manage a bunch of kids."

A bunch of kids. On this ranch. With this man. Regret overpowered the love in her broken heart, but he'd forced her to let go of that dream long ago.

CHAPTER 14

Mia arrived in Junction at the downtown office of Hill Country Banquets to find a closed sign on the door. She'd driven thirty minutes and was on time for her appointment, so being locked out in the midafternoon heat wasn't the welcome she had expected.

She pulled the paper Craig had given her out of her purse and dialed the number he'd written.

"Hill Country Banquets, this is Rocky," the woman answered.

"Hello, this is Mia Ellis. We had an appointment today."

"Don't leave!" Her plea sounded frantic. "I'm almost there."

Within minutes, a pearl white SUV pulled into the parking space next to Mia's Prius, and a fortyish woman, dressed in a floral chiffon dress that left little to the imagination, got out and headed toward her.

With an extended hand, she said, "You must be Mia."

"Yes," Mia said, shaking hands.

"I'm Rocky. Let's get inside out of this heat." She unlocked the office and held the door for Mia.

Standing a head taller than Mia, the strawberry-blonde had her hair in a soft, twisty braid that fell over her left shoulder, landing at the delicate cinch waist of her dress. She was braless and buxom in the deep V-neck chiffon.

Mia tried not to stare, but the well-endowed blonde, whose freckles trailed down through her cleavage, was a strikingly beautiful woman.

Locking onto Mia's focus, Rocky said to her, "I don't usually dress like this for business meetings. This was pure show for Clayton, my soon-to-be ex-husband, who made me late for our meeting today." She stepped back, a sweep of her hand presenting herself. "I just signed the final papers and wanted to remind him what he'd lost by carousing and cheating." She started for her desk. "The bastard was also my chef, hence the reason I need a new one."

"I see," Mia said.

Rocky motioned her to a chair. "Have a seat."

Behind the desk, Rocky took out a notebook, flipping through pages until she came to one scribbled with notes. She picked up a pen and, with it poised on the paper, said, "Craig tells me that you've just completed culinary school."

"Yes." Mia reached down into her leather bag at her feet and pulled out a printed résumé. She handed the page to Rocky. "I have an AA degree in economics and an AAS in marketing from Houston Community College, and then I also have an AAS degree in culinary arts from The Art Institute of Houston."

Rocky spent a moment scanning the paper but then

glanced up from the page. "Why in the world are you here? You should be in Austin or Dallas or back in Houston."

Mia smiled, knowing this woman understood the commitment she'd made and the work it took to get here. "Actually, I'm headed to New York for a culinary apprenticeship, but it doesn't start until the first of the year."

"Ah!" Rocky leaned back in her chair. "Now that makes sense." She laid the résumé on her desktop. "Can you work more events, or are you just interested in the Junior Livestock Show Charity Fundraiser in Legacy?"

"Just the fundraiser. I'm afraid that with my mother's health right now, I'm limited to Legacy. She has doctor's visits and rehab appointments, and she's not able to drive herself yet, so until I leave in December, I'm sort of her caretaker."

"I see," Rocky said as she stood. "That's a shame. I could keep you busy if you were able to travel." Extending her hand, she said, "I'm thrilled to have you onboard for the fundraiser."

Mia stood, too. "Don't you need to call my references before hiring me?"

"Craig recommended you, and that's the only reference I need. I'll be in touch with the details."

THE WEEKEND AT BOOMER'S BAR AND GRILL NEVER started slow, and this busy Friday night was no different.

Steve had hired Rooney, a goat rancher's son, to wash dishes after promoting Mia, but the teenager was too young to serve drinks and too inexperienced to cook. He was good at cleaning tables, though, and he was keeping up with the dishes.

"One cheeseburger, one hamburger. Both with fries," Steve shouted into the kitchen, waiting in the doorway for an acknowledgment.

Mia reached into a drawer to the right of the long stainless steel griddle, clean and hot, and pulled out an order book and pencil. She slapped it down on the serving counter. "Write it down, please?"

Steve stepped into the kitchen. "It's just two burgers and fries, Mia. Why do I need to write that down?"

She turned with both hands on her hips. "Because in a minute, you're going to be yelling for wings, and a minute after that, you'll be asking for chicken strips or jalapeño poppers or chips and queso, and while I'm in the walk-in getting it all, you're going to tell Rooney that you need something else, that's why." She pushed the order book toward him. "Write it down, Steve."

He grabbed the pad and pencil and wrote, *1 Hburger 1 Cburger 2 fries*, then slapped the pad back down on the counter.

Mia picked it up, read what he had written, and then handed it back to him. "Where do they go?"

"What the hell do you mean 'Where do they go'?"

"Which table?" she asked. "If you're busy, I need to be able to serve the food."

"The tables don't have numbers!" He took back the order pad, glanced into the dining room, then wrote, *Young guys in the corner wearing Cubs caps.* He slammed it down. "Jeez, Mia."

By quitting time, Mia reeked from grease and smoke. She needed a shower—and a raise.

With her once-white apron in her hand and her

leather purse slung over her shoulder, Mia went to the front register where Steve stood, counting out his cash drawer. She waited while he finished with the stack of hundred-dollar bills.

"Good night?" she asked him.

Steve glanced at her with a nod. "A really good night. Things ran smooth, too."

"Good," she said. "You realize I've been cooking for over two weeks, serving food, and managing your inventory on a dishwasher's pay, right?"

"You want a raise?"

"Yes."

"Okay. I'll give you a dollar an hour more."

"You'll pay me three dollars an hour more." She readjusted her purse. "And I want to talk to you about the quality of food."

"What's wrong with the food quality?"

"It's atrocious, Steve. Frozen everything. Most of it expired. I'm not trying to change your menu. I just think you should serve better food."

"Well, how will I do that if I don't change the menu?"

"Wings, for example. Instead of buying boxes of frozen prebreaded chicken, why not purchase fresh? I can make my own sauce. The flavor and quality will be ten times better. It's probably less expensive, too."

Steve thought for a moment. "Just chicken?"

"No, beef, too." She looked back at the now-empty dining room, clean and ready for the next day. "Your customers come in for drinks, and then they mostly order burgers and wings as an afterthought when they stay longer than they intended. Why not bring them through the doors for the food, too?"

"I'm running a bar, not a restaurant."

"Then why serve food at all?" Mia picked up a menu. "You're just drawing in customers who aren't hungry yet. A lot of them leave after a drink or two and go somewhere else when they need to eat. If the food here was good, they would stay, watch their sports on the big screen, and spend their drink money with you."

Steve thought for a minute. "And I wouldn't have to change the menu? Because I just had those printed last year."

"You wouldn't have to change the menu."

He slowly nodded. "It's a good idea, but I couldn't do it without you, you know?"

"So, give me that three dollars an hour more and let me take over the ordering for you."

He hesitated, then said, "I'll need to make a bigger profit to pay you more. I can barely afford you now. Why do you think I've been running this place by myself?"

"We can both earn more money with quality food and some advertising." Mia hadn't just excelled in food preparation; she had ranked top of her class in Food and Beverage Operations.

Still hesitant, he said, "Can you work five nights a week instead of four?"

Her mother was doing well, although she still couldn't drive, clean the house, or cook for herself, but she no longer needed a constant caretaker, especially when she retired to her room by eight o'clock to watch the nightly *Who Murdered Him?* television show from the comfort of her bed.

"Okay, but I'll need the last week of August off for a big catering event on September first. Deal?"

"Deal." Steve reached for a handshake. "Am I going to need more tables in here?"

Mia smiled. "Yes, you are."

The next day, Mia woke up early, got dressed in business-like attire, and then drove out to Boomer's to meet with Tom, the representative for Prime Purveyors.

The new order she placed looked much better than the last one he received, but when she handed the change order form to Steve for his signature, he just stared at it. Finally, he asked, "Where're the burgers?" He handed it back to Tom. "Add four cases."

Mia pulled the change order away from Tom and handed it back to Steve. "We're getting our beef from a local purveyor from now on." When Steve gave her a bewildered look, she said, "Folks will appreciate you buying local, and it's top-quality beef."

Answering with a doubtful cock of his head, he signed the new order and handed it back. "Sorry, Tom. If this doesn't work out, you'll get my beef order back."

"Understood," Tom told him.

WHEN DON GOSS CALLED JACE WITH THE NEWS that Cattlemen's Bank had approved his loan, he also placed a personal order for half a beef. "When you're able to take future orders, put me down for another half a beef in six months," he'd said.

With money in his account and the first order on the books, Jace drove to Home Depot, where he ordered twelve large chest-type freezers, arranged for their delivery, and then went to Dowd and Out Meat Processing, where he finalized plans.

By the time Jace got home, it was two o'clock, and he still hadn't called Melody for an update on the website.

First, though, he called Mia.

Hi, this is Mia. Leave a message.

Jace disconnected. He wanted to talk to her—the real her—not a recording. He searched his phone for Melody's number and pressed the key.

"Hey, Melody, it's Jace."

Before long, the red Mustang appeared on the dirt road, pulling into the driveway and parking beside his truck. The slender, long-legged woman got out and strode toward the door, wearing jeans and a sleeveless, low-cut white, turquoise, and pink paisley blouse. A black leather laptop bag hung from her shoulder.

Jace stepped out. "That was fast," he greeted her as she climbed the two steps to the front porch entrance.

Melody smiled. "You call, and I come. That's how it's supposed to work, isn't it?"

"Usually doesn't work that way for me." Jace laughed and then opened the door, inviting Melody inside.

In his office, they sat side by side, both laptops open.

"Can you change out this brown wood background on the website for something like a green pasture instead? I heard you could get one from an online site that sells stock photos." He clicked on the one he had saved from Mia's quick search. "Like this one."

Her attention was locked on Jace, not the photo. Behind her blue and brown tortoise eyeglasses, her gaze artistically sketched his seated outline before returning to his eyes, then she smiled. "I can do anything your little heart desires."

Uneasy, Jace straightened in his chair. "Great. Okay," he said, then cleared his throat. "A pasture it is."

The woman's flirtations hadn't gone unnoticed, but

Jace was trying hard not to adjudge this one. He had awarded himself a pro badge for his ambitious self-control, but when Melody slid her hand onto his knee, it was difficult not to be affected by it. No matter how hard he tried to keep his focus on his own laptop, it occasionally drifted to hers, where it escaped his restraint and shifted to her cleavage.

Jace forced his focus back to his computer, but instead, it landed on the spiral notebook he used for ideas and planning notes. He reached for it, flipping through several marked pages until he found where he had written *Prices and Packages*. Neatly, he folded back the page, then awkwardly offered it to the web designer for a look, but he fumbled the handoff, and it flew from his grip.

Melody grabbed for it, her hand netting the notebook instead of his knee. She raised her eyes to him. "You're either adorably clumsy or unexpectedly shy."

"I'm really sorry," Jace said, scooting his chair a few inches further from her. He took back the notebook, found the marked page again, and laid it on the desk between the two laptops. He focused on his roughed-out sketches, tapping his finger on each square drawn at the top of the page. "So, on the ordering page, I need buyers to be able to order a whole beef, half beef, or quarter beef, and I need prices shown exactly like this with the per-pound price, the approximate weight of the animal, and the deposit required." Then he slid his finger down the page, pointing to six more hand-drawn blocks beneath the heading *Boxed Beef Packs*. "If buyers want to order a combo package instead, the price and cuts are listed here under the pack's name." He glanced at her, relieved when he found her focus on the paper and not on him. "The order page is probably the most important one on the whole website, so I want it really easy to understand and use."

Melody nodded, then spent a minute clicking through to a stock photo site on her laptop. Together, they chose a photo of a Central Texas cattle pasture—a better one than his—that had either been irrigated or photographed after a good rainfall. It featured the legendary bluebonnets growing along the base of a metal T-post fence strung with barbed wire that looked a lot like his own fences.

While Jace watched, Melody used a template she'd named *Farr Reaches Quality Beef* to create a basic design for the ordering page. With his approval of the concept, she logged out, closed her laptop, and turned straight to face him.

Curling her dark, golden-brown hair behind her ears, she posed a prim posture, then said to him, "I was under the impression you were still single, but I'm getting the feeling that you're not."

Jace scooted his desk chair back and then stood. With a glance at Melody, he said, "I'm not married." He closed his laptop and then laid the spiral notebook on top of it.

"Okay." She stood, too. "A serious girlfriend, then?"

He shook his head, his hands landing on his hips. "It's not that," he said.

"Do you just not find me desirable, Jace? Because I've given you ample opportunity to make a move, and you haven't, so I'm a little lost."

Melody mirrored his stance with her hands plastered to her hips.

He intended his focus to stay on the floor, but a glance found those white leather boots that had some magical ability to enchant his gaze, drawing it upward, lingering at every curve along the way.

"You're a very attractive woman, Melody, but...I mean..." Jace stammered right into her words.

"Look, Jace, I've been attracted to you since the day I started high school, and seeing you again has reminded me why."

She took one long-legged step forward, her arms encircling his neck, and kissed Jace.

If he'd tried harder, he might have been able to force himself to push away, but instead, one arm wrapped itself around her willowy waist, and the other landed midback, tightening his hold, which summoned a groan of pleasure from her lips.

It was too late to turn back now.

Melody deepened their kiss, her body encouraging his hands to rove until Cowboy gave a double bark. They both jumped.

Twice again, the dog barked from the doorway.

Jace dropped his embrace. "Grandma's coming."

Melody stepped back, straightening her blouse as Hannah entered the room.

"Oh, hello," she said to Melody. Then, "Jace, I didn't know you had company in your office. I was just coming in for a book of postage stamps. I thought I'd get an early start on our Christmas cards."

When Melody laughed at her remark, Jace started toward his grandmother, serious. "It's not Christmas yet, Grandma." He put his arm around her shoulders, turned her toward the door, and walked with her. "Your birthday is next week, though. Maybe we'll go to the big July 4th fireworks show in town to celebrate." On their way out the door, he looked down, whispering, "Good boy," to the Aussie, but then to his grandmother, he said, "But I'll help you do Christmas cards later if you don't mind my scrawly handwriting."

"All right," she said, but then she stopped and turned, looking back into his office. "Jace, that's not the same girl who cooks, is it? You know the one I mean. The one who brought dinner out to us."

"No, Grandma, that's not Mia." He glanced back. "This is Melody. She's designing a website on the computer for us."

Jace walked with Hannah through the house. After he had her situated in the chair at the dining table, which was strewn with boxes of leftover holiday cards, he returned to his office.

Melody stood waiting, one foot tapping the floor, her laptop already in its black leather bag with its strap over her shoulder.

He stopped midway through the room. "Hey, I'm real sorry about that," he said.

"I can't believe you're still hung up on Mia Ellis. I didn't even know she was back in town." Instead of waiting for a response, Melody started toward the office door. "You should have just told me, Jace." She pushed past him on her way out. "If you come to your senses, look me up."

CHAPTER 15

The subject of Hannah's approaching birthday weighed more heavily on Jace than watching Melody drive away, dust roiling up from beneath her tires.

He grabbed his Silverbelly Stetson off the rack and fitted it onto his head, and then gave Cowboy a treat from the can he kept in his office. He went to find Hannah.

"Hey, Grandma," Jace said when he found her still at the dining table, flipping through the address book she used for Christmas cards. "I need to go into town for a little while. Do you need anything?"

"No," she said, but her head cocked in afterthought. "Unless you can bring another one of those beef pies home?"

Jace smiled. He was headed into town to find Mia anyway. She deserved to know that the bank loan had come through, and he needed to ask Josie about Hannah's birthday quilt.

"I'll see what I can do, Grandma." He leaned and

kissed her cheek, telling Cowboy to stay as he left the house.

Jace parked outside Mia's home at the curb, even though the driveway was unoccupied.

He knocked on the bright yellow door and waited. When it finally pulled open, he said, "Hi, Josie."

"Jace," she said, adjusting the crutches under her armpits. "Mia's not here, but do you want to come in anyway?"

"Yeah, I noticed her car was gone, but I wanted to see you, too." He stepped inside. When Josie made her way back across the room to her recliner, he closed the door and followed. "You're doing real good on those crutches."

"What's that?" Josie asked, scooting herself back onto the gray leather chair.

Jace went to the side table where the remote control was set and turned down the volume on the television. "I said, it looks like you're doing real good with your crutches."

"Oh, yes, I am, but I hate them." She rubbed her underarms. "Now I know how a saddle sore feels."

Jace settled himself on the loveseat—the seat closest to Josie. "I was wondering about the quilt you're making for Grandma. How's it coming along? Her birthday is in a few days."

Josie twisted in her chair to see him. "It turned out real nice. Didn't Mia tell you?" When he shook his head, she said, "Well, the colors look good together, and from those two pictures you showed me of Hannah's bedroom, I think she will like it. I had it almost finished when the car accident happened, so it just needed a few little things done to it. Mia helped." She pointed to her sewing room. "Go take a look. It's on the quilt rack."

Jace got up and went to the room. As soon as he opened the door, he spotted the quilt—he knew because in the center was his Circle FR brand.

From the living room, Josie shouted, "Did you find it?"

"Yeah," Jace called back. "I'm looking at it now."

The saddle-brown Farr Reaches brand was prominently set as the center of a compass star design, displayed on a smoke-white background. The more prominent patchwork points were in colors of dark chocolate brown, almond, wheat, cornsilk, and light cantaloupe. Jace fingered the quilt. The work was stunning and well worth the asking price.

He returned to the living room, motioning Josie to turn the volume down again. When she did, he said, "The quilt is perfect for Grandma. Thank you. I'll be proud to give it to her."

"I spent extra time on it since it was for you. Mia said she'd wrap it, just like I promised when you ordered it, but she needs to buy wrapping paper. I ran out."

"Can I pay the balance when I pick it up?"

"The sooner, the better." Josie turned with a confused squint toward him. "Did you know disability isn't a whole paycheck?" When Jace shook his head, she eased the TV volume up. "I'll tell Mia to bring the quilt out to you as soon as it's wrapped. You can give her the money."

"Where is she, by the way?"

"She left for her shift at that bar. This is the second time today that she's been out there. She won't be home until the ten o'clock news goes off."

Jace headed straight out Ranch Road North, passing the entrance to an exotic game ranch where a herd of Arabian oryx, white with long straight horns, gathered.

He pulled into the pothole-ridden lot of Boomer's Bar and Grill, parking his F-350 King Ranch between a Cadillac Escalade and a Range Rover. Other cars and trucks dotted the lot, too. Colorful neon signs flashed in the front windows even though daylight still lit the evening happy hour.

Jace opened the door and walked inside amid boisterous shouting directed at a big-screen television.

The elite game lodge clientele either loved the local dive or wanted to spend their money at the neighboring sports bar nearest the wild game because the place was packed.

There wasn't a Texan in the group, and it was obvious. Instead of the iconic cowboy hat or ball cap, most men there wore Panama Jack or Indiana Jones-style hats and drank beer out of a mug.

Jace stood at the saloon-type bar, waiting for the burly red-haired man cashiering at the counter. The smell of hamburgers hung heavy in the air.

When the man closed the cash register drawer, he made eye contact with Jace and started toward him.

"What'll it be?" he asked.

"I'm looking for Mia."

After a quick once-over, the man said, "She's paid to work, not talk. I'm Steve. I own this place. Can I help you with something?"

"I just need to talk to Mia for a few minutes."

Steve grabbed a menu and set it down on the bar in front of Jace. "Then order something. Soon as it's ready, she'll bring it out."

Boomer's Bar and Grill was just a few miles from

the Farr Reaches Ranch, but it was on a different road, so it wasn't a place that Jace frequented.

"Okay," Jace said, giving a tap to the menu. "I'll have a bacon cheeseburger with extra bacon and fries."

Steve wrote it on the order pad. "And to drink?"

Jace glanced around the bar again, then pointed to a red-and-white sign with a gold star on the wall. "Beer," he said. "The bottle is fine."

Steve clipped the order ticket to the stainless steel wheel at the cook station in the kitchen and then called out, "Bacon cheeseburger and fries." He turned to leave but then stopped and turned back, pointing to the order. "Extra bacon on that cheeseburger."

Mia had three other burgers on the griddle and a basket full of fries already in the hot oil, but she grabbed the order ticket off the wheel and looked at *Extra bacon* and *Guy at the bar in a Stetson*. The words jumped out at her like a flashing beacon. She stepped out of the kitchen and glanced down the length of the bar. Seated at the far end was Jace.

After plating the orders for three hamburgers and fries, Mia rang the bell for Steve. He never questioned her when she passed him on his way into the kitchen for the food pickup.

She walked behind the long bar, stopping in front of Jace. "Hey," she said. "I'm surprised to see you here."

Every time he laid eyes on her, Jace smiled. "I drove out to give you the good news."

"I have good news for you, too."

"You do? You first."

"No, you go first."

He leaned forward in a secret-to-be-told posture. "My bank loan was approved today."

"Is that all?"

"What do you mean 'Is that all?' That's kind of *everything*."

Mia laughed. "I never doubted that you'd get the loan, Jace. Not once. Which makes my news all the sweeter."

Steve squeezed behind Mia on his way to the cash register for a customer waiting to pay, his red hair in a sweaty frizz. He glared at Jace. "Mia, you got that bacon cheeseburger ready for this guy yet?"

Mia reached for Steve's arm, stopping him on his way past her. "This *guy* is more than a customer, Steve. He's your new beef supplier."

Jace straightened on the bar stool. "Me?"

"Him?" Steve asked. Then to Jace, he said, "Who do you work for?"

Jace stood and reached out his hand. "I'm Jace Farr. I own the Farr Reaches Ranch about ten miles from here."

Mia interjected, "Jace just started a new pasture-to-plate program, selling direct to consumers. You'll be surprised by the high-quality beef you'll be serving soon."

Steve wiped his hand on the white bib apron that covered his belly and then shook hands with Jace. "Steve Miller. Nice to meet you. How soon will our first order be delivered? We only got about two weeks of burgers left, and I don't want to run out."

Jace glanced at Mia, his look a questioning one, but then to Steve, he said, "You won't run out. I'll make sure you're restocked before then."

"Okay, good." Steve started toward the cash register again where his customer waited, calling back over his shoulder to Jace, "Looking forward to doing business with you."

When he was out of earshot, Jace turned his focus back to Mia. "You got an order for the restaurant from him?"

Her smile came with a nod. "Congratulations. Boomer's Bar and Grill just became your first commercial customer." She reached into the back pocket of her jeans and pulled out a paper, handing it to Jace. "I was going to talk to you about it today, but I ran out of time. I just jotted down an order, but we'll need it official so that I'll have a record and you'll have an agreement." With a raised brow, she whispered, "Don't you let me run out of beef."

Jace laughed. "I promise, I won't."

WITH THE GRIDDLE CLEANED AND THE WORKSTATION restocked and ready for the next day, Mia helped Rooney restack the clean mugs in the glass froster before having him clock out for the night. She was untying her apron when Steve returned to the kitchen with an order ticket.

"Sorry, but I told the guy you'd make him a bacon cheeseburger. I said the fryer was shut down for the night, though, so no fries. Do you mind making one more? The guy had car trouble, and he's waiting for Ramirez to show up for a tow."

"Not at all," Mia said, retying her apron. She reheated the griddle, then went to the walk-in and grabbed what she needed for the bacon cheeseburger.

The basket looked naked without fries, so Mia added a bag of potato chips. She carried the order out to the dining room where just four patrons remained. Without a table number or a description of the person who ordered the burger, she glanced at Steve, who pointed to a lone man at the table in the far corner, focused on his phone.

Mia crossed the room, setting the burger basket lined with red-checkered paper on the bare wooden table. "Here's your cheeseburger and a bag of chips." When she saw his glass was empty except for ice, she asked, "Can I get you another drink?"

Disinterested, it took a moment before he looked up. When his eyes caught sight of Mia, he sat back, setting his phone face down on the table. He smiled. "Yes, another iced tea. Thank you."

"Sweet or unsweet?"

"Unsweet."

She nodded, then started back across the room toward the bar. He was older, but he was a strikingly handsome man with hazel eyes, their specks of gold and green glinting in the glow of the neon window sign. Mia glanced back once, catching his unhindered focus, which was riveted to her.

The man had a quality air about him—one that radiated success. Older by maybe fifteen years, his hair and stubble had an early graying, but specks of black gave away his original color. He was hard to ignore, especially when he refused to release her from his gaze.

His Merino wool knitted open-collar polo shirt was too warm to be worn in Texas in the summer, but his jeans and boots kept him from looking entirely out of place.

While pouring his tea, she glanced out the window into the parking lot. She matched the white Mercedes S-Class sedan to him.

He watched Mia as she crossed the room toward him, carrying his tea.

"Here you go," she said, setting it down with a straw.

He reached out his hand. "I'm Ethan. And you are?"

"Mia," she said, accepting his handshake. "And I'm betting you're not from around here, but you don't look much like an exotic game hunter either."

He smiled. "Right on both counts."

When the other patrons paid and left, leaving the bar and grill empty, Steve locked the front door behind them. He called out to the last customer, "Take your time. I'm not tossing you out. We close at ten o'clock on weeknights but finish your meal. I have some accounting to do, so you have plenty of time. Ramirez should be here soon."

Ethan motioned to the chair beside him. To Mia, he said, "Sit, won't you? I hate to eat alone."

Why she agreed, she couldn't explain, but Mia pulled out a chair and sat.

CHAPTER 16

J ace had tagged four prime two-year-old heifers to start his pasture-to-plate program. When he arrived at the holding pen near the south pasture, Travis had the ranch's dark blue Ford F-450 with dual rear wheels hooked to a twenty-eight-foot stock trailer, and he had the cowhands ready to start loading.

On the way to the processing plant, Travis told Jace, "I've tagged two more cows, and six heifers like you asked. I can have the boys move them to the south pasture tomorrow if you think you'll need them soon."

"Good. Move those heifers but leave the cows for now. I only want prime for the startup, but as soon as we've got steady orders coming in, we can add the cows for choice grade orders."

While Jace drove, Travis used an app on his phone to take notes. "You want to look for a new bull for spring calving? I can go to Lampasas next Wednesday and pick one up at auction, or I can call Shay Henry over in Marble Falls and see what he's got."

"That's a good idea, Trav. Call Shay first. He had a

few Charolais bull calves last year. I'd sure like to have one or two of those if he's got 'em."

"Yes, sir," Travis said.

THE JULY 4TH CELEBRATION IN LEGACY HAD NEVER been small, even though the town itself was the epitome of small with a population of less than 25,000. Even the town's chamber of commerce boasted about the size of Legacy's patriotic parade, claiming it was the longest in four counties, which might have been true once upon a time, but it certainly wasn't true now. It was, however, long enough on too hot a day to fatigue Hannah, causing Jace to take her inside Shonda's for a donut and coffee. The air conditioner was a welcome respite from the 99-degree morning.

Jace handed her an apple fritter. "We're going to have birthday cake today, too. I asked Mia to make a hummingbird cake for you. We'll go by and pick it up on our way home."

"I think that's my favorite, isn't it?" Hannah took a bite of fritter with a sip of her coffee.

"It's always been your favorite. Remember when I was a kid, and you used to make it for us, and then you'd tease us about making your slice vegetarian?"

"Oh, Jace," she said, laughing. "You know that recipe doesn't have real hummingbirds in it!"

He laughed with her. "I know, Grandma. I'm just teasing. When we stop for the cake, I'll also pick up the birthday gift I bought for you."

Hannah sat back in her chair. "You shouldn't have bought me anything, Jace. I don't need presents. I have everything that I need."

"But this is something I want you to have," Jace told her. "Even though I know you don't need it."

When the parade ended and the main street through town had started to clear, Jace and Hannah walked back to his pickup truck parked in the strip mall parking lot, and then he helped her up into it.

At the start of the engine, Hannah pointed to the furniture store they faced across the lot. "What happened to the hardware store?"

Jace glanced to where her finger pointed. "You mean Hastings Hardware?"

"Yes, didn't it used to be there?"

Jace hesitated, but then he said, "Pete Hastings died almost ten years ago, Grandma. His wife sold the store to a family from San Antonio, but they turned it into a furniture store." He looked for the memory in her eyes. "Don't you remember? You helped Margie Hastings sell off the inventory. That's where we got our shelving units in the storage building and our generators. You bought out her supply of bird feeders, too."

Although her eyes drew a blank, Hannah said, "Oh, yes, I remember."

The vacancy in her memory tugged at Jace. Pete and Margie had been her close friends. He put the truck into gear and pulled out onto the main street.

He parked in the unoccupied driveway at Mia's house, then said, "I'll be right back, Grandma. You stay here in the truck with the air conditioner." A minute later, he returned with a wrapped box, setting it down on the backseat floorboard. "Just one more thing to get, Grandma, then we'll head out to the Farr Reaches." He closed the door and jogged back to the house, coming out with a cake in a clear-topped baker's box.

Hannah was unusually quiet on the drive back to

the ranch, steadily staring out the side window. Jace couldn't see her face, but he wondered if she was trying to remember Margie Hastings.

ALTHOUGH THE RED OAK MOTEL HAD THE NICEST rooms in Legacy, Mia hadn't remembered that its only food service was a pitifully scant continental breakfast, and they were located more than two miles from the Armadillo Diner, the nearest restaurant. Difficult for a man who had no car while waiting for his to be repaired.

But when she'd suggested the place to Ethan Cole, they'd both thought he'd just need the room for one night anyway. She'd been surprised when he called her the next day to say he'd be staying longer and wanted to see her. They'd been together every day since.

While waiting for Ethan at the motel, Mia looked out her car window, watching highly vocal wrens hopping up and down tree trunks, searching for insects and spiders. She was trying to count how many she saw by spotting their dramatic white brows when Ethan tapped on the passenger side window.

She unlocked his door. When he was settled and buckling his seatbelt, she asked, "Any word on the part from the Mercedes dealer in Austin?"

"Nothing yet. Day three, and all I keep hearing is that the solenoid is on order."

"Small towns are like that," she said, pulling out into the traffic headed to River Park. "It takes a while for parts to be delivered sometimes." She glanced at him. "Legacy doesn't have a Mercedes dealer on every corner, you know?"

Ethan gave a sarcastic laugh. "They don't have a Mercedes dealer on *any* corner." Then he shrugged. "The price you pay for the peace and tranquility of a small town, I suppose."

Mia invited Ethan to the Independence Day celebration in Legacy, which had been held at River Park for the past twenty-five years. The last time she'd attended, it had been with Jace.

In Houston, the Freedom Over Texas event at Eleanor Tinsley Park on Buffalo Bayou was so spectacular that Mia had been able to see most of the city's fireworks from the tiny side yard of her townhouse, making her feel like she was still a part of family festivities, even though she could never bring herself to attend in person. Attending the Legacy celebration with Ethan was a new feeling for her. With him, she wanted to do fun things again.

They parked in the lot beneath the Main Street Bridge and walked across the green lawn to the event entrance. Drought or not, the grass in the park was well watered throughout the summer. Admission was free to the public, but tickets to the "Best BBQ in Texas" cost ten dollars per person.

Ethan handed a twenty-dollar bill to the ticket booth attendant and then gave one of the tickets to Mia, who slid it into the back pocket of her indigo blue jeans. For the occasion, she'd bought a new pair of cowboy boots in white crackled leather.

"You look stunning today," he said, taking her hand in his.

Mia hadn't had the extra money for luxuries, but being with Ethan these last few days had reminded her how it felt to be grounded with a man, and she was enjoying it. She splurged and bought an Aztec-inspired brown V-neck top with tiered fringe, detailed with teal beads and white dreamcatcher feathers from a local designer her mother knew. Then, in an old keepsake box under her bed, she'd found her set of blue turquoise jewelry—a pebble necklace, matching bracelet, and feather dangle earrings.

"Thank you," she said to Ethan.

Though his New York style was undeniable, Ethan tried to blend in with his Paris-made denim jeans and the same Caiman boots he'd worn the night she met him. Instead of his wool knitted polo, he wore a short sleeve light-persimmon Henley, giving himself a more casual look for the fireworks event.

The way he held her hand awakened her soul.

AT THE FARR REACHES RANCH, HANNAH SAT ON THE edge of her bed, her hand skimming the Circle FR brand in the center of her new quilt.

"I'm glad you like it, Grandma," Jace said to her, arranging her many pillows at the high headboard after helping her remake the bed. "You've made this ranch a success for the last sixty years, and I want you to wake up every morning and remember that it's still here because of you. That brand is a badge of honor."

When a glistening came to her eyes, Jace changed the subject. Her tears had a way of softening his heart until they were both in a puddle.

He glanced at the wall clock. "You ready to go to River Park for the fireworks? It's after five. We can get a plate of barbecue and find a place by the river to set up our lawn chairs and watch the show."

Hannah stood, then she went to Jace with a hug.

"I'm worn out." She patted his shoulder after releasing him from her embrace. "I'm eighty years old today," she said, "and that's too old to gallivant around the countryside just to see a bunch of colorful flashes in the sky."

Jace nodded with a smile. He didn't see any reason to remind her that she was eighty-three today, not eighty.

"Okay then, let's go see what we can fix for dinner."

"You go on without me, Jace. You don't have to babysit me. Go enjoy the show."

He hadn't planned on Hannah wanting to stay home. Promoting Farr Reaches Quality Beef at the event had been part of the plan, and in the past, she had always attended the event, so he never doubted that she would go. Wherever she went, she drew a crowd. The whole county knew and loved her, and they all wanted to spend time with her. It was just another reminder that he was on his own.

"Are you sure, Grandma?"

In less than a week, a few thousand pounds of processed meat would be delivered to his freezers, and he needed some enthusiastic buyers.

Hannah reached for his hand and squeezed it. "I'll bet there's a pretty young lady there who would be glad to spend the evening with you."

He hoped so, but he didn't intend to voice it. Not yet, anyway.

Earlier, Jace had called Boomer's, finding out that it was closed the whole day due to the celebration in town, so he knew there was a slim chance Mia might attend tonight's event. If she was there, he planned to find her. He needed her back in his life, even if it meant her spending half a year without him in New York, working and learning in the mega-center of the culinary world.

In his bedroom, Jace went to his oakwood dresser where framed photographs were set—wedding pictures of his parents and grandparents. A photo of his mother, too. He hadn't put the photographs there, his grandmother had years ago, saying, "to remember your heritage means to look at it."

He pulled the hidden jewelry drawer open and took out the Tiffany blue box. Although it was more than five years old, the platinum ring inside was still stylish, and its two-carat diamond had maintained its brilliant shine.

Jace showered, changed into a clean pair of denim jeans, and then put on a short sleeve teal-and-tan ombré shirt with two snap pockets with a deep back yoke. He took the ring out of its box, dropped it into his shirt pocket, then tucked twenty business cards into the other pocket. He left the ranch in his brushed and buffed Lucchese boots and headed for River Park.

At the gate, Jace bought a ticket to the "Best BBQ in Texas" and then started for the row of red, white, and blue tents.

He spotted Trace and Cindy from the Armadillo Diner in line for the barbecue. "Hey, you two," he said. "I'm surprised you took the night off."

Trace turned with a handshake for Jace. "All our customers are here. What the hell would we do at the diner?" He laughed. "Besides, Bobby can handle the kitchen on his own for as slow a night as it will be."

Jace reached into his pocket, pulled out one of his new business cards, and handed it to Trace. "I'm offering Farr Reaches beef direct to consumers now. If you have some time this week, I'd sure like to come by and talk to you about it."

Trace and Cindy shared the card, reading it together. "You mean like a direct supplier?" Trace asked. When Jace nodded, he said, "When did you start that?"

Proud, Jace said, "Just now. I've got my first delivery of prime beef on its way, and I'd sure love to bring you some of it. I can supply whatever cuts you need, burgers, ribeyes, flank steaks, you name it. And you know I'm reliable because I'm already at your place four or five times a week for dinner anyway."

Trace nodded, serious. "Come by and see me tomorrow."

The two shook hands again just as Jace caught sight of Mia on the other side of the long line. She was the best boots and bling thing he'd ever seen.

"Hey, I'll catch you guys later," he said to them. "Spread the word, okay?"

Jace stepped out of line and started for Mia. Nerves jangled him. He was halfway to her when a man he didn't know pulled Mia to him and kissed her.

CHAPTER 17

Mia had been living like a woman alone on an island. She had no interest in male companionship since leaving Legacy. The attention of many had been steadily rejected based simply on the fact that they were not Jace. There had never been anyone who came close to taking his place, and she had given up hope that there ever would be. She had shut down her emotions. Her work had been her salvation, and she'd given it all her attention.

But Ethan was a whole other kind of man.

"When does the music begin?" he asked her.

"As soon as the food line slows down, I think." Then Mia gave him a who-knows glance, noticing that his gray stubble beard had grown a little in the last few days. "Remember, I've been gone five years. It could have changed."

"Yes, tell me about that." Ethan led her by the hand to a wood-slatted park bench beneath an old oak tree. "Why did you leave?"

Mia sat, allowing his alluring, hazel-colored eyes to pull the truth from her. "I had a broken heart."

Ethan sipped beer from a clear plastic cup, resting one arm across the bench back. "I've had many of those and never left New York."

"This broken heart was different."

"Different how? A broken heart is a broken heart, isn't it?"

Pensive, Mia smiled, her eyes downcast. "My heart was just the first thing to break, then came my soul. My existence in this place flipped upside down, and I became someone I couldn't live here with anymore."

Lights strung around the live music stage flicked on, and a band of five men wearing western shirts started to warm up.

Ethan took another sip of beer, its amber hue blending into what was left of the evening's golden sunset. With his arm draped behind Mia on the bench back, his fingertips gave a brush to her bare shoulder.

"So, tell me. Who was this thickheaded man who broke your heart?"

Mia shook her head, a simper of pardon on her lips. "I don't go there anymore, Ethan." There was no room in her mind—or in her heart—for those long-ago days. "I'd rather talk about you. And New York. I can't wait to get there."

"Well, from what you've told me, you'll be on the Upper West side, and I'm in Central Park South near The Pond. By Texas standards, we'll practically be neighbors." He smiled. "Call me when you arrive, and we'll go for drinks."

Jace stood, frozen to the spot, his eyes glued to Mia and the man she was with.

Whoever he was, he wasn't a Texan. It wasn't wholly the man's attire that gave him away but his mannerisms. It was the swagger he didn't have.

From afar, Jace watched the man lure Mia to her feet. With his hand low on her back, he escorted her onto the hard-dirt surface reserved for dancing. They were the first couple out for the band's opening two-step. Slowly, they swayed.

"So…" The feminine sound drifted over Jace's shoulder from behind. "Looks like Mia found a big-city man to play with."

The familiar floral scent turned Jace to Melody. Her light blue tee with white stars was tucked into her tight-fitting stonewashed blue jeans.

"Yeah." Jace glanced back at Mia on the dance floor, her arms around the man's neck as they slow-danced. "Do you know who that guy is?" he asked Melody.

"Nope." She sipped beer from a near-empty plastic cup. "But since you're not available, I might introduce myself. He's a nice-looking man, even if he doesn't know he's slow dancing to a two-step." She nudged Jace's shoulder. "Maybe I'll teach him how to do it."

Jace looked at Melody, a hardness in his eyes. "You should do that," he said. Then he grabbed hold of her hand and started for the dance floor.

Several couples had already taken to the hard-dirt surface in a quick, quick, slow, slow rhythmic walk, the women twirling into half turns and full turns.

Jace escorted Melody through the crowd, shielding her protectively from the dance spins. When they reached Mia, Jace tapped the man on the shoulder.

"Switch," he said. Then in one fluid movement, he exchanged Melody for Mia.

Jace pivoted Mia into a turn away and then stepped into the rhythm of the two-step.

In the steps that had Mia facing Jace, she said, "What are you doing?"

"Who is that guy?"

"Why do you care?"

"I care because you shouldn't be with him."

"Who should I be with, Jace?"

Jace eased Mia into a half turn, out and back again, progressing across the smooth ground of hardpacked dirt. "You should be with me."

They missed the spin when Mia stopped, dropping her hands to her sides. Other couples used a promenade to veer around the two of them.

"We're done, Jace. We've been done for five years."

Mia swept past him, maneuvering through the dancers, passing Ethan and Melody, who laughed after bumping each other, leaving Jace to stand alone in the middle of the dance.

She was still as stubborn as ever, but Jace couldn't shake the memories of them together when her heart belonged to him. He started after her, following her path through the crowd.

"Mia, wait," Jace called to her when they were out in the open, beneath the dim starlight that awaited darkness. When she stopped and turned, his hurried steps turned into a jog.

"Are you trying to ruin my life completely?" she shouted at him. "Wasn't dumping me once enough?"

"Mia," Jace said when he reached her. "I never dumped you. We've talked about this already. I thought it was what you wanted."

"I told you what I wanted, Jace."

Jace couldn't keep his eyes from tracing the outline of her. He knew what those curves felt like — he knew every inch of her. He knew the taste of her, the scent of her. He took a step closer and pulled her to him. He didn't care that another man's lips had been on hers moments ago. He intended to reclaim her.

She didn't resist when he kissed her, his need summoning a familiar tremble in her touch.

"Hello, remember me?" Ethan asked the two of them.

Jace turned with a fiery stare.

"I'm Ethan." He reached a hand out to Jace. "Mia's date tonight. Awkward, isn't it?"

Mia stepped back from Jace. "Ethan, I'm sorry."

Jace didn't take the offered hand. Instead, he told Mia, "You don't have anything to apologize for."

"Yes, I do, Jace. I came with Ethan." To explain further, she said, "I drove him here."

Ethan made a second offer to shake hands with Jace. "I'm Ethan Cole. From New York."

Jace glanced back and forth between them. "New York?"

"Yes," Ethan said. "That place on the East Coast. You've heard of it?"

His sarcasm hadn't been lost on Jace. "I've heard of it. Isn't that the big ol' state that's a little smaller than the city of Houston?"

Ethan laughed, dropping his focus to the ground. "Yes, that's the one." He looked back at Jace again. "I take it you're the man Mia has told me about." He glanced at Mia.

"Yes," she said. Her hand casually swung from one

to the other. "Ethan, meet Jace Farr. Jace, meet Ethan Cole."

Ethan did not offer his hand to Jace again. Instead, he stepped back, giving Jace the once-over, hatband to boot. "I've recently come from Houston on business, and I'll be on my way to Dallas soon, but I must say, you're the first *cowboy* I've met in this state."

"If that's true then you never made it off the main roads," Jace said.

"That's true," Ethan admitted. "Just trying to get from here to there, you know? I prefer big cities and fast freeways."

"So, I guess Mia was just a detour?"

Ethan glanced at Mia with a smile. "Yes, I suppose she was."

Jace's fingers balled into a fist.

When Mia saw the white-knuckled hand, she shouted, "Stop!" and stepped between the two men, backing Jace up a step. "Ethan had car trouble," she explained. "He has a Mercedes, and the repair shop is waiting for the part to be delivered. That's the only reason he's here."

"Well, it might be why I'm here, but it's not the only reason I stayed." When she shot him a curious look, Ethan gave Mia a shrug. "Let's face facts, I could have easily boarded a flight, flown to Dallas to purchase a newer Mercedes, and then continued on my way. I'm not emotionally attached to this one. It's just that I wanted to see some of this wonderful country that I'm responsible for promoting abroad."

"So, she's actually more of a tourist stop." Jace pushed the narrative, intending to back the man into a corner.

Ethan laughed. "A tourist stop?" He glanced at

Mia, who stood in wait of his answer. "No. Mia is actually quite lovely. Worth much more than a stopover. A refreshing breath of fresh air, as they say." His attention reverted to Jace. "I plan to see more of her when she comes to New York."

Jace tossed a questioning glance to Mia.

"I *am* going to New York, Jace," she said to him. "It's been my plan all along."

He knew that was true. She had never led him to believe that she might stay. It was his own heart that couldn't let go, not hers.

In a low, restrained voice, Jace said, "Right." A nod came when he stepped back. "That's right." He stared at Ethan a moment longer, wanting to challenge the man's right to Mia, but he wasn't sure how well he could take her rejection if she chose the New Yorker instead of him. "I guess I'll see you in a few days with the beef delivery."

Jace turned and walked away, back toward the community gathering beneath a burst of fireworks lighting the night sky, keenly aware that the brilliance of the ring in his pocket was dimming.

CHAPTER 18

The phone call from Dowd and Out Meat Processing came seventeen days after Jace and Travis delivered the first load of cattle to them, but it was still one day past the date Jace had promised meat to Steve at Boomer's Bar and Grill.

As a peace offering, along with their initial order of bulk ground sirloin and hamburger patties, Jace threw in six prime ribeye steaks.

With rain strafing the roof like bullets, Jace backed his truck up to the rear entrance, but instead of exiting his truck, he dialed Steve.

When his call was answered, he said, "Hey, Steve, this is Jace Farr. I'm at the back door with your meat delivery. Can you open up so that we can unload this beef?"

In no more than a minute, the back door swung wide. Steve scooted a cinderblock out to prop it open. When Jace and Cade exited the truck, Steve yelled, "You need help?"

Rain pelted the men, but Jace raised his hand, shouting, "We got it, but thanks!"

When they had the boxes inside, Jace asked, "Where do you want them?"

Steve pointed. "The walk-in freezer." The two men followed him with their boxes, setting them inside the big freezer where indicated, coming out after straightening the stacks.

Jace closed the stainless steel door, then removed his felt hat with an unintended splatter of rain. "Sorry about that," he said, reaching for a handshake. "Good to see you again." He motioned toward Cade, who stood wiping his face with a red bandana. "This is Cade, one of my ranch hands."

Cade straightened, stuffing the wadded-up kerchief into his back pocket. He reached to shake hands. "Nice to meet you, sir."

After shaking hands, Steve looked at Jace. "Appreciate the call yesterday, but we ran out of burgers by five forty-five last night."

"It won't happen again," Jace said to him. "It was our first delivery, and I guess I didn't add enough leeway to the timetable." Jace reopened the walk-in and then used his pocketknife to open the smaller box he had set on top of the others. He pulled out a single vacuum-sealed steak and handed it to the owner. "I brought a half dozen prime ribeyes to apologize for being late with the delivery, but I assure you, your orders won't be late again." He intended to make sure of it because the cost of those free ribeyes was almost as much as two boxes of burgers.

Steve took the clear package and turned it over and back again. "Good enough," he said. "I'll have Mia cook one up for me tonight before we get busy." He tossed the frozen steak onto the work counter.

Jace hadn't heard from Mia since July 4th, which was more than a week ago. "You want to do an inventory before we leave?" he asked Steve.

"Yeah. Let me get the clipboard."

When Steve left the kitchen, Cade asked, "Should I stay or wait in the truck?"

Jace pulled the keys out of his pocket. "Truck is fine."

Cade took the keys and left the building, closing the back door behind him.

While Steve and Jace were marking off the inventory inside the walk-in, Mia pulled open the stainless steel door. Her honey-highlighted brown hair was wet with rain, but the sight of her jumpstarted Jace and his heart.

When her gaze landed on him, Mia said, "Oh, I didn't know you were here. Where's your truck?"

"He parked out back to unload," Steve said, oblivious to the looks between them. "Mia, why did you order bulk ground sirloin? We've already got burgers in patty form. You want him to take it back?"

"No," Mia said. "I'm doing a Saturday Special with chili, and ground sirloin is the beef I want." Then she looked at Jace. "Is it in a chili grind?"

"Yeah," Jace told her, sliding the box around so she could read the label. "It says so right here."

Steve looked at Mia. "You never said anything about making chili. In fact, you promised me I wouldn't have to change the menu."

"You won't. I'll just put up a 'Today's Special' sign. Saturday is your busiest day, so we can start there and offer it. We don't have to commit to it every week if no one's buying it," she explained. "But I make great chili. It's a weakness of mine. I love it, and your customers will, too. The real stuff, though—the true 'Bowl of Red' chili. That's what we're going to serve."

The opening of the front door sent Steve hurrying out of the kitchen.

After an awkward silence and a throat clearing from Jace, Mia said, "So, how are you?"

He shrugged. "I've been better. You?"

"I'm good." Her nod lingered too long. "I'm fine."

"That's good," Jace said. He straightened the delivery boxes again before pointing to the clipboard Steve left on the walk-in shelf. "I need a signature."

"Oh, yes, of course," Mia took the clipboard and pen and signed her name, then tore off the duplicate sheet and handed it to Jace. "Thanks for delivering in this rain."

Jace nodded. "You want the same order on the first of the month?"

"Yes. Same order." Her voice was quiet. "Thank you."

"Sure enough." Jace folded the paper and then started for the back door. He wanted to say more, but the fact of the matter was, there was nothing left to be said.

ETHAN DEPARTED WITH A KISS AND A PROMISE TO stay in touch, both he and Mia ticking off the dates on their calendars. New York was waiting for her, and so was Ethan.

In the meantime, she intended to make the best of it in Legacy, and elevating Boomer's Bar and Grill to a decent place to get burgers and chili was at the top of her list.

Using an app on her computer, Mia created marketing flyers, and then she ordered fifty, printed in full color. In big letters across the top was the name, address, and hours of the bar and grill, and just below was a tagline that read: *Serving local beef from the Farr Reaches Ranch*. When the flyers arrived, she took them into the closet-sized office where Steve was working and presented them to him.

"I've made a list of places that need one of these flyers hand-delivered." She gave him the paper.

Steve silently read it, then pulled a high-gloss page out of the bound pack. With a nod, he said, "This looks really good." He looked up from the flyer. "How did you learn how to do all of this stuff?"

Still not ready to admit to being a chef with restaurant marketing skills, she said, "This is all easy. Anyone with a computer can do it." Which was true.

He stood. "So, you want me to hand-deliver these to all the places on this list?"

A scan of him had her shaking her head. "Maybe Rooney could go?" As an owner and a bouncer, Steve fit the bill just fine, but as the public face of the place, he lacked the look needed.

Steve glanced down at himself, giving an upward tug to his loose-fitting pants stained by oil and food. "I get it," he said. Then he gave Mia the same scan she had given him. "You look good. Why don't you go?"

Mia had put more effort into Boomer's Bar and Grill than she had initially planned—although, frankly, the place was beginning to grow on her—but this wasn't how she wanted the townspeople to think of her. She wanted to be thought of as a highly trained professional chef, schooled in Houston and New York, not as a dishwasher turned fry cook.

"No," she told him. "I've designed the flyers, printed the flyers, and paid for the flyers." She reached into her pocket, pulled out an invoice, and handed it to him. "Which, by the way, I need to be reimbursed for. And I've come up with a list of places for them to go. Now you need to send Rooney out to deliver them. With his blond hair and dimples, he'll have this place filled in no time."

"All right, fine." Steve picked up the telephone. "I'll tell him to come in early and deliver these today."

"Good," Mia said. "Oh, and ask him to dress nice."

The marketing flyers immediately impacted the popularity of Boomer's Bar and Grill, attracting more clientele from the exotic game ranches and pulling in the local ranch hands after hearing that beef from the Farr Reaches had made its way into the restaurant business. Curiosity had a way of drawing a crowd.

With the arrival of six new tables and chairs, all but the three most popular arcade game machines were moved into storage so that the pool table could be relocated farther back instead of taking up room in the middle of the dining area.

When Mia finished with a few final touches, she stood back, her hands planted on her hips, and said, "Now this looks like a place that even I might come and hang out on a Saturday night."

"I don't know about those tablecloths, Mia," Steve grumbled beside her. "What was wrong with the plain old wood tabletops?"

She glanced at him. "Trust me, Steve. Everyone loves the Lone Star, whether the customers are tourists, transplants, or locals. It's *so* identifiable and comfortable." She folded her arms across her chest, admiring the new look of the room. "It's got a rustic Texas welcome now."

Wholesome buns, crisp vegetables, fresh chicken, and local beef—combined with Mia's golden touch as a highly trained cook—had filled the diner from open to close the last five days.

And it didn't seem to matter that the late-July heat was bearing down, the chili sold out within hours the first day it was offered, and customers had been requesting it every day since. Postcard-sized placards were added to each table advertising *The State Dish of Texas* served every Saturday. But on the days when she needed to escape the chaos of her mother's home, she would go to work early to clean, organize, or experiment with making different varieties of chili, without any advertisement, serving it when a diehard chili fan requested a bowl.

JACE HADN'T EXPECTED THE VOLUME OF ORDERS SO soon, but he was pleased with the reception Farr Reaches Quality Beef had received from the community. He'd had Travis and Cade haul another load of cows and heifers to the processing plant while he stayed back, recording more orders, doing the bookkeeping, and increasing the herd. Having money in the bank was a much better feeling than just scraping by, but he knew that sometimes you had to spend money to make money. Within a week, he'd purchased two new bulls from Shay Henry's herd. He had high hopes that he might have the ranch back on track by spring.

He was totaling the new orders when his phone

rang. Without taking his eyes off the calculations, he answered, "This is Jace."

"No sweet 'Hello' or anything?"

Jace stood. "Melody, hi." She had a deep, flirty voice that he couldn't help but feel all the way to his core. "How are you?"

"I'm good. I just called to let you know that I found a job in Dallas with an NFL-themed golf club. Grapevine, actually. I'll be leaving next week."

Jace sat back down. "That's good." He held the phone closer to his ear. "Congratulations. I didn't even know there was an NFL golf club."

"Well, there's only one in the world, which is why it's an amazing opportunity for me."

"Yeah." A softness he hadn't intended settled in his tone. "That's really impressive, but then you're very good at what you do." He scooted himself closer to his desk, a hand on his forehead. "Seriously, congratulations."

"Thanks," she said. "So, I thought I would check and see if you needed anything before I leave?"

He cleared his throat, then said, "Any chance you could help me figure out how to do an email newsletter before you go? This stuff is like a foreign language to me."

"Of course. I can come out anytime. And don't feel bad. Those are harder than most people think."

Thoughts of Mia raced through his brain. Memories of her kissing Ethan Cole, knowing she would be leaving to be with the man in just a few months was more than he could handle right now. He needed to focus on the ranch. To be the man he was meant to be. Before he knew it, he'd asked Melody, "Can you come tonight?"

Her silence held for a moment, then, "It's eight o'clock, Jace. Are you sure?"

No matter how much he still loved Mia, she wasn't in love with him. She was leaving, and so was Melody. "I'm sure."

~

WITH THE JUNIOR LIVESTOCK SHOW FUNDRAISER less than three weeks away, Steve reneged on his promise to give Mia a week off.

"I just can't do it." Even though it was five minutes past eleven, Steve hadn't unlocked the front door or turned on the neon *Open* sign. He ignored a persistent knock by keeping his focus on Mia. "I didn't know I'd be depending on you for just about everything by now." He slapped his hand down on the bar top to emphasize the problem. "Who's going to cook while you're gone? Who's going to make the chili you've got everyone coming in here to eat?"

"We had a deal, Steve." Anger raised the level of Mia's voice. "I agreed to cook for you five days a week as long as I got the last week of August off for this catering event."

Steve straightened his posture, his belly pushing into the bar. "Well, I've changed my mind."

Mia took off the apron she had just tied around her waist and put it on the bar top. "Then I quit. I made a commitment, and I don't make those lightly."

"You can't quit," Steve said as Rooney knocked hard on the front window, peering inside.

Through the glass, Rooney shouted, "The door is still locked!"

Steve started around the bar, keys in his hand.

"Fine, you can have it off. But if the event is just one night, why do you need the whole week?"

The start of her culinary program in New York was still more than three months away, and that meant she needed to keep this job. Besides, the bar and grill had grown on her. So had Steve and Rooney. And she'd have nowhere to go but home if she wasn't working.

When Steve opened the front door, Rooney walked straight to the switch for the *Open* sign and flicked it on. "Did you guys forget to open up, or what?" He headed toward the kitchen. "I'm not gonna get docked for being late because I couldn't get in, am I?"

Steve looked at Mia but shook his head at Rooney. "No, you won't get docked," then, to Mia, he said, "So what about it? Can we compromise?"

"I need time to prep the food and assist with setup. It's not like I can just walk in and start cooking. It's not just a one-day commitment. It's an *event*, Steve."

"So, how about two days off?"

Mia sighed, her silent stare boring into him, causing him to shift uncomfortably.

"Okay, four days," he said. "But that's my final offer."

"All right," she said to him. "Thursday, Friday, Saturday, and Sunday." She would be exhausted, she knew.

"Okay, but those count as your days off. This place will be falling apart by the time you get back."

Mia went to the cash register and reached over the counter to the cubby underneath. She pulled out a notepad and pen, scribbled on it, and then handed it to Steve. "Sign it," she said.

Steve read the note, then looked up. "You're going to make me sign an agreement?"

"Yes, I am." Her hands went to her hips. "You went back on one promise already."

Steve slammed the paper down on the counter and signed his name to it. He slid it back to her.

"Four days off instead of your regular two days off." He grumbled as he walked away, stopping just once to look back at her. "I can't even run this place without you anymore. What the hell have I done to myself?"

CHAPTER 19

With the fundraiser fast approaching, Mia was nervous about not hearing from Rocky Hill. She dialed her number, leaving a message at the prompt.

"Hi, Rocky, it's Mia Ellis, your Legacy event chef for the Junior Livestock Show Charity Fundraiser. I haven't heard from you, so I just wanted to check in to make sure everything is still a go. Let me know, okay?"

It wasn't until Mia was making lunch for her mother that the return phone call came in.

"Hi Mia, it's Rocky." The catering owner didn't wait for a response. "I'm sorry for not staying in touch like I promised, but it's been a nightmare here trying to sort through the mess of suppliers and vendors. Clayton destroyed the records as soon as the divorce was finalized, and I have no idea who's supposed to be supplying what for my upcoming events. He's sabotaged it all for me."

"I'm sorry," Mia said to her. "You didn't keep any records of your own?" It had slipped out unintentionally. She clapped a hand to her forehead. "What I meant to say is, he can't legally do that, can he?"

Rocky laughed. "It's okay. You're right. Sometimes good sex knocks the common sense right out of a woman. I'm the owner and business manager, and it was my responsibility to keep my own records." She sighed. "Point is, I can't find a supplier with enough beef at this late stage to fulfill my obligations for the Legacy event or the next one in Menard. Basically, I'm screwed, and not in a good way."

"Maybe not," Mia said.

"Maybe not? What does that mean? Tell me you know something I don't know."

"The Farr Reaches Ranch in Legacy has a new pasture-to-plate program, selling direct to consumers now. Jace Farr might have what you need."

"I've heard of the Farr Reaches…" Rocky said hesitantly, "but I hadn't heard about their direct operation. Do you know how I can reach them?"

"Yes," Mia told her. "I can give you Jace's phone number."

"Better yet, can you set up a meeting? Today? And I'll need you there to help me sell my desperate need without it costing me an arm and a leg."

Mia hadn't seen or talked to Jace in weeks, but she couldn't afford to lose this catering job, and she knew it would be a good business opportunity for him.

"Yeah." She looked at the clock. "I can call him for you, but I have to be at work by five o'clock, so can you meet us at Boomer's Bar and Grill on Ranch Road at maybe four?"

Rocky's tone changed into a hopeful one. "You got it. I'll see you at four o'clock."

JACE WALKED INTO BOOMER'S DRESSED IN HIS BEST pair of Wranglers and a long-sleeved white dress shirt. When Mia stood, it caught his eye. He started toward her table, taking off his hat when the blonde-haired lady at the table rose to greet him.

"Hi, Jace," Mia said to him, her gaze lingering. "Thanks for coming."

Rocky reached for a handshake. "I'm Rocky Hill, the owner of Hill Country Banquets. I really appreciate you coming out here to meet with me today."

"Jace Farr," Jace said. He couldn't look at Mia because when he did, he just wanted the world to go away and leave the two of them alone together.

"Can I get you something to drink?" Mia asked him.

"No," he said. "But thanks." He pulled a chair out from the table.

Before reseating herself, Rocky's gaze scanned Jace, head to toe. In a mumble, she said, "My God, if I was just ten years younger."

Jace took his phone out of his pocket, set it on the table, and then seated himself. "So," he said, focused on Rocky. "I hear you need beef for the fundraiser on the sixteenth."

Rocky nodded. "Yes, sirloins and ground beef."

Jace leaned forward, his forearms on the table. "Sirloins? How many do you need?"

"Two hundred."

Jace sat back in his chair. "That's a lot of sirloins on such short notice."

"I know," Rocky said. "That's why I'm in a bind." She reached down into her satchel, pulled out a printed page with a list of menu items, and handed it to Jace.

"This is the approved menu for the charity event. It's been signed off on, so I don't see how I can substitute and still stay within the confines of the agreement. One hundred and ninety-three attendees have been confirmed, but I can't tell you how many times people forget to count themselves or their board members, so I'll need at least two hundred sirloins to make sure we don't run short."

When Jace picked up the menu, Mia scooted her chair closer, scanning the items with interest.

"Oh, I like your vegetarian option," Mia told her. "I usually see a pasta dish or a meatless lasagna, but if you did that, you would need to add an alternate gluten-free item, too. By serving cauliflower steaks, you're covering both options."

"Exactly," Rocky said, an approving lilt to her voice. "And my recipe is excellent."

Jace gave a questioning glance to Mia. Quietly, he said, "What's a cauliflower steak?"

Mia patted his leg beneath the table, letting it rest there. "It's *literally* cauliflower, thickly sliced like a steak."

Jace nodded as if it mattered, but the feel of Mia's hand was the only thing that mattered to him at the moment. He started to reach down and take hold of it when she eased her hand back onto her own lap.

Jace laid the menu faceup on the table, giving a finger tap to the list of appetizers. "So, I'm guessing you need the ground beef for these meatballs?"

"Yes," Rocky said. "I'll need forty pounds. Do you think you'll be able to supply all of this in time?"

"Let me make a call before I commit." Jace picked up his phone.

Mia and Rocky waited while Jace sat through three

rings, the phone pressed to his ear. "Hey, this is Jace," he said when his call was answered. "Is Blake there?" Then, "Yeah, transfer me back, will ya?"

Jace snuck a glance at Mia while he was on hold. The sun, streaming through the window behind her, gave a shine to her shoulder-length brown, honey-highlighted hair. She'd been the woman of his dreams for as long as he could remember. When Blake picked up the phone call, Mia was asking the catering owner about the menu.

"Blake, I've got a big order," Jace said, "so I was wondering about the ETA on those ten head Travis brought in last week." He listened with a nod, then asked, "Do you think we can get two hundred sirloins out of those?" Then to Rocky, he asked, "What size sirloins?"

"Twelve ounces," she said.

Jace repeated it to Blake, then said, "Okay, great. When can they be picked up?" He looked back at Rocky and said, "Is the thirteenth okay?" When she nodded, he thanked Blake and ended the call.

Rocky reached across the table and grabbed one of Jace's hands. "You're a real lifesaver. I swear you'll get all my beef business from now on!"

Jace was feeling like a successful businessman, not just a rancher. "So, you want to talk about the Menard event?"

"Yes." Rocky reached into her satchel again and pulled out a different menu with an approval stamp and initials. She handed it to Jace. "It's a company appreciation banquet, so I'm committed to sixty attendees." She pointed to the entrée section of the menu. "I need eight-ounce filets. What do you think?"

"That's no problem, but I only deliver within fifty

miles, so you'll either need to pick up the steaks your-self from Dowd and Out, or I can deliver them to you in Junction."

"Junction is fine. As long as you can assure me that I'll have sixty filets by the first of September, we can work out the details later."

"That works," Jace said. "Anything else?"

"Yes," Rocky said as she tucked the menus into her satchel. "I have an event in Junction the end of September and another in Mason in mid-October, but I don't have the signed contracts back yet."

"Can you give me an idea of what you might need?"

"Skirt steaks and more filets."

"Okay." Jace stood. "Just let me know as soon as you can." He handed her a business card and asked, "Do you have a card?"

"Oh, yes." Rocky pulled a pink and green business card out of her satchel and then stood, handing it to Jace. "As soon as I have the signed contracts back, I'll call you with the details." She glanced at Mia. "Sure wish I had you working for me full-time."

Rocky left in a sashay that even caught Steve's attention. Once she was out the door, Mia asked Jace, "Do you have a few minutes?"

Jace hesitated but then nodded. "Okay."

Mia motioned him to sit again, but instead of reseating herself in the chair closest to Jace, she took Rocky's seat across the table from him.

"I'm sorry we haven't talked in the last few weeks, but I really appreciate you coming out today and meeting Rocky on such short notice. She was in a real bind."

"Well, thanks for calling me," Jace said sincerely. "She could be a real good customer. I need to get the ranch name out there more. Do you think she might be able to say that she uses Farr Reaches beef?"

"Maybe. That's a great idea."

"Yeah," Jace said with a nod. "I think I'll ask her about it." Then, after a moment, he said, "Did you need anything else?"

He hoped she did because he wasn't ready to leave her yet. It'd been too long since he'd last seen her, and it hadn't ended well. Maybe they could smooth things over.

"No." Mia stood. "Nothing else, I guess."

Jace stood, pushing back his chair. "Okay. Well, I'll have another delivery for you on Monday, but I guess that's your day off, isn't it?"

"Yes." Her glance held his gaze. "Will you be at the fundraiser?"

"Yeah," he said with a nod. "We never miss it."

"Maybe I'll see you there."

"Maybe so." Heartache settled inside him—the place it had belonged for so long. He picked up his Stetson from the empty chair and fitted it onto his head. "Thanks again for the opportunity, Mia."

Jace left without looking back.

On the drive out to the Farr Reaches, Jace called Melody. He hadn't even said hello yet when she said, "Hey, handsome cowboy. I've missed you."

"I've missed you, too. There's still two days before you leave for Grapevine, right?"

"Two days, but three nights, if you count tonight."

"I want to count tonight."

At the next opportunity, Jace turned the truck around and headed back into town.

≈

Saturdays had become extra busy for Mia at Boomer's Bar and Grill by her own doing. With the popularity of her chili, she'd started arriving early to work, mixing and matching powders and spices until the aroma in the diner was so scent-laden it could have drawn customers in right off of Ranch Road, even with their car windows closed.

When Mia had the big kettle full of chili for the day, she returned home to tend to other duties, returning for her evening shift. Steve managed lunch. Dinner was her charge. Whenever the chili sold out, it was gone for the day.

"See you in a few hours," Mia called out to Steve on her way to the front door.

"Hey, Mia, come look at this before you go." Steve had the newspaper spread out on the bar top beside his coffee. "You could make us famous."

With her leather purse slung over her shoulder and her car keys in her hand, curiosity walked her to Steve. "How can I do that?"

"Look." He flipped the paper around until it faced Mia, then he pointed to a quarter-page advertisement. "I'll bet you could win this chili cook-off, and if you did, it would put this diner on the map."

She leaned, silently reading the ad. "Yeah, if you win Terlingua, you win the world." She straightened up, looking at him in all seriousness. "Not literally the world as in world champion, but in Texas, it's close enough."

"So do it!" Steve stood. "I'll pay the entry fee."

Mia laughed. "There's more to it than just paying the entry fee. You need points."

"Points?"

"Points. It's a road you pave." She shrugged. "I've

already won three chili cook-offs this year with my Houston team from culinary school. I was the head cook in all three competitions, so I probably have enough points to enter, but I'm not going to." Mia gave a pat to Steve's hand, whose finger was still pointed statue-like at the ad when she turned to leave.

To Mia's back, he said, "So, you have enough of those points to enter?"

"Probably," she called over her shoulder, then pushed open the door and walked across the parking lot to her car.

Competing for the things she loved no longer seemed worthwhile.

CHAPTER 20

"Well, Hannah Farr," Craig called from the Feed and Seed's front counter when he spotted the quintessential Texas woman who'd once taught him all about ranching. When her gaze found him, she smiled.

"Craig," she said, crossing the entrance and reaching for his hand. "It's good to see you." Then, "On the way over, Jace told me that Mary wasn't feeling well. How is she?" When his gaze dropped, she patted the hand she held. In an understanding tone, she said, "Well, you tell her that I asked about her, will you?"

A few steps behind was Jace—his red Aussie postured beside him. "Craig, do you mind if Cowboy comes in with us, or is that long-haired mouser on duty today?"

"Bring him in." Craig waved them inside. "The General has been napping in my office all morning." Then he pointed to the far wall where a WILD-FLOWERS sign hung. "Jack's in back if you want to go and say hi."

Jace and Cowboy started through the store, leaving Hannah and Craig talking together.

At the TXUS SEEDS spinner display, Jace spotted his cousin restocking seed packets. "Jack," he said, reaching for a handshake and hugging the man. "Good to see you."

Jack Brown was aging well, not that his cousin was much older than him, but his short-boxed beard with mustache, well-groomed at the edges and framing his lips and jawline in high-box style, gave him a mature, corporate-like look.

"I was just thinking about you," Jack said to him. "How's the ranch doing? And how's Grandma Hannah?"

Jace's father, Jacob, and Jack's mother were distant cousins, but Jace and Jack had grown up close.

"Grandma's doing okay," Jace said, pointing to the front of the store. "She came to town with me today. I left her upfront, talking to Craig. It's hard to get her out of the house anymore."

"You're lucky to have her," Jack said. "I still miss Gramps and Grammy. It seems like yesterday that I inherited their house and seed farm, but it's already been over seven years."

Jace knew better than to ask, but he did anyway. "Have you seen your folks lately?"

"No." Jack shook his head, almost crushing the seed packets he held in his hand.

"Well," Jace shifted, "I thought about driving over or meeting up with them at a rodeo, but the ranch has kept me busy."

Jack filed the packets back in their box, focusing on them like they were made of gold, without responding.

"You seeing anyone?" Jace asked him. He suspected he knew the answer to that question, too. Jack had fallen in love with Kaitlin the moment he'd met her, but she'd been killed in a car wreck just a few years after they married. That had been almost four years ago. They'd had one child together, but another had been on the way at the time of her death.

Jack glanced up. "Kaitlin was my one and only, Jace. She always will be." He smiled, easing the tension. "True love only comes along once, you know?"

"I'm beginning to think you might be right about that." Life without Mia had changed everything for Jace, too, but losing Mia had been a different kind of loss. Hope had never died.

"C'mon now," Jack said. "Of the three of us, you were always the one who had the girls following him all over the place."

Jace laughed. "Yeah, owning a ranch with free horses to ride was a big draw."

Jack straightened up, his height a head taller than Jace. "I thought you would be married by now. What are you? Twenty-five? Twenty-six?"

Jace nodded. "Twenty-five."

"So, are you seeing anyone?"

"Yeah," he said, looking down at his feet. "But she just moved to Dallas." He looked up, an embarrassed smile creasing his face.

"Jace, it's hard to see somebody who is a five hour drive away." Then taking a more thoughtful tone, Jack asked, "Was it serious?"

"Not really," Jace admitted. "I feel kind of like a heel about it if you want to know the truth."

"Why is that?" As kids, it had always been Jack's

brother who'd taken the big brother lead, but with him out of the picture, Jack had become a natural in the role.

"Do you remember Mia?" Jace asked him.

"Yeah. I always thought she was your one and only. Everybody thought you two would get married. You were an item forever."

The memories made Jace smile. "Well, she's back in town. For a while anyway."

"Are you getting back together with her? I thought she moved to Houston years ago."

"She did, but her mom was in an accident, and Mia came back to take care of her for a while. She's been back most of the summer."

"Are you two serious again?"

Jace shook his head. "No. She's been really helpful, but she's got another guy in New York. She's moving there in December."

Jack gave an understanding squeeze to Jace's shoulder. "Sorry, man."

A change of subject was needed before he admitted things he didn't want to admit. "Hey, how's that little girl of yours? You know, Grandma would love to see you both."

Jack's eyes lit up at the mention of his daughter. "Juli's great. She's about ready to start kindergarten." The girl was his whole world now.

"You should bring her out to the Farr Reaches next time you're in town. Maybe we could grill out and spend some time together. You could stay the night. We could ride up and show Juli the lambs on Old Duke's farm." Jace shifted into his standard forewarning. "Grandma's memory has gotten a lot worse since you saw her last, though. Some days are better than others, but it's just like a light switch. Don't worry if she doesn't remember you. She would still enjoy the visit, and sometimes people have a way of bringing her memory back for a while, just like it was never gone."

Jack gave a slow nod, a hard focus on him. "You were handed some big responsibilities when your dad died, Jace. I just want you to know that I'm real proud of you." Jack reached out for Jace's hand. "We need to stay in closer touch."

Jack had a true Texas heart. A family trait, it seemed.

Mia met Rocky at the Ag Barn Exhibit Hall on Thursday morning, before Saturday's fundraiser to familiarize herself with the kitchen and dining setup and to discuss the prep work needed for the charity event.

"Hey, you can't use those tables!" Rocky shouted to a trio of men, moving a dining table for eight to the wall. She started across the room toward them. "Those are our dinner tables."

The men set the table down. The two younger ones, wearing T-shirts and ball caps, waited while the older man in a cowboy hat explained, "We're doing the setup for the auction items."

"I don't care," Rocky said. "The round tables are mine."

"Who are you?" he asked.

"I'm the caterer," she pointed, "and all of those round tables are mine for the event."

The man's gaze shifted from Rocky to Mia. "Aren't you Mia Ellis?"

"Yes," Mia said, studying the man. "Are you Diana's dad?"

"Sure am." He walked toward Mia. "Does Diana know you're back?"

"No," Mia said, hugging him. "I thought she moved to Austin."

"She did for a while. College Station, anyway. Soon as she graduated from Texas A & M, she came back home. She's managing the antique shop now."

"The Well Remembered shop?"

"Yeah, you should stop in and see her." He shot a glance to Rocky before it veered back to Mia. "So, what are you doing here?"

"I'll be the chef Saturday night, cooking your dinner."

He gave a side nod to Rocky. "You work for her?"

"Yes." Mia glanced at Rocky when he did. "Rocky, this is Sam Duren. He owns Brown Buffalo Auctions."

Rocky barely suppressed a sigh before reaching out for a handshake. "Rocky Hill of Hill Country Banquets. Can you put my table back, please?"

"Yes, ma'am," Mr. Duren said. He turned to the table and grabbed hold of its edge, saying, "Let's move it back, boys."

When the catering van arrived and started unloading table linens, napkins, chafing dishes, serving trays, coffee urns, refrigerated drink dispensers, dishes, and cooking pans, Mia helped set up the kitchen.

"Will there be centerpieces for the tables?" she asked Rocky.

"Not our problem," Rocky said. "They have

someone making floral arrangements for the tables, and then they're planning to auction them off after dinner."

By midafternoon, the initial setup was complete, and sponsor signs for the event and the auction had arrived. Mia had her purse over her shoulder, ready to leave, when the crew hung the sponsor sign for Farr Reaches Quality Beef. The man who had shied away from putting his own name on the company business now had his face plastered in the upper left corner of the giant sign. And it looked good. Really good.

She stood, staring at the signboard, when her cell phone rang. Without taking her eyes off the oversized photo of Jace—hung so prominently on the wall—she answered, "This is Mia."

"Hello, Texas lady."

"Ethan?"

"Yes." His naturally sexy voice carried a smile. "I've been thinking about you."

Mia pressed the phone closer to her ear, closer to him. "I've been thinking about you, too."

He was the only man she had ever known who could take her mind off Jace.

"I was wondering if you might want to fly up and spend a few days. I have enough airline miles to fly you cost-free. I could show you around, and maybe we could look at a few studio apartments while you're here."

"I can't, Ethan. Mom still needs me, and I have the charity fundraiser this weekend."

"Oh, that's right," Ethan said. "And why are you doing that again?"

Mia suppressed a laugh. "Money, for one thing."

"And what's the other thing?"

"I need to practice my culinary skills. I hope these

rehearsals will pay off when I get to New York." Then, she said, "Maybe you could fly back to Texas next week?"

"No good. I'm flying to Brussels on Tuesday and taking a tour of Bruges, Ghent, and Dinant to gain insight into the history and heritage of the cities before deciding whether to add the places to the Belgium tour."

While lots of other businesses were scaling back, Ethan's international tour company was expanding and booming. It seemed a tour-guided vacation was the remedy for the stress in the world.

"You know," he said. "I'm in need of a culinary expert for my tour guests. The position requires a chef. Like you. As part of the salary, which is quite good I might add and has fantastic travel benefits, the company will provide a furnished one bedroom near Carnegie Hall. Would you be interested?"

Mia was stunned into silence for a moment. "Ethan, that's an amazing offer. Thank you, but I need to stay on track with my plan. I've worked hard to be accepted into the apprenticeship program. It's an incredible opportunity for me."

"Yes, I understand," he said. "But think about it, won't you? If I don't hear from you, I promise the subject will come up again between us."

When she arrived home from the charity set up, her mother was shouting before Mia even had the door unlocked, but her words were barely perceptible over the blare of the television.

"Is that you, Mia?"

"Yes," Mia called back. Without putting down her keys or purse, she hurried through the living room and into her mother's bedroom. The first thing she did was grab the remote and turn off the television. Her mother was sitting in the wingback chair across the room. On the floor a few feet away lay her crutches.

"This is why you can't run off and leave me alone, Mia." Josie was angry. "I've been trapped here in this chair for over an hour!"

Mia picked up her mother's crutches and carried them to her. "How did they end up on the floor so far away?"

Josie pointed. "I tripped over those dirty clothes and nearly fell!" She took the crutches from Mia. "Help me up."

Mia helped her mother stand and waited while Josie positioned the crutches beneath her arms.

"I'm sorry," Mia said. "You should have called."

Josie disappeared into the bathroom. "My phone is on the nightstand. I couldn't reach it either."

Mia straightened up her mother's bedroom, picking up the clothes and trash off the floor. She carried the blouses, pants, pajamas, and socks to the laundry room but then returned, helping her mother to bed even though it was midafternoon.

"Mom, I have the catering event this weekend. I'll be gone a lot for the next two days. You need to be more careful. I won't be able to run home and check on you."

Josie swept her overgrown blonde bangs out of her eyes, her stare landing on Mia. "I can't be left alone that long. You said you'd take care of me, Mia. You can't just run off whenever you get bored with me. I'm a person, too. Don't you think I want to go out sometimes and have fun like you do?" Josie pulled the bedsheet up to her waist and reached for the TV remote. "I mean, just look at me, Mia. What if I'm crippled for life? What are you going to do with me then? Just throw me out?"

Mia felt the catch in her chest. She drew a breath and held it, drawing in every ounce of energy and patience from it before releasing the air. The stress of being her mother's daughter was wearing hard on her.

CHAPTER 21

J ace took his ranch hand, Cade, with him early
Friday to deliver the two hundred sirloin steaks
and forty pounds of ground beef to Rocky at the
Ag Barn kitchen. The meat was frozen rock hard,
so he wanted to bring them as early as possible to thaw
for the next night's charity dinner.

He knocked on the rear entrance door and waited.

"Want me to go around front?" Cade asked when
no one answered.

"No." Jace nodded toward the cars parked alongside the building, recognizing Mia's Prius. "They're
here." He knocked again, louder this time.

After a moment, the door pushed open.

"Thank God," Rocky said at the sight of him.
"You're earlier than I thought. Just bring everything
in."

"Yes, ma'am," Jace said, turning back toward his
truck while Cade stood staring. Jace nudged him.
"Come on. We've got to unload this order."

He understood the mesmerized look on the young

ranch hand's face. Rocky wore ultra-tight blue jeans, a big silver belt buckle with a coral heart, and a sleeveless white cotton blouse with a plunging neckline. She was a knockout in any man's eyes.

Cade stumbled into step with Jace, whispering, "Is she the caterer?"

"Yeah," Jace said, opening the truck's back door. He picked up the first box of frozen meat.

Cade leaned in close. "So, she's your girl?"

Jace set the box down on the seat and turned to Cade. "What are you talking about?"

"Everybody says the caterer is your girl."

Jace sighed. "They're talking about Mia, not Rocky, who's got to be ten or fifteen years older than me, Cade. You can see that, right?" Jace had a hard time seeing it himself, but he tried not to look too closely.

"Yeah, maybe," Cade said, glancing back at the long-haired blonde who waited in the doorway. "But if she's not yours, she's sure somebody's girl."

Jace picked up the box again and started for the open kitchen door. "Grab a box, Cade."

Inside the kitchen, Jace spotted Mia aligning meat racks and trays. He set his box on the counter, and when she glanced at him, he nodded a silent greeting before returning to his truck for a second box. He carried it inside.

This time, Mia was at the counter, waiting for him. When he set the box down, she said, "You know, I hate this."

"Hate what?" His hands went to his hips.

"Us seeing each other and not talking. It was easier when we weren't running into each other all the time."

Jace held her gaze. "This wasn't my idea, Mia. It's never been my idea."

"Well, I wasn't expecting to stay so long when I came home. It never occurred to me that I would run into you so much or that this would become a problem. But it has."

"So, seeing me is a problem?" He knew his tone was turning ugly. "Mia, you got me this contract with Rocky. I'm here because of you. What do you want me to do? Call first to make sure you're not around?"

"That's not what I mean, Jace." Mia finger-combed her shoulder-length brown hair back over the crown of her head, which she only did when she was feeling stressed. "I'd just like us to be friends again, you know? Like when we were working on your bank proposal."

"I thought we were more than friends." There hadn't been a single moment in their lives when they'd simply been friends and nothing more.

"I mean now. Friends now."

"I meant now, too…" He wanted to dispute the differential, but Mia took hold of his hand and pulled him toward the event center dining room. When he balked, she shushed him. When he argued, she shushed him again.

Finally, he listened since she would not listen to him.

"Look," Mia said, pushing open the swinging kitchen doors. She pulled him along until they stood in the middle of the room together. She turned and pointed to the sponsor sign on the wall.

"You used your photo." She smiled at him, nodding her approval. "I really like it."

Jace stared at the sign. "It's bigger than I thought it would be." He studied it a minute longer. "The picture was Melody's idea. She's real good at advertising and marketing."

Mia dropped his hand. "It was Melody's advice you took? I'm the one who suggested you use your own name so you'd get the credit for the new business. Why would you use her marketing ideas but not mine?"

He hadn't meant to say it, but sometimes broken hearts bled mean words. "Because she's willing to sleep her way to the top, and I like her there."

Mia's face drained of color.

Jace immediately took hold of her arm. "Mia, I'm sorry. I shouldn't have said that."

"No," she said, clearly shaken. "It's okay. You have every right to sleep with whomever you want." A glistening moistened her eyes. "Friends probably isn't a good idea, is it?"

She used her fingers to loosen his grip on her arm and then she stepped back. "So, I'll see you at the charity dinner tomorrow, okay?" Without waiting, she turned and walked back into the kitchen.

HANNAH WAS IN THE LIVING ROOM, WATCHING THE early news on television when Jace came looking for her.

"It's four thirty, Grandma. Do you want to take a shower before we go? Dinner is at seven, but if we get there early enough, we can browse the auction items and see a few folks before we're seated."

She glanced up at him. "Are we going somewhere tonight?"

"Yeah," he said, kneeling at her chair. "Tonight's the Junior Livestock Show Charity Fundraiser. Did you forget? We talked about it this morning. Travis is going, too, and he's bringing Ameree." When her brows furrowed, he said, "Ameree is Travis's wife. And the ranch is one of the big sponsors. I did it just like you taught me—we're supporting local causes and giving back to the livestock community. They're even serving our beef tonight."

Worry settled into the vacancy in her eyes. "I guess I did forget." She patted his hand—her thoughts searching him. "Why don't you go on without me this time? Take a nice girl on a date tonight."

Jace stood and reached out his hand to her. "You're my date, Grandma."

The parking lot of the Ag Barn near the event center was more than half full when Jace and Hannah arrived. He parked as close as possible to the entrance and helped Hannah down from the truck.

She was a stylish woman, wearing cognac-colored boots and dressed in a burnt orange three-quarter-length dress with a brown, long-fringed shawl lavishly embroidered with fall-colored flowers. Her gray, short-layered hair was sprayed to maintain its style for the evening.

Jace slipped her arm through his as they walked across the lot to the entrance.

At the door, Oaks Bradley, a tall, well-built man, took their tickets. "It's good to see you, Miss Hannah. You're looking lovely tonight."

"Thank you." Hannah smiled and patted his hand as if he were a child. A few steps in, she asked Jace, "Do we know that nice young man?"

Jace nodded to her. "Oaks used to haul our cattle to market."

"Oh, yes." She held a little tighter to his arm without more being said.

A table near the front had a tent sign *Reserved for the*

Farr Reaches Ranch on it, but instead of sitting, Jace and Hannah walked the line of tables, looking at all the silent auction items.

"Do you see anything you like, Grandma?"

She pointed to a pencil sketch framed in charred wood. "I like that cowboy sketch, don't you?"

"Yeah," Jace said. "It's real nice. You want to bid on it?"

"Oh, I don't know." She glanced at him. "It doesn't serve much of a purpose, does it?"

"It does if you like it. Where would you hang it?"

"By the back door, I think. So that I can look at it when I refill the bird feeders." Her fingers brushed the glass over the sketch. "It looks a little like your father on…What was his horse's name?"

"Pitter-Patter," Jace said. He took the pen off the clipboard and wrote his bid down on the lined sheet. "Let's see if we can get it."

The last table of auction items featured a full-color flyer slid into a clear stand, offering the "Bandit Pack" from Farr Reaches Quality Beef—the steak lover's package. He glanced at the bids and smiled when he saw its most recent bid was three hundred over the minimum.

At a slap on his back, Jace turned to see Trace and Cindy from the diner.

"Heard we're eating your beef tonight," Trace said.

"Yeah, sirloins," Jace told him. I guess there are appetizers around here somewhere, too. We supplied ground beef for the meatballs. Have you had any yet?"

"Oh, yeah." Cindy patted Trace on the stomach. "We ate more than our fair share, but the chicken satay with that jalapeño sauce was killer good. I'd eat a whole plate if they offered it to me."

"Jace," Hannah said to him. "I might like to try one of those."

"You would?" Jace glanced back at Trace and Cindy. "Hey, do you guys mind staying with Grandma while I go and get us a plate of appetizers?"

"No, you go right on ahead," Cindy told him, tucking her blonde waves behind her ear.

Jace was stopped several times by people congratulating him on his new Farr Reaches Quality Beef startup and asking questions about the ordering process. The dinner and auction were stirring up the interest he'd hoped it would.

With a variety plate of appetizers—prime meatballs in peppercorn sauce, chicken satay with smoked jalapeño aioli sauce, and mushroom crostini, Jace worked his way back across the room to where Trace stood a good head taller than everyone else. He was an easy man to spot in his twenty-year-old black felt cowboy hat with a bite out of the brim.

"Where's Grandma?" Jace asked them.

Cindy turned with a smile. "Oh, I don't know, darlin'." She motioned toward the back wall. "She wandered off that way a while ago."

With his heart skipping beats, he scanned the crowd for a petite, gray-haired woman. If she was in the room, she was overshadowed by the hordes of people. He started across the room, weaving in and out, asking almost everyone, "Have you seen Grandma?"

When he came to their reserved table, he set down the plate of appetizers and looked for any sign that she might have been there, but every napkin was in place, and not a single glass of water had been moved.

He turned to see Travis and Ameree. "Trav, I can't find Grandma."

"Where've you looked so far?" Travis asked him.

Jace pointed to the most obvious black hat in the room. "I left her over there to go for a plate of appetizers, and when I came back, she was gone."

"Okay," Travis told him. "We'll make our way back to the entrance, and if we don't find her, we'll start looking through the parking lot." He held up his cell phone. "Call if you find her."

Jace started for the stage area. He should never have brought her. She hadn't wanted to come. He knew she was uncomfortable in overcrowded places, and being out in public confused her.

"Sam," Jace called to the auctioneer who was setting up a sound system speaker. He shook hands when offered but then said, "Can you get on the microphone and ask Grandma to come up to the stage? I can't find her, and I'm worried."

"Yeah, hang on," Sam said and took the steps up. He turned on the microphone and waited for the squeal to die down. Into the mic, he announced, "Could Hannah Farr please come to the stage? Hannah Farr to the stage, please."

Jace scanned the crowd for movement, glancing at Sam Duren, who was doing the same thing.

"I don't see her, Jace. You want me to do it again?"

"No, but can you stay here for a few minutes, just in case she answers the page?" He glanced at the nearby swinging doors. "I'm going to check the kitchen."

A frenzy of servers and staff swarmed the kitchen without anyone noticing him. He dodged a few white-aproned waiters carrying oversized trays of appetizers to the dining area, and then he squeezed by a lady filling pitchers of ice water and tea. He spotted Rocky filling salad plates and Mia at the stove. On a bar stool beside her sat Hannah.

Jace walked toward her while he pulled his cell phone out of his pocket. He dialed Travis. "Hey, I found her," he told him when he answered. "She's in the kitchen. We'll be out in a few minutes."

The smoke from Mia's station had a five-star restaurant aroma. She dropped two sirloins into a cast-iron skillet with butter for finishing, searing them until a brown crust formed, and then put each on a serving plate manned by an assistant.

"Grandma," Jace said when he reached Hannah. "You scared me. Are you okay?"

Mia glanced at him. "Glad you're here," she said, working steak after steak. "I was afraid she might wander outside, so I asked her to wait here with me until I could take a break and help her find you. I had a stool brought in for her." Mia smiled. "She's been keeping me company."

"Jace," Hannah said. "Did you know that a pan-seared sirloin is more flavorful than a grilled sirloin?"

"No, Grandma. I didn't." Jace smiled at her ease. "But if Mia told you that, I'll bet it's true." He reached and helped her down off the stool. "Let's let Mia get back to work. Travis and Ameree are waiting for us at our table."

Guiding his grandmother back past Mia, Jace leaned in and whispered, "Thank you."

CHAPTER 22

A storm had been threatening to unleash a torrent since four in the morning, sending thunder booms and lightning flashes to the ground, but so far, only a sprinkle of rain had fallen on the Farr Reaches.

Jace stood, his coffee cup in one hand, looking out the front windows toward the horizon, waiting to see if the rising sun would burn through the darkening storm. He hoped the clouds would win today, break open, and pour down a deluge. The drought needed a good dowsing.

"Good morning, Jace," his grandmother said, much of her vocal strength absent. She crossed the room in her pajamas and robe in a slower and more unsteady gait than yesterday.

"Mornin', Grandma." When she was close enough, he leaned and kissed her cheek. "You want some coffee?"

"Yes, I would." She inched toward her favorite easy chair by the window.

"Are you doing okay?" Jace asked, following her to the chair. "You're moving a little slow this morning."

Hannah sat and then scooted back into the comfort of her swivel glider chair. "My lower back is hurting today. I can't imagine what I did to it to cause it to be so sore."

"Well, you danced two dances with me last night at the charity auction. Do you think that could have done it?"

Hannah glanced up at him and smiled. "That's right. We did dance last night, didn't we?"

He nodded. "You still got it, Grandma."

"Oh, stop." She laughed. "Would you mind bringing me that cup of coffee?" Her gaze was drawn to the window. "Quite a storm last night, wasn't it?"

"Loud, but not more than a quarter-inch of rain." Jace left and returned with her coffee, setting it on the side table. "We might run into Dr. Evans at church this morning. Maybe we can ask if there's something he can give you for your back."

"Oh, no, I don't want to do that," Hannah told him, taking a sip of coffee. "I think I just need to rest today. Maybe I'll stay home. The reverend will understand."

She deserved the rest. The charity fundraiser had been a big event for her, mentally and physically.

Jace saddled Ghost and rode toward the irrigated south pasture where Travis and the hands had moved the pasture-to-plate prime beef, and also twenty cows raising June and July-born calves.

For a moment, Jace sat his horse, taking in the sight of a herd on the rise. The calves looked good and healthy, and the weight of it all didn't seem quite so heavy on his shoulders today.

"Trav," he called to his foreman. When Travis

climbed down off the fence railing and started toward him, Jace dismounted. "They're lookin' good, aren't they?"

"Yes, sir," Travis said, smiling. "It was a good idea to irrigate this field when you did."

"Yeah, I had a feeling we might need it." A soft breeze blew beneath the dark sky, but the thunder and lightning had subsided a while ago. Jace pointed to one of the men on horseback. "How's the new man working out?"

"Good," Travis told him. "I think, anyway. We'll find out tomorrow when we brand those Charolais. He came with good references, but you never know."

"I'll ride out with you in the morning to get those calves sorted and into the pen. I want them vaccinated, too, and the bulls castrated, then we'll turn 'em back out with their mothers." Jace was pleased with the stock. "I'll tell you the truth, Trav, this is the best-looking herd I've seen in a few years on this ranch."

"It is," Travis agreed. "After we're done with the branding here, I want you to ride up to the north pasture with me and have a look at the Brangus that need branding, too. We've got some work to do up there if you're planning to crossbreed 'em again with these Charolais."

"Okay. We can ride up Wednesday morning," he pointed to the new man again. "We'll take Nash. That big Oklahoma ranch he came from was Brangus heavy. Let's find out if he was worth that raise in pay."

On the ride back, the sun was working hard to force its way through the day, often giving the storm clouds a brilliant silver lining. It didn't take long for Jace to see it as a sign. He leaned forward, raising slightly out of the saddle, sending Ghost into a gallop.

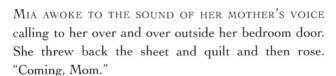

MIA AWOKE TO THE SOUND OF HER MOTHER'S VOICE calling to her over and over outside her bedroom door. She threw back the sheet and quilt and then rose. "Coming, Mom."

When she unlocked and opened her door, Josie had a glare aimed at her.

"Why did you lock your door? It's just me and you here."

"Habit, I guess. I've lived alone for so long that I don't even think about it anymore."

"Why would you lock the door to your bedroom if you live alone? Who do you think would be coming in?"

Mia shook her head. "I don't know. An ax murderer, maybe?" More awake now, she asked, "Did you need something?"

"No." Josie readjusted her stance on crutches. "You overslept, that's all. Are you going to fix me breakfast?"

"Oh, I'm sorry. What time is it?"

"It's after ten. I made the coffee myself. You should come get yourself a cup. Can you fry me an egg with a slice of bacon while you're in there?"

"Yes." Mia yawned and turned back to her room. "Let me get dressed, and I'll be right out."

Mia hadn't arrived home from the charity fundraiser until after three in the morning, and she was exhausted. She had today off, expecting to sleep her Sunday away, completely forgetting her mother would need help to get through the day. Her focus had been on the event, not on real-life responsibilities.

Mia sat at the table drinking coffee while her mother ate an egg, bacon, toast, and jam.

"Did you cook good last night?" Josie asked her.

"Yes. Lots of compliments." Mia smiled. "I saw my friend, Diana, after dinner. She came back to the kitchen afterward."

"She's managing the antique store now," Josie told Mia. "She went all the way to Texas A & M college just to come back here and manage the shop she worked at in high school." She took a sip of her cold coffee, then said, "But look at you. You went all the way to Houston for school, and here you are, back in town, working at a bar." She kept eating.

Mia set down her cup. Her eyes were on her mother. Tears welled, but she blinked them back.

When the doorbell chimed, Mia jumped up from the table and went to the front door, glad for a reason to leave.

Even though the morning sunlight blazed blindingly into the house through the open door, there was no mistaking who rang the bell.

"Jace," she said when she saw the silhouette of a cowboy. Without another word, Mia stepped outside and pulled him into a hug.

"Are you crying?" he asked.

"No," she lied. After a minute, Mia looked up at him. "I need to get out of here."

Jace glanced down at her silky, lemon-yellow shorts, white tank, and sandals. "Go put on your boots and jeans."

"I can't go back in there."

"Yes, you can," he said. "I'll keep Josie busy while you get dressed. Meet me at the truck."

It was just like high school. Jace—just in time. Her tears broke free.

"Go on now. Hurry up." He stepped into the house, closed the door, and started for the kitchen.

Inside her room, Mia grabbed a pair of already-worn-once-this-week blue jeans and some socks. She put them on and then slipped her feet into her cowboy boots. She threw on a red, white, and blue short-sleeved plaid over her tank top, ran a brush through her hair, and hurried out of the house with only her cell phone in her pocket. Once inside Jace's truck, she honked a single short honk.

Before long, Jace was on his way out the door, headed for his F-350.

Under a mostly blue sky spotted with puffy, cotton-white clouds, Jace drove out of town. All along the road, the heads of sunflowers, thistle, and golden tick-seed had lifted in response to the storm. Even the switchgrass and bluestem stood tall as if just a quarter-inch of rain had been all they needed to flourish.

Mia never questioned where they were going. She trusted Jace. She almost always had.

When he turned off the farm-to-market roadway onto the unpaved road that would take them to the Farr Reaches Ranch, relief flooded her. The sight of the family home with its fences, barns, corrals, and round pen felt like home. At least it did while she was with Jace, but that was something she could never admit.

After parking in the drive near the house, Jace got out of the truck. He started around the front end to open Mia's door for her, but a barrage of excited high-pitched barks turned him. He braced against the front grill guard.

Cowboy was in a dead run toward the truck, pouncing against Jace and bouncing back into twists and spins, yipping at every turn.

Mia smiled at the sound of Jace's laughter. It had never changed. It was the love of a boy and his dog. It came from deep-seated happiness that she had only known a few times in her life, always here, on this ranch.

After Jace hugged, playfully scratched, and petted the frenzied Aussie, he rewarded him with a treat from his pocket, then glanced back through the windshield at Mia. "Sorry." He held up a wait-one-minute finger. "I just need to get something." He trotted to the front porch, up the steps, and then into the house with the red dog beside him.

Mia got out of the truck, waiting. There was a *feeling* here. A strength that drew sadness out and tossed it away. Just that easy.

When Jace reappeared, he carried Mia's straw Stetson. He brought it to her and handed it over. "You're gonna need this."

Mia didn't balk. She took the hat, fitted it onto her head like she'd never been without it, and fell into stride alongside Jace.

Although he didn't take her hand, the two walked together across the yellowed summer lawn to the gate in the perimeter fencing that separated the residence from a pasture. Jace opened the wood gate, holding it for Mia before closing it, and then they started over the bare ground on a trail walked by the men and women of the Farr Reaches for a century.

The sandstone-colored wood exterior of the horse barn blended into the natural landscape of the Hill Country ranch. The scent of hay, worn leather, and dirt had never smelled as good.

Mia stopped midway through, closed her eyes, and inhaled. "I love the smell of a horse barn."

Jace laughed. "You're the only girl I know who likes the smell of horse manure."

Mia opened her eyes, taking in the sight of him. *God, he was beautiful.* His rich chestnut brown hair beneath his Silverbelly Stetson and his honest, earthy-brown eyes moved her almost to tears.

Even though the first week of September was still warm, Jace wore a long-sleeved white cotton shirt thinly lined in blue and brown. The shirt had pearl snaps and a single back yoke. But he wasn't fooling her —he'd always understood she was a sucker for a cowboy in a dress shirt and jeans. He'd seduced her into admitting it many times.

She hadn't meant to, but her gaze dropped down the length of Jace before she could pull away. Redirecting her focus, Mia held her hand out to the smoky-gray dun, who'd been watching them from his stall.

"Ghost doesn't look a day older than when I left." The horse touched her palm with his nose, allowing Mia to stroke his muzzle.

"Would you ride Hardtack today?" Jace asked, moving to another stall. "He's kind of a ladies' man, and Grandma doesn't ride much anymore. It's hard to find someone to give him the exercise he needs."

Hardtack, a dappled gray Quarter Horse with a slate-colored mane, had a calm demeanor, solid and sane. Hannah had sworn that the horse preferred women.

Mia walked to the stall and offered a hand. Hardtack stepped closer, nodding.

"I think he remembers you," Jace said. "Or else it's been so long since Grandma has paid attention to him that he's just glad to see a pretty woman."

Tenderly, Mia said, "Hi, Hardtack." She rubbed his

soft muzzle. "Looks like I get to ride you today. Will that be okay?"

When Hardtack gave a soft nicker, Mia looked at Jace. "I can't think of a better horse for me to ride. How old is he now?"

"He's probably about twenty. I think Grandpa gave him to Grandma about a year before he passed away."

Mia looked back at the horse. "Let's go for a ride today, boy."

The rugged land, with its rocky outcroppings and open fields of native grasses, chiefly grew live oak and post oak, with mesquite minimal in this northern part of the ranch. Mullein, though, was plentiful. The horses plodded over its broad velvety leaves, which somehow flourished in even the most unforgiving soil.

But time had a way of changing things in both man and nature.

One hundred million years ago, an ocean had covered this land. When the water receded, the magnificence of the Edwards Plateau was revealed.

In time, rivers, creeks, freezes and furnaces, wind, rain, and hail cut through its limestone and shale, eroding the plateaus and transforming the land into rolling hills, steep slopes, and flat-bottomed valleys.

The grasslands that had once been home to herds of bison and antelope now saw white-tailed deer, Texas longhorns, and a variety of good cattle that supported the ranches and the people within the state, too.

The Farr family had taken its place here in the late 1800s when land cost one dollar and fifty cents an acre, and the Comanche were still a threat. It had never been easy, but when given a chance, they had taken it. Never for granted, though. Always grateful with an eye toward future generations.

The significance of its history had never been lost on Mia, nor Jace, she knew. Jace was living a legacy, and if she'd been asked to guess, she would say the honor was more important than life itself to the man who now held the reins.

Saddled and mounted, Jace reined Ghost northward with Mia and Hardtack alongside them. The horses seemed to know exactly where they were headed.

CHAPTER 23

Low in a valley near Sleepy Creek, Jace dismounted, leading Ghost forward to a wash that rarely flowed unless heavy rains over-flowed the creek. He knelt on one knee, picking through the white rocks with his fingers, finally dislodging a thin, corner-notched point. He stood and held it up for Mia to see.

"That rain must have been enough to wash up this arrowhead from between the rocks." He slipped it into his shirt pocket and walked back to her. "Or else I just missed something real obvious all these years."

There was something she'd missed all these years, too. "Is that old cabin still standing?" It'd been the place they used to go when she wanted the world to go away.

With his hat shading his eyes beneath the afternoon sun, he said, "Yeah, you want to go there and get in out of the sun for a while?"

"Yeah," she said.

"I was hoping you would. I did some work on it a

few years back. The boys use it as a shelter now if they're caught out here in a storm, and I still come up every chance I get." He had a proud grin. "Trav even helped me get the water well working on a pump handle."

"Does it still have that big field of bluebonnets and firewheels?"

"Well," Jace glanced northward, "probably not in September, but I bet there'll be some sunflowers and maybe a few thistles left." He mounted Ghost, then glanced at Mia again. "Let's go see."

Amid the rock and native grasses, the prickly pear and the sumac shrubs, elevations dropped and then rose again, taking them across a landscape of granite uplifts and limestone plateaus.

Hidden down in a canyon on the south bank of the James River stood the rustic cabin. It looked livable now with its new tin roof and restored front porch with cedar support logs, but it was still definitely off-grid. No road. No electric lines. And the outhouse hadn't been torn down, so she knew other things were the same, too.

There was a rail at the rear of the cabin, resembling an Old West hitching post. It stood solidly in the ground not far from a giant old oak, right where it had always been, but the water trough nearby hadn't held more than a sheeting of rain after the storm.

Jace dismounted, wrapping the reins over the post, and then went to the rock water well and set a bucket on the limestone stand beneath the pump handle and filled it.

When he did, Mia eased out of the saddle and waited for Hardtack's turn to drink, and then she gave him a scratch behind his ear. "Good boy."

After emptying the bucket, Jace reached for Mia's hand. "Come on. Tell me what you think."

When she took his hand, he started up the porch steps where there was a crude handmade bench and a wrought iron chair pushed up snug against the exterior cabin wall. Jace took hold of the old original doorknob and turned, opening the door.

"You first," he said to her.

The one-room cabin looked entirely different inside than it had more than five years ago. The interior now had plywood walls, and the windows were new with screens and locking wood shutters. The old cast-iron stove was the same, though, used for both cooking and heating.

Mia pointed to the furnishings. "How did you get a futon and bunk beds up here?"

"Four-wheel drive," Jace said, laughing. He turned, glancing at the room. "Looks better than when you last saw it, huh?"

She nodded. "Lots." Then her gaze fell on a photograph of an early morning sunrise, clearly taken from the front porch of this cabin. Mia walked to the wall near the door where it hung and studied it. "Who took this picture?" She didn't turn around, instead, her scrutiny stayed riveted to the photo framed in rough wood.

"I did," Jace answered quietly.

Mia turned to him. "Why?"

She knew why—she had tried to block many of the memories that would have haunted her soul otherwise, but this one had never found its way out of her heart, and maybe it hadn't his either.

"Well," he tried to laugh, "it wasn't for the boys." But her focus firmed, so Jace started again. "That's how I remember the sunrise looking the first time you told me you loved me." He motioned to the front porch. "We were right out there, and you said you never wanted to leave this place. Or me. And I guess I don't ever want to forget that day."

Mia went to Jace, took his face gently in her hands, and kissed him, lingering in his breath, inhaling the soul-nurturing air he'd always given to her.

"I thought you didn't want..." he started but then stopped when her lips met his again.

There had been a time in life once when all Mia wanted or cared about was Jace in her arms and her in his. A time like now, in this cabin that no longer bore the dust and dirt associated with a secret love affair. Not that their love was a secret, but their lovemaking had been. Just the two of them had known they'd been each other's first and only.

In the hours after, at daylight's dimming, Jace rose, pulling Mia to her feet, her arms draping his bare shoulders. So natural. So freeing.

"We should get back before dark," he whispered to her, sweeping strands of her brown, honey-highlighted hair behind her ear, clearing a spot for another kiss.

"No," she whispered back. Her gaze lifted. She brushed her fingertips over his lips. "I want to watch the sunrise from that porch again. With you."

Jace held her gaze a moment, then softly kissed her before leaning to pick up his jeans. He pulled them on, then took his phone out of the front pocket. He held it up. "There's no cell service here. We can't tell anyone where we are."

She smiled. "How great is that?"

He laughed. "Josie will be worried."

"I don't care." Her mother probably deserved to worry about how she'd driven her out again.

"Mia, I can't leave Grandma alone."

Second-choice hit her square in the heart. It's what had sent her running once before. Mia turned, grabbed her jeans, and pulled them on. "You're ruining it again." Braless, she took her white tank and slipped it on over her head. "You always choose the ranch instead of me." Other than the truth, her words hadn't meant to be harsh.

"Mia, don't..." Jace stopped her from putting on her plaid overshirt.

"Choose, Jace!" she shouted, inches from him. "Me tonight, or the ranch?"

"Don't go. I'll stay. We'll stay. I'm sorry if it sounded like a choice I was making. That's not how I meant it." He pulled her to him, kissed her, then held her in his arms until she stopped trembling.

As the haze of darkness crept over the horizon—its thin line of sunset-orange fading—Mia went outside with Jace, him leading Ghost, and her, Hardtack, to the corral behind the cabin out past the old oak where an enclosed lean-to stood. They removed the saddles and bridles and uncinched the horses, then Jace tossed hay from a bale to them. He watched them for a minute, explaining to Ghost that they'd be staying the night.

Before returning to the cabin, Jace reached into his saddle bag and pulled out two carrots and then a pouch. He fed one carrot to each horse, then carried the pouch inside with him, laying it on the small square table for two.

"I'll get us a bucket of water if you'll check that camp coffee pot. The boys never rinse that thing out."

When Jace headed outside to the well, Mia went to the cast-iron stove and picked up the blue-speckled pot, removing its lid. It was getting dark, so she stepped outside onto the porch for more light to see inside it.

"It looks clean," she called to Jace, who was on his way back with the pail of well water. As he neared, she held it out to him. "Can you just pour a little in so I can swish to make sure?"

Jace did and then waited for Mia to swirl the water and dump it out, both of them going back inside together.

Mia set down the pot. "So, I'm guessing you have coffee stashed somewhere?"

"Yeah." Jace went to an unfinished cupboard—installed on the wall near the little eating table with two chairs—unlatched the critter-proof hook on the double door and opened it. Inside were six coffee cups, a package of percolator filters, a dozen cans of sardines in oil, two cans of ground coffee, one opened and one not, and a big strike-on box of matches. On the top shelf, face out, was a hard plastic first-aid kit.

Jace turned to her. "I didn't plan for a romantic night up here. You want some sardines?"

"No, thanks," she said, shaking her head, disgust curling her lip.

He lit the oil lamp that hung on a hook by the door. Its light lit the cabin with a glow that ignited urges in Mia that she hadn't felt in a long time until today. She went to him, encircling his neck with her arms.

In response, Jace held her around the waist, pulling her close and kissing her.

"Looks like no romantic dinner for us tonight," she said softly.

"No?" He grinned. "I have jerky in my pouch. And two more carrots that I brought for Ghost and Hard-tack, but I'd bet they'd be willing to share."

Mia laughed, kissing him again. "Let's make some coffee and go outside. City lights ruin dark skies, and I want to star gaze with you tonight."

Jace took the oil lamp outside with them and hung it on an iron plant hook nailed to the far cedar post — lowering its glow just enough to deter most of the nightlife who might venture too close without it.

The wrought iron chair had been there on the porch for as long as Mia could remember. She took her place in it, and Jace took his on the handmade bench that had no arms or back.

In the distance, coyotes howled, owls hooted, and cricket songs found their way to them. The rest of the world was quiet beneath the celestial heavens as star after star popped out of the darkness.

"The universe talks to me out here. Does it talk to you, too?" she asked him.

Jace took a breath so deep that it turned his face downward. "The only thing I ever hear out here is my heart telling me that I messed up big time with you."

In the solace of seclusion, Mia took hold of his hand. "I never meant for this to happen." Her gaze settled on him. "I never expected to see you again. To be with you again. When I came home for Mom, I thought I'd only be here a day or two." Comforted by the feel of his skin, his scent, his energy, she said, "If this doesn't feel right to you, or if it's too much too soon, you should tell me now because losing you was the hardest thing I've ever done."

Jace glanced at her, then dropped his focus back down to the wood plank floor. "What about New York?" He hesitated. "What about that Ethan guy?"

Truth had a way of pushing itself out of Mia.

"I don't know, Jace. I'm not sure about anything anymore."

When a look from Jace landed on her soul, she reached, grabbing his hand. "Oh, I didn't mean Ethan. I meant New York—I'm not sure I can give up New York. I've worked so hard to get there."

Jace stood and pulled her into a stand with him. They searched each other's eyes. "I don't want to be away from you for one second ever again. Five years was way too long."

Mia kissed Jace, her sensuality consuming the two of them. He responded by sweeping her up off her feet and carrying her back inside the cabin.

Even before daylight, Mia awoke. Light from the quarter moon barely cast any radiance onto the man sleeping so soundly beside her. She sat up, feeling for her clothes beneath the quilt. After finding them, she partially dressed before reaching for her footwear that she'd stashed on the side table. She'd learned long ago that she wanted nothing to do with things that had less legs than her or more than her horse—and scorpions, tarantulas, centipedes, and snakes often found a way into places where they were not welcome.

After shaking out her socks and boots, she slipped them onto her feet before sliding off the futon bed.

Quietly, she took down the oil lamp and struck a match to light it. When she did, Jace stirred but did not wake. She lit the lamp, then went outside with it.

Here in this place where nature had not been rearranged by the hand of man—where the land had so many things to say—it was hard to decide what it was saying to her, except to know that it was where the chance to start again began.

She listened to the silence, waiting for the dawn

chorus. Birds were always quiet until then, maybe because they knew what she knew — it was when loneliness and uncertainty were the strongest.

It was the moment when she doubted everything about her own existence and questioned the reasons why she was here at all. Like the birds, she would wake Jace when the chorus began, just to be sure she wasn't alone in the world.

CHAPTER 24

Jace rose just before sunrise—the time of day when everything was luminous but not clear. Mia was gone from the bed, but he heard no sounds of movement. Not even a breeze tapped the loose metal cap of the stovepipe. He put on his jeans and boots and went to the door, opening it to the lamp light. He stepped out, knowing Mia was there.

"Mornin'," he whispered.

Mia turned with a smile from where she stood at the far post beneath the dim glow of the lamp.

"I was just coming to wake you," she said.

He went to her, wrapping his arms around her from behind after sweeping her shoulder-length hair to the side and pressing a kiss onto her neck. "Are the birds singing yet?"

"No," she whispered back, "but the crickets have quieted down to barely a chirp."

"Should be any minute then."

They stood wrapped in love, waiting in silence.

At the first bird call, Mia gave a soft caressing

squeeze to his arms. Wrens, sparrows, titmice, towhees, and chickadees slowly, sporadically, began to call, then sing.

Amid the songs, dawn became sunrise—a yellowish blue with slashes of dull orange and gray. Before long, slanted sunbeams painted the ground, while others speared the land through narrow spaces where limbs and leaves hindered its passage, giving promise that there would be no rain today.

Mia turned in his arms. Softly, she kissed him. "Thank you for this." Her fingertips traced the outline of his face, her gaze studying every inch. "I'm so afraid to say 'I love you,' but I do."

"I love you, too, baby. I always have. I've never stopped."

When they rode out of the canyon that morning, it was ordinary daylight with glistening dew still clinging to the low grasses.

But crossing the limestone studded pasture east of the homestead sent a bristle through Jace. Even though they were still a half mile away, the horse barn, round pen, and the main home had an air of quiet that didn't sit well with him.

Hardtack and Mia continued onward toward the barn, even though Jace and Ghost had stopped. He stared at the silence within the distant house.

After a moment, Mia pulled up on the reins, glancing back at Jace.

"Is something wrong?" she asked him.

"I don't know. It's quiet, isn't it?" The most haunting of instincts strangled the life flow to his heart.

Mia turned toward the house, listening before she turned back to Jace. "It's still early. They're probably asleep."

Jace glanced at the barn again, turning an ear toward the land. He shook his head. "Sun's up. Something's not right."

He sent Ghost into a gallop.

Jace rode the horse into the round pen, dismounted, leaving Ghost saddled. Crossing the pen, he said, "Cowboy should be here." He headed for the gate he'd opened, closing it after Mia and Hardtack entered, saying, "I need to check the house."

He never looked back, focusing on the porch entrance instead. His stride was long and strong all the way to the back door where a turn of the knob found it locked.

Heart racing, Jace turned and ran back to Ghost, mounting him without a word to Mia, and rode for the bunkhouse.

On approach, Cowboy bolted from the opened door in a frenzy. Ray, Nash, and Cade came out after him.

"Sir," Ray said to Jace. "Me and the boys looked everywhere for you."

Jace dismounted, not even noticing Cowboy's frazzled demeanor. "What happened?"

Ray shifted from one foot to the other, his gaze grazing the ground before he lifted it to Jace again. "Miss Hannah had an accident."

"What kind of accident?" He went to Ray, Cowboy bouncing against him the whole way. "And where's Travis?"

"Travis and Ameree went with the ambulance to the hospital in Junction, but before they left, Trav drove Cowboy here." Ray gave a nod to the Aussie. "He's the one who came and got Travis for help, but then when the ambulance left with her, the dog tried to follow it.

He told us to keep him locked up here 'til you got home."

Jace remounted. "Keep Cowboy a while longer," he ordered. "Don't let him follow me."

THE SPEEDOMETER READ FIFTEEN MILES OVER THE speed limit, but now wasn't the time to advise Jace on how to drive safely. Mia simply pulled her seatbelt tighter and held onto the right grab handle.

From the ranch, the hospital was thirty-eight miles —every mile being quieter than the last, except when Jace would call Travis. At every voicemail response, Jace asked the same question, "Why isn't he answering?"

"It's the hospital, Jace. Cell phone reception is terrible inside." She lay a hand meant to comfort him on his arm. "Let's not assume the worst."

"I never should have left her alone." His focus stayed on the road. "I never should have done that." Then under his breath, his whisper was to himself but still strong enough for Mia to hear. "I wasn't there when she needed me."

Mia knew—it was *her* fault. Worse, Jace knew. She was the one who had set the demand at the cabin. She had forced him to choose, and for once in his life, he had chosen her. This was not the result she'd wanted. If she apologized now, she would become an unwanted distraction.

The sound of tires on pavement became their silence.

The miles had Mia searching the recesses of her mind, trying to find something she knew about life that might help her reach out and touch the soul of this man who she had never stopped loving, something to keep her close to him, but there was nothing she could say or do that would change the outcome of her unforgivable ultimatum.

The two-story limestone block hospital looked no different today than it had the day she drove into the parking lot in search of her mother. Although Jace held tight to her hand on their walk across the lot, the connection was only hand-to-hand, not heart-to-heart. Mia couldn't deny the chilly wall that was between them.

"I'm Jace Farr," he announced halfway to the front desk. "I'm looking for Hannah Farr."

"Jace," Travis called from the waiting room.

With a turn, they both started toward the other, Jace dropping his hold on Mia's hand.

"How's Grandma?"

"Ameree is with her. They only wanted one person in the room while they did another exam, and I figured she's better at this stuff than me."

"What room is she in?"

Travis pointed. "She's in ICU. Room 8."

Jace started for the corridor, never looking back.

Travis glanced at Mia. "You want a cup of coffee or something?"

"No," she said. "Thank you." Her heart was breaking, and a flood of tears threatened. "I'm sorry it took Jace so long to get here."

"Wasn't your fault," Travis said.

Yes, it was. "Do you know what happened to Hannah?"

"She was in the shower before bed last night, and she slipped and fell, I guess. The EMT said she hit her head on the tile bench seat. She was unconscious when we found her." His focus stayed on Mia. "Cowboy ran all the way to the house for us, but I don't know for sure how long she lay there under that spray of water. It was almost midnight when he woke us up, barking at the door like the house was on fire."

"Have the doctors said anything about her condition this morning?"

"Yeah, she's awake and talking. That's a good sign, but she didn't know Ameree or me for a while. She just kept asking everyone to call John."

"John?" Mia asked.

Travis nodded. "Jace's grandfather. Her husband."

"Did you tell them that he died probably twenty years ago?"

"Yes, ma'am. I did. They believe me, but Hannah doesn't. She's pretty upset about things right now."

Jace came down the hall, head down, walking toward Mia and Travis in the waiting room.

"Jace, how is she?" Mia met him halfway with Travis.

"They're going to take her back for a CT scan in a bit." He looked at Travis. "She's comfortable with Ameree, and she knows I'm here. Would you mind taking Mia home?"

"Home?" she asked.

Jace glanced at her. "You have to work today, don't you?"

"Yes." She nodded. "Later though."

"I'll probably stay here with Grandma. Travis can take you home."

"Mr. Farr?" A nurse called to Jace from the reception desk. When he turned, she said, "The nurse asked me to tell you that they're getting ready to take your grandmother back for the scan."

"Thank you," Jace told her, then he turned back to Mia and Travis. "I gotta go."

~

THE MOMENT MIA OPENED THE FRONT DOOR TO HER house, her mother was yelling.

On her crutches, Josie made her way into the living room where she had the TV blaring. "Where were you? Why didn't you come home last night? Why didn't you answer your phone?"

"I'm sorry," Mia said to her, and because of Hannah, she truly was sorry they hadn't come home. "Jace's grandmother had an accident."

Josie stood quiet for a moment, then asked, "Is she dead?"

"No," Mia said with a disconcerting stare at her mother.

"Good." Josie started for her recliner. "I'm glad for Jace. He paid a lot of money for that quilt he bought for her birthday. It would have been a big waste of money." She lowered herself onto the chair and then set the crutches aside. "And I can't give him a refund. It has their cattle brand on it, you know? No one else would buy the quilt with their brand on it."

Mia walked past the recliner, into her room, and slammed the door, feeling like a trapped and broken teenager again. *She didn't belong here.*

"Mia?" Josie called to her. "Are you coming back out?"

When Mia didn't answer, her mother called again.

"Mia? I called a lawyer last Friday. I've been waiting to tell you."

Curious, Mia turned toward the closed door, calling out, "Why did you call a lawyer?"

"He told me I should sue the driver of that other car. He said I could get a lot of money. He wants to talk to us."

Mia opened her bedroom door. "You mean he wants to talk to you."

"No." Josie shook her head. "Both of us. He said he needs a statement from you since you've been paying the bills."

She stepped out of her room, but when her phone rang, she stopped, looking at the caller ID. "Mom, turn down the TV!" then she turned away, answering, "Hi, Steve."

"Mia, where the hell are you? Are you coming in or what?" Her boss had zero finesse.

"Yes, I'm coming in." Mia spoke softly even though his voice was booming. "I've been at the hospital in Junction. A friend of a friend had to drive me home to get my car."

"The hospital?" His voice was lower and calmer than before. "Is everything okay? Are you okay?"

"Yes, I'm fine." Mia nodded. "I just need to shower and put on some clean clothes," she glanced at her mother, "and make sure things are okay for the rest of the day, and then I'll be in."

"Well, okay," he said. "But it's already noon, and two guys just left because they came in for a bowl of chili and there wasn't any."

"I'll be there, Steve," Mia said, then she disconnected the call.

Josie sat glaring at her. "You spent the night at a

hospital with someone who isn't even your own mother, and now you're going to leave me so that you can sling hash at a truck stop and bar? You're not making very good decisions, Mia."

"Stop it!" Mia shouted. She dropped down onto the couch, head lowered, and clenched handfuls of her hair. "I can't take this anymore!"

The problems she had caused Jace were unforgivable and inexcusable.

Josie quieted, even muting the TV herself without being asked.

Quelling a sob, Mia looked up at her mother. "I'm moving out."

"You can't move out. You said you didn't have enough money."

"I have a new job offer in New York, and it includes housing. There's no reason for me to be here anymore."

Mia stood and pulled her phone out of her pocket. On her way to the bedroom, she dialed Ethan Cole.

CHAPTER 25

How do you tell a person who has lost most of their memories that the one person they remember best died twenty years ago?

Jace sat beside the empty, unmade hospital bed with his head lowered into his hands. To Ameree, who was across the room, he said, "Do you know how long this scan takes?"

"Maybe thirty or forty minutes?" She glanced at the time on her cell phone. "She should be back soon. Are you okay?"

Jace leaned back, surrendering his attention to Ameree. Her coal-black hair, long and straight, was pulled back into a low-set ponytail, and her soulful, dark brown Native American eyes offered him comfort, compassion, and understanding.

"I suppose you've done this a hundred times, huh?"

"No." She shook her head. "School nurses don't spend a lot of time in hospitals."

"I guess that's true," Jace said. "I appreciate you and Travis coming to help Grandma last night. Sorry I wasn't there when it happened." He didn't want to ask the question, but he had to know. "Do you know how long Grandma was unconscious in the shower before you got there?"

Ameree was hesitant, but then with a supportive smile, she said, "Jace, it was probably a while, but you could have been home, working late in your office, and never known she'd fallen. This wasn't your fault."

"Oh, I would have known." Jace stood and started to pace. "I always check on her before I go to bed, and even if I hadn't, Cowboy would have come for me." He stopped and glanced at her. "Thank God he came for you."

The door pushed open, and a nurse wheeled Hannah back into the room. Her short gray hair was mussed, and she had on tan slipper socks and a blue and white hospital gown that didn't even cover her knees. She looked thinner than she did just a few days before.

"She did real good," the nurse said, then she helped Hannah up out of the wheelchair and back into bed. "I'll have a late lunch sent in for her."

"Do you know when the results will be back from the scans?" Jace asked.

The short, stocky nurse never looked at Jace when she answered. "The doctor on call will need to look at the reports first. She'll probably be in sometime this afternoon to talk to you."

After the nurse left, Jace took hold of his grand-mother's hand. "How are you feeling?" His gaze veered upward to the blackish-purple bump with a stitched gash on her head. "Do you need anything?"

Hannah gave a light squeeze to his hand. "No, I'm just glad you're here. Were you able to get a hold of your grandpa and your dad for me? No one seems to know how to reach them. I don't want them wondering where I am and worrying about me."

Jace glanced at Ameree, but then he looked back at his grandmother. "You just need to focus on getting better so we can go home, okay? Dad and Grandpa are right where they were yesterday, but I promise I'll stay here with you."

Hannah put her hand on his cheek and patted. "You're a good grandson, Jace."

A knock on the door preceded Travis peeking his head inside the room. "Okay if I come in?"

"Yes." Ameree went to the door. "They've finished the tests. We're just waiting for more information now. I'm glad you're back." She kissed him quickly, then led him to the foot of the bed. "Hannah," she said. "Travis is here to take me back home. Jace is going to stay with you. Do you need us to do anything at the house?"

"No, I don't think so. John can water the plants, but oh, will you remind him to feed the birds? I can't remember if I fed them this morning."

No one wanted to tell her that she hadn't been home this morning and John no longer existed except in her heart and in her memories.

"We'll make sure the birds are fed," Travis promised, then he reached out to Jace for a handshake. "We'll take care of things at the ranch. You stay as long as you need."

"Thank you," Jace said, then, "Trav, can you pick up Cowboy from the bunkhouse and let him stay with you 'til I can come and get him?"

"Yeah," Travis said. "We'll make sure he stays with us until you get home."

AN HONEST AND ENTHUSIASTIC LILT IN ETHAN'S voice raised Mia's spirits, even though the goodness of the feeling bypassed her heart.

"That's tremendous news," he told her. "I'll be out of the country next week, but as soon as I return, we'll set up your flight to New York." When she didn't respond, Ethan said, "You're sure about this?"

"Yes," Mia said. Her voice bore so little strength. "I'm sure."

After her shower, Mia dried her hair and then dressed, glancing at her phone every few minutes. *No calls.* Every minute that passed without Jace needing or wanting her broke her heart a little more. Most likely, he hadn't given her a second thought. And why should he? The ranch came first—it always had until last night —and right now, *first* meant Hannah. Ranch and family were synonymous to them.

The diner had two customers when Mia walked through the door of Boomer's Bar and Grill. She stopped and scanned the room for Steve, but when she didn't see him, she started for the kitchen.

There, Steve stood at the fry station, waiting on an order of French fries.

"Where is everybody?" she asked him.

With a glance up from the bubbling oil, Steve said, "It's been this way for two days. Soon as the customers realized you weren't here, they stopped coming in." His glance had an element of alarm. "It happened just that fast."

Rooney approached, drying his hands on the apron tied around his waist. "Everybody's been asking for you. They think you quit."

"You've been gone four days, Mia. *Four days* and this is what I get—two customers for lunch today." He raised the fry baskets out of the hot oil. "If you ever quit, I'll have to sell this place."

Mia hesitated, giving a "get lost" side nod to Rooney, who took the hint and retreated to the triple sinks where his dishes were drying. She knew he was still watching and listening, but it couldn't be helped. The kitchen just wasn't that big.

"Actually, Steve, I need to give my notice."

The big, burly, redheaded man rehung the fry basket onto its hook and turned to face her fully, eyes wide, a catch in his breath. No words came.

Mia moved in front of him, took the metal fry basket, and emptied the French fries into the burger baskets where two ready hamburgers waited. "Rooney, can you serve these, please?" She handed them to the busboy, who carried them into the dining room.

With her and Steve alone in the kitchen, Steve said, "You can't quit. Not now. You said you'd be here until the first of the year. I'm counting on that."

"I know," Mia said. "And I intended to be, but a job offer came up in New York that I can't refuse, so I'll be leaving the week after next. I can teach you how to make my chili before I go."

Mouth agape, Steve stood, staring at her.

Mia picked up a clean apron and tied it around her waist. "It's slow today. Let's make some chili together."

Without waiting for Steve to agree, Mia went to her spice racks and pulled four different chili powders, ground pepper, and more spices, then she carried tomato sauce and cartons of beef broth to the workstation and set them beside the other ingredients. When

Steve's involvement became uncomfortably absent, she turned with a glance.

"Don't you want to write this down?" His silence sent Mia into the office. She came back with a notepad and pen and set them down on the work counter. She gave them a push toward him. "You'll end up with your own favorite spice mix after a while, but I'd start with my recipe first." She tapped the notepad. "Come on, write it down."

"I can't do this, Mia."

"Of course, you can, Steve. It's actually really easy to make great chili. But keep in mind, competition chili is different from restaurant chili in a lot of ways. Competition chili is based on a great first bite, whereas restaurant chili needs to be great for a whole bowl. And even though I hate to do it, I always keep a separate pot of beans ready so that if some out-of-stater comes in and complains that there are no beans in his chili…" she turned to Steve again, "which there aren't any beans in *real* chili, right? I hope you know that by now. Anyway, you can always spoon a ladleful of beans into his chili to make him happy, but be sure to charge more. Not because your cost is that much higher, but because anyone who thinks beans go in chili should pay the price for their ignorance."

She went to the walk-in, took out the chili-grind ground beef, and then returned to the workstation with it.

"Mia…" Steve stopped her. "I mean I can't go back to how it was before you got here. I just can't do it. I was working sixteen-hour days and didn't have enough customers to sustain the place. Then you came along, and all of a sudden this place turned into a profitable venture almost overnight. Hell, Mia, I don't even like Texas." He shook his head. "No. I can't do it."

Boomer's Bar and Grill had become her safe haven in Legacy. It was the place she came when she needed to put herself back together. And right now, there seemed to be a lot of missing pieces to find. She'd depended on the place to help her get through her culinary depression, and she'd developed a strong affection for it. She didn't want it to fail because of her.

"And by the way," Steve said on his way out of the kitchen. "That no beans in chili thing is only true in Texas. I'm from Ohio, and we eat beans in our chili."

Mia went to the door, frustrated at his lack of fight for the place, calling out, "There's no beans in chili, Steve! Texas literally invented chili—and there's no beans in it." She turned to her workstation, still brazenly calling out to him, "It's the official state dish of Texas. We know how to make it!"

CHAPTER 26

The following morning, Jace stood opposite Dr. Jemison, across his grandmother's hospital bed, while the doctor spoke more to him than to Hannah.

"The results of yesterday's PET scan and CT scan indicate the dementia is progressing beyond mild cognitive impairment." She glanced at Hannah with an acknowledging nod. "With your grandmother's permission, I called and spoke with Dr. Evans in Legacy, who said he's been her physician for over thirty years, is that right?"

"Yeah," Jace answered. "What did he say?"

"He agrees that her condition is worsening, Mr. Farr."

"So, what does that mean? Does she need new medicine?"

Dr. Jemison, a petite Black woman with close-cropped hair, held her clipboard tighter to her chest. "There are things we can try. For instance, an improved diet might help, but the fact of the matter is, your grandmother will need closer supervision—more assistance with daily things like showering." She glanced at the clipboard, made a note on Hannah's chart, then pulled it up close to her chest again. "I'll have the dietician visit today. She'll give you a list of foods that might help if added to her daily and weekly menu, which might benefit her cognitive abilities."

"Oh, Jace does just fine with our food," Hannah assured the doctor. "He usually brings something home from the diner for us. I don't eat much anyway."

The doctor focused on Jace. "Diner food won't be on the dietician's list."

Jace stepped back from the bed, head down, eyes focused on the floor. "I don't know how all of this is supposed to work, but I can't cook, and I have a ranch to run." He pulled his gaze up. "I don't know how to do what you're asking me to do."

After a quiet moment, the doctor said, "There are care facilities available."

"No." Jace shook his head. "I'm not putting her into a home."

His heart was breaking. This woman had been his world. His rock. A friend and the only person who had stayed a constant in his life. She was the matriarch of his family. The one who held things together.

"Well," the doctor said. "Take some time to think about it. A social services worker can talk to you about your options."

Jace struggled to maintain a steady voice. "If Grandma is okay to go home, I'd like to get her checked out of here today."

"I'm going to keep her for one more night, Mr. Farr. It's difficult to determine how much of her cognitive failure was present before she fell and hit her head, and what might actually be new symptoms that developed after the fall." The doctor checked Hannah's scalp and the stitches there. "She should be able to go home tomorrow."

When the doctor left the room, Jace went to the hospital recliner and sat, leaning forward with his hands clasped between his knees. His mind wandered to an unforeseeable future. There had been a time when he'd known exactly what his life would be, but that was long ago, and circumstances had been different then.

Slowly, everything and everyone was vanishing from his life.

MIA WAS LOST IN THOUGHT, DRIVING THE ROAD TO the Farr Reaches Ranch. She had trapped Jace into saying he loved her, but for a while, she actually believed that he did. There could be no other outcome when you're alone together in paradise, loving each other like newlyweds in lust.

Not everyone would see an ages-old cabin with no running water and only an outhouse as paradise, but that's how she saw it. It was the place where the world went away, and only good things lived in her heart. She understood life there. She understood herself.

Twenty-four hours had come and gone without a word from Jace, and he hadn't answered or returned any of her phone calls. One way or another, she needed to tell him she was moving to New York earlier than expected, and she didn't want to do it over voicemail.

Cutting ties sooner rather than later was for the best.

The windshield of her Sea Glass Pearl Prius was

covered in dust when she stopped in his driveway and parked. She got out of the car, hearing faint, faraway-sounding voices. Mia started around the house toward the back.

Although her approach had gone unnoticed, she saw that it was Travis and his wife whom she'd heard in the backyard. Mia stopped quietly at the edge of the house, watching the husband and wife, lingering a moment in the memory of the love and pride that had always existed here, before pushing herself out into the open, calling, "Hello."

In a turn, Travis saw her. "Mia." He hung the hummingbird feeder he had been holding then walked toward her. "Jace isn't here. He's still at the hospital."

"I haven't been able to reach him at all," she said. "I've left messages."

"Darlin'," Travis said to her, "he never left the hospital. I'll bet he hasn't moved an inch from Hannah's bedside, and they won't let anyone use their cell phones in ICU."

"Have you talked to him?"

Ameree came closer, reaching out her hand in greeting. "Mia, it's been a long time since I've seen you."

Mia reached, received her hand but then stepped into a hug. These two people were not blood relatives, but they were the closest thing to family that Jace and Hannah had now. "It's good to see you, Ameree."

"We left the hospital a little after noon yesterday," Ameree told her. "But we didn't hear from Jace again until after ten when he stepped out of ICU to let us know that he planned to stay the night with Hannah."

"We haven't heard from him today," Travis said. "Do you want us to give him a message when he calls?"

After his father's death, Jace had become a different

man. He'd immersed himself in the ranch and his new role as the descendant owner of a Texas Century Ranch. Other than Cecelia, his sister who now lived in Colorado, he'd withdrawn from almost everyone he knew except Hannah, Travis, and Ameree.

Inheriting the ranch and its responsibilities at just nineteen had changed him from a teenager into a man she had no longer known. He hadn't needed her. Hadn't wanted her help. She'd become invisible to him. Sadness, regret, and discontent were the only things left in her heart when she packed up and moved to Houston. The culinary school was the reason she was able to rise above those lonely feelings of insignificance.

Yesterday, at the hospital, she saw that man again, and the empty feeling of inadequacy reemerged. She couldn't survive it a second time.

"I'm leaving," she told them. "I'm moving to New York. I just wanted him to know."

Travis stiffened. "That's the kind of thing you need to tell him yourself. He shouldn't hear something like that from us."

"That's why I drove out here. It was to tell him."

"Why don't we have him call you," Ameree suggested. "That way you two can talk."

"I don't want to do it over the phone."

"No, phone breakups are no good," Travis said, a shake of his head driving his opinion home.

"When we see him, we'll ask him to call you," Ameree said. "Maybe you can arrange to meet somewhere." Then she went to Mia, taking both of her hands gently in hers. "Are you sure about this? Second chances don't come along often."

Mia nodded, not wanting to look into her eyes. "I'm sure."

THE WELL REMEMBERED ANTIQUES SHOP SOLD more than antiques. Spinners at the front counter held greeting cards, postcards, blank cards, and notepads, all with an old-fashioned theme. When Jace entered beneath the tinkling bell, he intended to buy a get well card for Hannah, but an unusual wooden box, displayed on a Victorian library table, drew his attention.

He went to it, touching its polished wood lightly so as not to leave any fingerprints on its glossy surface.

"That's a nineteenth century writing slope. Beautiful, isn't it?" Diana asked on approach.

Jace glanced at her. "A writing what?"

"Slope," she said again. "I only have one."

"What's it used for?"

"Think of it as a personal writing desk. Look," she said, opening it trifold. "This one is made from mahogany and olive wood. Writing is easier on an angle, which is why it's called a *slope.*" She brushed her hand over its burgundy velvet writing surface, then she lifted its hinged lid, revealing storage for pens and papers. "Were you thinking of it for Hannah?"

"No." Jace shook his head. "Someone else."

"If it's a gift, I can wrap it for you."

"Does it come with a pen and writing paper?"

"No." Diana laughed politely. "But I have the perfect notepad." She closed the box. "Come take a look."

While in high school, Diana had been Mia's best friend, but then they'd both left Legacy with a different dream in mind. Many of their mannerisms and vocal inflections were still the same.

At the counter, Diana chose an eggshell-white notepad with a feathery sketch of a quill pen in the upper left corner. She set two pens on the counter, too. "What do you think?"

Jace nodded. "Okay. I'll take them," then, "Oh, I actually came in for a get well card for Grandma." He went to the spinner and turned it round until he found a column of get well cards.

"Is Hannah sick?" Diana asked.

Jace focused on the cards. "She fell in the shower, but she's doing better. The hospital is releasing her in a few hours. I just needed to get some things ready at the house before bringing her home."

"Oh, I'm sorry to hear that, but I'm glad she'll be okay. Why don't I wrap the gift for you while you're looking through the cards."

He stopped. "Hey, can I write a note and have you put it inside the box before you wrap it?"

"Yes, of course," Diana said. "Why don't you pick out a blank card and use it for your note?"

"Yeah," Jace said. "That's a good idea."

Diana took the pens and the notepad and started around the counter. "Do you have a color preference?"

"Color for what?" He asked without looking up from the cards.

"The ribbon and wrapping paper."

"Oh. No, you go ahead and pick it out, Diana. Thanks." Jace pulled a card off the rack, but then waited until Diana took the wood box and disappeared into the back with it. He set the card on the counter and then used a pen from the cash register to write inside the card before he slipped he into its envelope, sealing it. He walked to the back room, calling to Diana through the curtained doorway. "Hey, I got the card ready."

"Come on back, Jace," she answered.

At a craft table, Diana had a length of wrapping paper laid out beneath a cardboard box. She lifted a corner of the paper, revealing a tan and white polka dot design. "You didn't say if this was for a man or a woman. Neutrals work for both. I can use a white bow."

"Yeah, that looks good." He handed her the sealed card. "Can you put this inside the writing box?"

"You don't want to use it as a gift tag?"

"No, I want it to go inside, where that velvet lining is."

"Okay." Diana opened the writing slope and set the card on the burgundy velvet before closing it again, then, using cushion packaging, she set the writing slope inside the outer box and sealed it. She finished the wrapping and attached a bow.

"Let me get you a gift tag."

"Don't need one," Jace said. He picked up the package and carried it to the front counter for Diana.

After Jace paid, Diana slid the get well card for Hannah into a bag and handed it to Jace, then she hurried to the front door, opening it for him while he carried the wrapped package out to his truck.

Instead of driving back to the ranch, Jace drove to Mia's house, pulling his truck into the empty driveway and parking. He knocked, opening the door when Josie yelled, "Come in!"

"Hey, it's me. Jace," he called into the house before stepping inside.

"Come on in, Jace!" Josie called back.

Unable to take off his Stetson while holding the gift

box, he stepped inside wearing it. When he saw Josie in the kitchen, supporting herself on crutches, he went to her. Using the edge of the box, he scooted dirty dishes away, clearing just enough room on the table to set the gift down.

"Do you need some help?" he asked her.

"No, I'm about done now," she said.

"Mia's car isn't in the driveway. She's not here?" he asked.

Josie's toast popped up. "She's hardly ever here anymore." She took the toast, buttered it, then held up a slice. "This is what my daughter—the cook—leaves me to eat." She dropped it onto the clean paper towel with the other slice, then wiped her buttery hands on the knee-length robe she wore. Pointing to the gift, she said, "Did you bring that for me?"

"No." Jace picked up the box again, maneuvering it away from Josie's fingers. "Sorry. It's for Mia." He glanced at the clock on the wall above the kitchen sink. "It's not even ten yet. Is she at work?"

"That's where she always is. She doesn't appreciate the home I've made for her." Josie wrapped the toast in the paper towel like she was diapering a baby, slid it into the pocket of her rose-colored robe, and then started toward the living room, navigating through the clutter of dropped magazines, crumpled paper towels, and single socks strewn across the living room on her way to the recliner.

There, she retrieved the toast from her pocket and set it on the end table beside the chair before she sat, clicking on the remote. She pressed the volume button until the sound bars were fully lit across the bottom of the TV screen.

Jace walked the gift to Mia's bedroom door. To

Josie, he said loudly enough to be heard above the blare, "I'm going to leave this in Mia's room for her, okay?"

He didn't wait for Josie's permission, instead he just opened the door and went inside.

The small room was clean, her bed was made, and the pillows were arranged against the wall instead of at the iron headboard. Even if his eyes had been closed, he would have known he was in Mia's room by the sweet scent of her orange and thyme candle. He set the gift-wrapped box in the center of her bed, then he left the room, closing the door.

Jace went to Josie, putting a hand on her shoulder. "I left a message for Mia this morning, but I haven't heard from her. Will you let her know that I came by?"

Josie swallowed a bite of toast. "I'll tell her, but I don't know when I'll see her again." She pointed to the kitchen. "Will you get me a cup of coffee before you go?"

"Sure," Jace told her. After delivering the coffee, he patted her shoulder again, saying, "See you, Josie."

Until he'd left the hospital earlier, he hadn't known he had phone messages from Mia. He should have called her before today, but his mind had been on his grandmother. As soon as he saw her missed calls, he'd sat in his idling truck in the parking lot, listened to her simple "call me" voicemails, and then called her back, but she hadn't answered. He wanted to see her. To hold her. To be with her again. But he needed to get Hannah home from the hospital and settled first.

At the house, workmen finished the shower bar installation and put in Hannah's new slip-proof mat. They were cleaning up when Jace went to check on them.

"Looks good," he told them, testing the sturdiness of the metal bar. "Appreciate you guys coming out on such short notice."

There were still things left to do on the "Safety List for Seniors" that social services had given to him, but the shower was ready, and the red emergency call button was installed in the bathroom and another in his grandmother's bedroom. It was the best he could do before bringing her home from the hospital this afternoon.

Jace knew Travis was up in the north pasture, branding the Brangus bought at auction, but even though there was no cell reception in the area, he called him anyway. He left a message to say he was bringing Hannah home today.

CHAPTER 27

It was nearly midnight when Mia got home from her long shift at the bar and grill. The house was dark, which meant her mother had fallen asleep before the timer shut off her television. A sigh of relief came, knowing she wouldn't be met by yelling or the blare of a late-night talk show.

The plug-in nightlights lit the way across the quiet house, but not well enough to prevent her from stepping on magazines strewn on the floor. She stooped, picking them up as she came to each one, stacking them together before setting them neatly on the table beneath the television.

Inside her room, she closed the door and then turned on her overhead light, finding the waiting gift on her bed. She set down her purse, keys, and phone and went to it, looking beneath the big white bow for a tag. Finding none, she stood at the bed and unwrapped the package.

The polished box inside was a stunning antique. Diana was the only person she knew who understood the worth of such things, so she suspected the gift had come from her.

Mia moved the empty carton to the floor, then sat on her bed to inspect the unusual box.

When she lifted the larger of the two lids, she found an envelope, unmarked with no name written anywhere on it. She opened the card inside and read:

> *Dear Mia,*
>
> *There were so many stupid things I did that pushed you away. I blame most of it on being young. I never wanted to be the one who ruined your dreams, so if you have to go to New York, I want you to take this with you and write down every dream you have while we're apart. Keep them here in this box, and then when you're ready for me, I'll do my best to make them all come true.*
>
> *Jace*

Mia burst into a sob, curling up on her bed. It had started all over again.

∼

EVEN THOUGH HANNAH HAD BARELY STIRRED overnight, Jace had tossed and turned. He had checked on her almost every hour, his attentiveness almost waking her once.

It was too early to call Travis and Ameree, so Jace brewed a cup of coffee for himself, and then stood in the kitchen drinking it and watching the big clock on the wall.

Cowboy was at his feet, hyper-focused on his every move, sending Jace to the kitchen table where he sat, calling the Aussie to him. He scratched the dog behind his ear.

"Are you waiting for me to say I'm sorry for leaving you here alone with Grandma?"

The dog's ears perked and his head cocked.

"Well, I am sorry and I'm gonna make sure it doesn't happen again. You saved Grandma, you know that?"

When Cowboy sat back on his haunches and put both front paws on Jace's knee, Jace hugged him.

At straight up six o'clock, Jace called Travis, hoping he hadn't left for the bunkhouse yet. When he answered, Jace said, "Trav, are you still at home?"

"Yeah, just finished breakfast. Everything okay?"

"Yeah," Jace told him. "But, hey, I was wondering if you and Ameree could come to the house so I can talk to you about Grandma."

"Yes, sir. Give us a couple of minutes. You got coffee on?"

Jace glanced at the nearly empty pot and got up from the table. "It'll be full when you get here."

Hannah was still sleeping when Travis and Ameree arrived, so they gathered quietly in the kitchen with their coffee.

Seated around the table, Jace said, "I can't leave Grandma alone anymore. The doctor and the social services people suggested assisted living, but I can't take this house away from her. This has been her home for most of her life, and she loves the ranch. She remembers things when she's here." He glanced at each of them, hoping for a reaction that might indicate their thoughts on the subject, but both sat quietly, listening, nodding, and sipping their coffee.

"So, I was thinking," Jace said, turning his focus to

Travis. "The ranch is doing good with this whole pasture-to-plate thing. Better than I expected. And you've got the herd lookin' good, especially with those new Brangus. I think we might have a real good year. Maybe the best in a while, don't you think so?"

"Sir, I don't know what the books look like, but we're sure moving stock faster than I can remember in the last five years. We've got lots of interest in our heifers and bulls, especially now that the local folks have started eating our beef. It's like they never knew about us before."

Jace nodded, a smile creeping in. "I know."

"So, what are your thoughts on Hannah?" Ameree asked, serious.

"That's something I need your help with, Ameree."

She sat up straight, sitting down her cup. "How?"

"You're more experienced in this stuff than me, and you know Grandma better than almost anybody." His gratitude sent a smile to her. "So, I was hoping you'd help me find one of those nurses that can come to the house and take care of Grandma every day so that I can keep running this ranch. It would have to be somebody we can trust. And somebody who will show Grandma the respect she deserves. I don't want her treated any different than she is now." He handed her three brochures that the hospital had given to him. "Do you think you can call and maybe interview some of them for me?"

Ameree sat back in her chair, holding the brochures. She nodded without looking at Jace. "Of course. Yes. I can do that."

He'd upset her, he could tell. It was an unfair request. Jace reached across the table for the brochures. "I'm sorry, Ameree. That was a lot to ask. I shouldn't have burdened you with it."

But instead of handing them back, she held tight to them. "No, that's not it."

Travis said to her, "Why don't you just ask him?"

Ameree glared at her husband.

"Ask me what?" Jace said.

She held up the brochures. "Do you have your heart set on a licensed caregiver?"

"Is there any other kind?"

"Yes," Ameree said, glancing at Travis first before she leaned in, closer to the table, and laid down the brochures, looking directly at Jace. "What about me?"

Jace set down his coffee cup. "Do you mean it?"

"She's been going crazy since she retired last year," Travis told him. "And you know me, sir, I don't ever go anywhere unless it's on a horse, so those trips she was hoping we would take aren't looking very promising."

"I've given this a lot of thought, Jace," Ameree said. "I would really like the job, if you think it would work."

"Well, hell, yes, it'll work!" He stood and went around the table to where Ameree now stood. He hugged her.

"Jace," Hannah said, entering the kitchen. "Foul language belongs outside. You're picking up bad habits from those boys in the bunkhouse."

His smile was big and wide. "Grandma, we've got some news." He went to her and lent a guiding hand, pulling out a chair for her from the table.

Hannah pointed to the coffeemaker. "Could you get me a cup of coffee before this news just busts out of you?"

He laughed when Travis and Ameree did. "Yes, ma'am."

Jace poured her a cup of coffee and then took it to her, sitting down beside her. "Ameree is going to come and stay with you every day while I'm working. Isn't that great news?"

Hannah glanced at Ameree. "Well, what in the world are you going to do here every day with me?"

Ameree reached for Hannah's free hand, took hold of it, and smiled at her. "I'm going to help you feed the birds."

Outside, Jace shook hands with Travis. "I can't thank you two enough."

"It's good for both of us, sir." Travis put on his hat, then asked, "Did you get a chance to talk things through with Mia?"

Jace looked at him. "Talk things through? What do you mean?"

Travis lowered his head but then raised it again. "Sorry, sir," he said. "She came out here to tell you that she's leaving."

"Yeah," Jace said. "I know about that, but it's not until the first of the year."

"No, sir. It sounds like she might be leaving right away."

Jace grabbed his keys off the hook inside the house and was out again fast. He was at his truck with the door open before he noticed dust from an approaching car. Recognizing the Prius, he shut the door and waited.

After Mia parked, he walked toward the car, intending to open her door, but she pushed it open herself and got out, her face tear streaked.

She threw the card at him, shouting, "What are you doing to me, Jace? Huh? I'm not going to do this with you all over again!"

Jace bent and picked up the card. He shook off the dust and held it up. "This feels like one of those déjà vu things, except this isn't a Stetson. What are you talking about, Mia?"

"The box!" She pointed. "That card!"

Tears started, so he moved forward, reaching for her, but Mia backed away.

Jace stopped and took a breath. He needed composure. "Okay, before we go any further here, you want to tell me what I did that upset you so much? I thought you'd like the box."

"I love the box! Damn you!"

"Mia, calm down. Just talk to me."

"You can't do this to me again, Jace. You make me fall in love with you, and then you push me away. When you're done feeling sorry for yourself, you reel me back in. And don't act like you don't know you do it —*you know*!"

Her face was red and wet, and it looked like she hadn't slept at all last night, but she was still the most beautiful woman he'd ever known.

"Look, Mia, maybe there's no fixing me. Maybe I'm never going to be a good enough man for you, but I'm trying as hard as I can." He took a step closer. "Just tell me what I'm doing wrong."

Shouting still, she said, "You want to know what you're doing wrong?"

Her question was a line drawn in the sand, and he knew it.

"Yeah, I do!" He shouted though he wasn't even sure why he was yelling. "Tell me what I've done that is so wrong you have to drive out here just to yell at me and throw things."

Mia stepped back, wiped her face dry on the hem of

her T-shirt, and then straightened into a face-off. "You've made yourself a martyr for your family and this ranch."

Jace's hands landed on his hips at the site of his tooled leather belt—his glare hardening at the words *ranch* and *family*. He'd expected her to say he'd slept with another woman, which he had, or that he'd given her a box instead of a ring, which he had also done, but she hadn't said either of those things. Fumbling with the truck keys in his hand, he didn't release the breath he'd been holding until she finished, but when she did, his exhale sent his gaze to the horizon and the land he loved before looking back at her with a disquieting air of calmness.

"It'll be a sad day when a man isn't willing to be a martyr for what he loves and believes in. I would have been one for us, too."

His spirit had taken enough bashing. Jace got into his truck, started the engine, and closed the door. He had somewhere he needed to go.

THE FARR FAMILY CEMETERY WAS NOTHING MORE than a square of land with an iron spike fence atop a knee-high rock wall. It was almost two miles from the house in an open field of short grass and mesquite, where deeper soil made grave digging easier.

The first of his family to die on this land had been his great-great-grandfather, Justin. His death had come as a result of a fight over the ranchland. With a Colt .45 pointed at him, all Justin Farr had to do was sign a deed handing over one thousand acres of the forty thousand he owned, but he had refused. The land was rightfully his, and no bullying thief was going to scare it away from him. His wife and sons buried him where he fell—a single shot through the heart serving as a reminder of how much he loved this ranch. The private cemetery had been established for him.

Jace removed his hat and then opened the gate and went inside. He stood looking at the headstones belonging to his family. His great-great-grandparents, his great-grandparents and their sons, his grandfather and his brothers, and his own father beside his mother, Laura. Jace knelt on one knee at her grave.

"Mama, all these men lyin' here next to you taught me all they could, and I swear, I'm doing the best I can, but not one of them taught me near enough about women. Grandma gave it a try, but I think she rode with the men too long. She doesn't have the softness you had. I sure wish you could've stayed longer."

He felt a well of tears, but he didn't intend to cry in front of his forefathers.

"The thing is, Mia is the only woman I'm ever going to love. I know you're thinking I'll find somebody else, but I won't."

Jace lingered there but then stood, patting his hat against his thigh. His gaze went far and wide before he glanced back, discontent moving his focus from one headstone to another. "Not one of you loved this land more than me, yet all of you had the woman of your dreams here with you. What am I doing wrong?"

A breeze blew through, tickling the tips of the native bunchgrass and bluestem, but other than a rabbit outside the rock wall, not a sound was made.

"Well," he said, fitting his hat onto his head, "I'm gonna need a sign from somebody, so y'all need to work it out."

CHAPTER 28

Behind Boomer's Bar and Grill, Mia stood out back, focused on the thick line of persimmon pink that marked the sky between dusk and the vanishing blue of day. The dining room was busy, but today, she didn't care.

From the ridgeline, the diner overlooked an escarpment of savanna-like terrain that drew exotic game hunters by the thousands each year. The ranches did some manipulation of the natural landscape for guest clientele purposes, but it didn't need much in this semi-arid region of the Edwards Plateau. The nearby ten-thousand-acre game ranch already resembled the native habitat of many exotic animals. Herds of gemsbok, gazelle, blackbuck, and oryx now grazed where buffalo had once roamed.

Mia heard Steve calling her, but she ignored him. This place had so much potential, she couldn't understand why he was willing to give up on it just because she'd given her notice.

"I know you can hear me out here," Steve shouted from the back door.

Mia turned and walked back toward him. When she got to the door, she said, "Why does everyone yell?" She pushed past his big belly into the kitchen.

Steve closed the door. "You yelled at me about the beans in chili thing the other day."

She stopped and faced him. "Why would you want to sell this place just because I'm leaving?"

He pointed to the grill. "You've got orders up."

"I'm serious, Steve."

He sighed, then said, "Because my wife left me and took the dog. She hates Texas."

"Your wife took Boomer? No wonder I've never seen him around here. I thought you just made that up about naming this place after your dog."

Steve shook his head. "I thought if I could make a big go of this place, she'd come back and bring Boomer with her, but without you, I just can't do it. I know that now."

"Hey…" Rooney came from the dining room into the kitchen with a tray of bussed dishes. "That guy who ordered the hot wings is getting mad. He said he's been here for twenty minutes without getting his food or his beer."

Steve stared at her. "I'm just not very good at this, Mia. I wanted to be, but I'm not."

Mia's thoughts bounced from one concern to another for the rest of the night without any reprieve. As soon as she forced the diner from her mind, dreams of Jace would drift in, and when she shook those fantasies from her head, visions of her mother struggling to recover seized her sensibilities. Her only peace came when she thought about New York and her life as a chef.

She had one week to wrap things up in Legacy before she could put her life back on track and board that flight to New York.

First, though, she needed to settle things with Jace so that her heart could finally rest.

It was just before midnight when Mia got home from work. She much preferred the quiet of the house when her mother was sleeping, so she stepped lightly through the living room and into her bedroom, closing the door with barely a click.

She desperately wanted a shower, smelling the diner's smoke and grease on her hair and clothes, but with the only bathroom located in her mother's bedroom, she chose to forego being clean and feeling fresh tonight.

With her candle lit, Mia clicked on her desk lamp and sat, opening the polished writing slope, her fingers caressing the burgundy velvet that had probably felt a century of joys and tears from letter writers just like her.

She took a note paper and pen and wrote:

> *Jace,*
>
> *Thank you for the night at the cabin and for helping me find myself again. I was doubting all the things I knew were me until then. I'd lost my balance, so I will always be grateful.*
>
> *To be honest, after that amazing night, I thought about asking you to leave this place and come with me to New York in a crazy plan to run away together, but I know you have to stay, and your family and the ranch will want you to stay, and I can't blame them.*

But for my own well-being, I've got to get out of here.
I'm planning to leave next week. It's sooner than expected,
but my dreams are a million miles away.

Though we were born in the same place, we're from
very different worlds. I knew they had to collide again.

Saying this is the hardest thing I'll ever do, but I'm
gonna let you go so that I can walk away—for the last
time, this time. I'm burning the bridges between us so that
we can get on with our lives.

You're the best part of my past.
Mia

She folded the letter and slipped it into its envelope, wrote *Jace* on the front, but then set it aside, fearing her falling tears would smear his name.

Tomorrow morning, she would drive to the ranch and put the envelope inside his mailbox at the road. She couldn't face him. Not when she needed all of her strength just to leave him.

"You want to drive the dually to San Antonio this morning or the F-350?" Travis asked Jace.

"My truck is fine. I've got a full tank, and we're not hauling anything. We're just looking today."

But it wasn't just stock horses Jace was interested in—he'd been asked to consider a new ranch hand, too.

Eighteen miles north of San Antonio was The Lost Lonesome Ranch and judging by the number of trucks with trailers near the barns and corrals, it wasn't lost or lonesome today.

"Are we watching the kid in the ring first, or talking to him first?" Travis asked.

"Watching." Jace pointed. "His dad is meeting us at the office and then taking us out to the rail to watch him ride."

They parked and then got out, heading toward the white building framed in red, skirting more buyers joining a sea of cowboy hats. Jace knocked on the office door and then opened it. Inside were several men gathered around a desk, but no one gave Jace or Travis a glance when they entered.

"Sorry to interrupt," Jace said loudly, "but is Sid Crisp here?"

"Yeah," a man called back, maneuvering through the bunch. He emerged with his hand outstretched. "Good to see you again, Jace. Let's go outside so we can talk."

Sid was a diminutive man with a bushy strawberry blond mustache, wearing a striped dark pink and pale pink button-up collared shirt and a dirty cowboy hat. Though he was a small man, his voice was not.

"Have you seen him ride yet?" Sid asked once they were outside.

"No," Jace told him. "We came straight here to the office."

"Well, come on."

Sid led Jace and Travis through the throng of spectators to the main pen where the cutting horses were already in full show. The three men stood at the galvanized pipe corral, watching the horses and riders inside the ring. Sid pointed to a sorrel gelding with a seasoned rider.

"That one is Banjo. He might be just what you're looking for today," Sid said. "He's a natural cutting horse, but he needs another twelve months to be the best he can be. He's never gonna be show ring material, but he's got a good temperament, and he's agile and confident. Kid could do a lot with that one for you."

The horse looked good, but Jace was just as interested in hearing about Kid. He wouldn't hire just anybody to live and work on the ranch, and even though Sid Crisp had a reputation no one dared to challenge, that didn't mean his son was as trustworthy. Jace had seen it before, and he wanted no part of anyone's rogue, hard-to-handle offspring. He had enough problems already.

"Tell me about Kid. Why are you shipping him off to work another ranch instead of your own?" Jace asked, then he motioned to the crowd of buyers and admirers that surrounded them. "You've obviously got enough work for him right here."

Sid adjusted his stance. "You're probably too young to really understand this, Jace, but you were different from Kid. You were obedient and hardworking, and you didn't get messed up by running with the wrong crowd. Your dad never had to worry about you." Sid pointed to the cowboys, poking and joking with each other at the chutes. "See that boy 'bout my size in the straw with a black shirt?"

"Yeah," Jace said. The straw cowboy hat resembled the one Sid wore, but it was newer and not near as beat up.

"That's Kid. He's up next." Sid leaned forward, forearms on the railing. "He's riding Thyme's Right today. Your checkbook probably doesn't have enough zeros to buy that one," he grinned at Jace, "mine sure doesn't, but watch how Kid handles the ride."

Midway through the performance, Jace glanced at Travis, who gave him a raised brow and an approving nod.

"So, lay this out for me, Sid. What's the story on Kid?"

Sid straightened off the railing and tilted his head to look up at Jace. Serious, he said, "Kid is smart. Always has been, but he got bored in school and got kicked out. He's got no real ambition to do anything other than ride and work a ranch, which would be okay with me, but he's hardheaded, and he's got a mind of his own as to how things should be run. I can't teach him. He's not going to listen to his old man. But you..." he tapped Jace on the shoulder, "you're still young. You're smart, too, and you're doing a helluva job running the Farr Reaches. You took over at nineteen like Kid is right now. He might listen to you." Then Sid kicked at the ground with the pointed toe of his boot. "And I got to get him away from his no-good friends." He looked back at Jace. "I'm losing him."

The Farr Reaches was a two-hour drive, probably too far for a group of teenagers to come and hang out with a buddy they'd probably forget as soon as he was gone.

Jace nodded. "Okay, let's go meet him."

Kid Crisp came from around the backside of the chutes, chaps and hat almost bigger than him.

Jace reached for a handshake. "Hi, Kid. I'm Jace Farr. You had a nice ride today."

"Thanks," Kid said, taking his hand. "I got another one coming up in about fifteen minutes."

Jace nodded and then introduced Travis to him. "I'm sure your dad told you that we're looking for a hand at the Farr Reaches. Are you interested?"

Kid looked down, but after a minute, he pulled his focus back up. "Yes, sir. I guess so."

"There's no 'guessing' about it, Kid," Jace told him.

"I understand you'll want to come back to The Lost Lonesome at some point, but until you do, I need a committed man." He looked at Travis. "Trav has room for you in the bunkhouse, and I'll make sure you're fed and paid, but it's got to be your choice, or this will never work. What do you say?"

"Okay." Kid nodded and reached for another handshake. "Is Monday all right?"

"Yeah." Jace shook hands with the nineteen-year-old again. "Monday's fine. Bring your gear," Jace turned to Sid, "and that sorrel called Banjo."

"Glad to hear it," Sid said, then he looked at Kid. "We'll settle up on Banjo and be back in time for your next ride, son. You made a good choice," he said to Kid, not Jace.

It was almost three in the afternoon before Jace and Travis pulled onto the unpaved road leading home, but as soon as Jace turned off the highway, he stopped the truck and got out to grab the day's mail from the mailbox. He got back in, setting the bundle on the console between him and Travis, and then continued down the road toward the main house.

"I wonder how Ameree did with Hannah today?" Travis said.

"For the first time in a long time, I wasn't worried at all about Grandma while we were gone," Jace told him. "I can't tell you what a relief it is to have Ameree staying with her."

When Jace parked, shutting off the engine, Travis opened his door, saying, "Well, let's go in and see how it went."

Jace and Travis found Ameree with Hannah at the dining table, putting together a jigsaw puzzle. It was half finished and had the colors of a forested mountain bathed in the sun's early morning light.

"Hi, Grandma," Jace said, giving a kiss to his grandmother's cheek. "How was your day?"

Hannah glanced up at him. "I think it was a good day." She looked at Ameree. "Wasn't it?"

Ameree smiled at Hannah. "Yes. It was a very good day. We even repainted two of the older birdhouses for the wrens this morning, didn't we?"

"Oh, yes." Hannah looked back at Jace. "We painted birdhouses."

His heart warmed. His grandmother might not remember as much of the past as he hoped but recalling what she'd done today was proof her memory still functioned, and he didn't intend to take that for granted.

Hannah reached for the mail tucked under his arm. "Did we get any Christmas cards in the mail?"

Jace took the delivery out from under his arm, but he held onto the bundle. "I don't think so. It's still a little early, Grandma."

She pointed. "Well, look through those before you take them to your office, just in case."

To appease her, Jace flipped through the bills, reminders, mailers, and offers, saying, "No holiday cards, Grandma." But the envelope at the bottom of the stack stopped him cold. It bore just his first name — written in Mia's cursive. He glanced at Ameree. "Was Mia out here today?"

"No," Ameree told him. "No visitors or deliveries today." She pointed to a green puzzle piece for his grandmother. "Try that one," she said to her.

Jace set the other mail on the table beside the jigsaw puzzle, and then he opened the envelope, turning away to unfold the letter. Silently, he read through to the last word.

You were the best part of my past.

His heart was beating too fast, trying to keep up with his thoughts. He turned, his focus landing on Travis. "Hey, I forgot something in town, I think." Jace glanced up at the clock on the wall, then to Ameree he said, "There's a pan of frozen lasagna in the freezer. Can you put that in the oven at five if I'm not back?"

"Of course," she said, helping Hannah fit a piece into the puzzle. "Take your time."

But Travis followed Jace out onto the porch. "Who was that letter from?" he asked.

Jace turned to him. "It was from Mia." He blinked away the moisture in his eyes. "I think I've lost her for good, Trav."

Travis shifted his stance. Head down, he said, "Boss, I've known this family most all of my life. I was working this ranch with your granddad and your dad when you were just a knee-high boy learning how to ride, so I hope you won't take offense to what I'm about to say."

"You know I won't. What is it?"

"Heart failure killed every man with the Farr name, except your great-great-grandfather who took a bullet to the heart, so one way or another, they all died from a broken heart. But not one of them had their heart broken by the woman they loved." Travis motioned to the vast ranch land. "They saved this for you, but the thing they couldn't give you was the thing that meant the most to them. That one you're gonna need to do all by yourself."

The understanding rolled through Jace. "I need to tell Mia that I still love her." His voice shook. "I can't let her leave without knowing how much."

Travis motioned to his attire. "No disrespect intended, but you look like you spent the day in a stock barn. Maybe you should put on a clean shirt first and stop at the florist for some flowers."

Jace raised his arm and took a whiff. "Yeah, okay." He reached out and squeezed the man's shoulder. "Thanks, Trav."

CHAPTER 29

J ace took a fast shower, dried off, and then put on a light-colored, short-sleeved shirt and a clean pair of jeans.

The stress of Mia's letter had him replaying every word, and when he couldn't remember the lines, he'd unfold the paper and read it again. *Run away together. Burning bridges. Different worlds.* He had no idea what to say to Mia other than to tell her he loved her, then if him loving her, and her loving him, wasn't the dream she dreamed he couldn't force her to stay.

He glanced through the glass doors in his bedroom to the land. If he had to choose—*had to choose*—between Mia and the ranch, which would it be? His emotions took a tumble, and his breath came roaring out in the pain of a broken heart.

Jace reached for his Stetson on the dresser and pulled it toward his head—the cuff of his short sleeve catching on a handle, yanking him back like a phantom hand, toppling his mother's photo and jerking open the top drawer. He grabbed the frame and reset it, his focus falling to the hidden drawer within a drawer. He glanced again at the picture of his mother. Her earthy-brown eyes, so much like his, sternly held his gaze.

Jace pulled open the jewelry drawer and took out the Tiffany blue box, lifting its lid. The smooth platinum two-carat ring inside belonged to Mia. It always had. He'd bought it over five years ago, and he'd kept it just for her. It would never belong to anyone else. Jace slid the ring box into his jeans pocket, donned his Stetson, and left the house through his double bedroom doors.

The bar and grill was just ten miles from the Farr Reaches Ranch on a back country road, but it was Friday night and the exotic game traffic was stopped bumper-to-bumper on the way to Boomer's. Jace had left the house at three forty-five and it was now four fifteen. He was already nervous about showing up unannounced on a busy work night to see the woman of his dreams, and this wait proved to be too much.

Jace pulled off onto the right shoulder of the road and drove his F-350 truck through the tall grass and sunflowers, passing Mercedes, Lexus, Jaguars, Land Rovers, obvious rental cars, and other pickup trucks headed toward Boomer's full parking lot.

When Jace walked into the diner, a path through the people seemed to magically clear for him. Maybe it was the hard focus of his determined demeanor, but those standing in line for a table simply moved aside as his stride carried him toward the kitchen.

"Hey!" Steve yelled from the cash register. "You can't go back there!" When Jace kept walking, Steve left the customer holding a credit card and started down the length of the bar. At the kitchen door, he came face to face with Jace, blocking his entrance.

"You can't go in there to talk to Mia right now. Don't you see all the customers in here?"

With an unyielding stare, Jace said, "I'm talking to Mia, Steve. You should move out of my way."

"Now, Jace? You have to talk to her right now while she's got more than a dozen orders cooking all at once? Can't it wait?"

"No," Jace told him, nudging the man's bulk aside. "It can't wait." He pushed through the swinging door.

Mia stood at the grill, flipping a dozen beef patties while two deep fryers bubbled hot oil over hand-cut French fries. Next to her was a vat of sizzling oil cooking hot wings. She had six bowls next to the chili kettle with a ladle, and at the workstation, she had buns and cheese plus twelve single servings of lettuce, tomatoes, and pickle spears.

Rooney worked, readying dozens of serving baskets with red-checkered liners.

For a moment, Jace stood watching. She wasn't flustered at all. She was balanced and beautiful.

He could see clearly now. This was not where she belonged. Mia belonged in a high-class five-star restaurant with crystal and white linens where her talents could shine like a work of art, just like her. She deserved New York.

He was still riveted to her when she looked up, catching sight of him.

"Jace, what are you doing here?"

He took off his Stetson and held it to his chest. "I need to talk to you."

The fryers beeped, but she stepped away anyway. "Rooney, get those fries out, please?" To Jace, she said, "I can't talk right now."

But he knew Mia, maybe better than she knew

herself sometimes. Her tone had a softness to it that told him she would talk if he pressed her.

Jace went to her and took her by the hand, leading her toward the back door.

"Rooney," Mia called, looking over her shoulder at the busboy. "Tell Steve he needs to finish those burgers."

Jace opened the back door and pulled her through with him. When the door automatically shut, he pulled her to him and kissed her, lingering in her willingness.

"I got your letter," he said to her.

"Then you shouldn't be here."

He loosened his embrace. "It's why I'm here, but I'm sorry it took a letter to do it. Mia, I love you."

She pushed herself back, turning away. "Don't, Jace. I'm going to New York."

He gently took her arm and turned her back to him. "If that's your dream, then I'll dream it with you. We can make this work."

Jace reached into his pocket and pulled out the Tiffany blue box. He opened it. "I want you to marry me, Mia. I want you to love me for the rest of my life."

She glanced from the ring to Jace and back again. "You bought a ring?"

"Five years ago. I bought this ring before you left for Houston. I should have given it to you then."

Jace brushed a strand of her silky, honey-high-lighted brown hair away from her blue-gray eyes, glassy from welling tears, wiping a single teardrop from her cheek in the process.

"So, will you marry me?"

Mia looked down at the ring. "And if I go to New York?"

"Then you go to New York." Jace removed the ring

and then slid the box back into his pocket. "I don't want to be without you a single day, but I'll wait for you, Mia. However long it takes. And if you decide you need to stay in New York to make your dreams come true, then we'll figure out how to make one of those long-distance relationships work." When she didn't say anything, Jace took her hand and slipped the ring on her finger. "This is yours either way, but I'd like to know. Will you marry me?"

"Yes," she said through tears. "Yes." Mia pulled Jace into an embrace and kissed him, flinching when the back door flew open.

"Mia, there's too many orders!" Steve shouted. "I can't run this whole place by myself. Are you coming back in here to help me, or what?"

She eased back from Jace, but her gaze, flowing with emotion, stayed fixed on him. "I thought we'd burned every bridge we had left between us."

Softly, he wiped her tears. "Baby, our bridge is never gonna burn. Not ever."

IN SPITE OF WANTING TO STAY IN JACE'S ARMS TILL the dawn of time, Mia had a diner full of customers. She couldn't leave Steve in a lurch on the busiest night Boomer's had ever had.

"Three more orders of hot wings," Steve yelled as he clipped the ticket to the stainless steel wheel at the cook's station, disappearing back into the dining room.

It was ten o'clock before the food orders slowed down. That's when Steve noticed the diamond ring on Mia's finger. He grabbed her hand and pulled it up for a closer look.

"You weren't wearing this when you came in tonight."

Mia smiled. "No, I sure wasn't."

"Jace proposed?"

Mia nodded. "And I accepted."

Steve released her hand. "Does this mean you're staying?"

"I love him, Steve. I've loved him since I was ten years old."

"So stay! We can have the wedding reception right here. I won't even make you cook that day." He laughed, then he hugged Mia. "I'm happy for you." When Rooney came back with a tray of dishes, Steve said, "Rooney, did you know Mia got engaged tonight?"

Rooney set down the black bussing tub and came to where Mia had her hand held out, displaying the ring.

"Is that why you went outside with the meat delivery guy?"

Mia laughed. "Yes. And his name is Jace."

Rooney glanced at her. "He didn't take you out for a nice dinner or something first?"

Steve swatted Rooney on the shoulder. "Stop causing trouble." He pointed to the triple sinks. "Go wash those dishes."

When Rooney walked away, Steve looked back at Mia. "I suppose you want out of here early tonight so you can celebrate."

"No." Mia gave him a reticent smile. "Jace is with his grandmother, and I don't really want to go home."

"I thought every girl wanted to tell her mother she was getting married. Don't you want to show that ring to your mom?"

Mia shook her head. "Tomorrow."

"Well, I'm sure she'll be glad you're staying. I know I am."

Staying. The word summoned nausea, a rise that rolled in like high tide in Trinity Bay, slow but steady. Mia held her hand to her stomach and looked at Steve, serious.

"I'm never going to have my own restaurant if I let this opportunity in New York slip away."

"You're still taking that food job for the travel company?"

She shook her head. "My spot in the apprenticeship program is still reserved for me. It starts January first. I'll stay here until then, but after that, you're on your own again. Deal?"

Steve nodded, but a smile crept in. "Are you gonna make me sign a paper about it?"

His snark made her laugh. "No, not this time because we're not negotiating this one."

IT WASN'T THE SUNLIGHT STREAMING THROUGH THE slit of the blackout curtains that woke Mia, it was the sound inside her dreams, or so it seemed.

"Honest, Josie, Mia won't be mad if I wake her up."

"If it was anyone but you, Jace, I'd say no," Josie said.

Mia sat straight up in bed, threw off her sheet and quilt, and bolted for the door, tossing it open.

The sight of Jace in his boots and Stetson, wearing dark rinse jeans and a long-sleeved white and cobalt blue grid-patterned shirt, sent Mia sprinting barefoot across the living room. She leaped into his arms, wrapping her bare legs around his waist, kissing him with her whole heart.

After a moment, Mia eased out of the kiss, her gaze landing squarely on his beautiful, earthy-brown eyes. "I love you, Jace Farr."

He pulled off his Stetson, mussing his chestnut-colored hair, and tossed the hat onto the gray leather loveseat. With her still wrapped around him, Jace rotated in the sunlight that blazed through the front windows. "I love you, too, Mia Ellis."

"What is going on with you two this morning?" Using crutches, Josie turned away and started for the kitchen. "Come get some coffee," she said.

With her arms still encircling Jace's neck, Mia released her legs and lowered her feet to the floor. She gave a side nod to the kitchen, smiling. "Are you ready?"

He kissed her once more, then said, "I'm ready if you are."

Jace went to the kitchen table and seated himself across from Josie, accepting the cup of coffee when Mia handed it to him.

"Mom, would you like another cup?"

Josie held out her thick ceramic cup to Mia. "Just half. Will you make French toast and put on some bacon while you're standing there?"

Jace turned with a look for Mia. "I could eat some bacon."

Mia laughed, pulling out a new one-pound package of smoked mesquite bacon from the refrigerator.

Not turning around, Mia said, "Mom, we have some news."

"What kind of news?" Josie asked.

"Hang on a second," Jace said. He reached across

the table for Josie's hand. He met her curiosity with a no-nonsense look. "Josie, I'd like to ask for your permission to marry Mia."

Josie returned his look with a hard stare. "It's about time, but you know I can't pay for a wedding. That's the father's job, and I haven't seen him since the night we made Mia."

Jace sputtered a laugh but reeled it back in. "I'll take care of the cost, Josie. Do we have your blessing?"

Josie glanced at Mia. "Did he give you a ring yet?"

Mia held her hand out to her mother. "Last night."

Josie reached for Mia's hand, pulling her close for a better look at the two-carat platinum ring. After a moment, she gave an approving nod. "Okay then."

CHAPTER 30

A man had a right to change his mind, didn't he? The wedding was still a day away, so Jace had time to make amends if he told Mia now.

He knocked and waited for an answer, taking off his hat, then putting it back on again. When the door pulled open, he took his hat off again.

"Hi, Josie." He glanced over his shoulder. "Mia's car isn't here. Is she gone?"

"There's things that need doing before a wedding, Jace. Did you find someone to drive me?"

"Yeah." He nodded, but he didn't want to talk to Josie about the wedding. He wanted to talk to Mia about the days that would come after tomorrow. "Do you know where she is?"

"No, but she said something about the diner, and Diana, too. She bought a pantsuit for me yesterday because I'm not wearing a dress with this big black medical boot. Do you want to see it?"

"No," Jace said, putting his hat back on his head. "But I'm sure you'll look great, Josie. If she comes back, will you tell her I'm looking for her? I need to talk to her."

"I'll tell her," Josie said. "But you're sure you got somebody to drive me tomorrow?"

Jace had already turned away and was heading for his truck, but he called back, "I've got somebody to drive you. Don't worry."

Diana was set to be the maid of honor for Mia, so it sounded plausible that they'd likely be together on the day before the wedding.

Jace parked in front of Well Remembered Antiques and went inside. When the bell above the door tinkled, a brown-haired girl, high school age, greeted him.

"Can I help you find something today?" she asked.

Jace glanced at her name tag. *Oma,* Diana's niece. "Is your aunt around?" he asked.

"No, she took the afternoon off." She stared at him a moment. "Aren't you the guy who's getting married tomorrow?"

"Yeah," Jace said.

"Aunt Diana went to buy boots for the wedding. She said she should be back from San Antonio by closing time."

"Do you know if Mia went with her?"

Oma shook her head. "She didn't say."

"Thanks," Jace said, leaving the shop.

They'd had two weeks to get the wedding planned, so why everyone was doing things at the last minute made no sense to him. Then again, he'd had two weeks to talk to Mia himself, but he hadn't, and now wedding jitters had him thinking crazy thoughts.

The only place left was Boomer's Bar and Grill. Surely, Mia wouldn't be working on the eve of her wedding, but Steve might know where to find her.

Lately, she'd spent more time with him than she had with Jace.

Instead of the usual traffic on Ranch Road North, it was just semi-trailer trucks hauling cattle or grain and a few pickups in need of washing.

Jace pulled into the empty parking lot. It was almost five o'clock, yet there wasn't a soul in sight. He got out of his F-350 and walked to the door, trying the handle before he noticed the closed sign.

Standing at the locked door, he pulled his phone out of his pocket and dialed Mia again. When her voicemail answered, he pressed disconnect, then checked the time. He had promised Ameree he would be home by five to take care of his grandmother, so he was already late, but he walked to the back of Boomer's empty parking lot anyway and stood looking out across the land that had once, long ago, belonged to his family. The acreage had been part of their original forty thousand, now whittled down to just a little more than five thousand.

They had made mistakes. Maybe selling this part of their land had been one of those, he would never know, but what he did know was that he was tired of letting things go.

Jace didn't want Mia to go to New York. He wanted her to give up that dream—for him. For the ranch. It was suffocating him, knowing she'd chosen to continue her culinary training even though their life together was waiting. He'd promised her they could make it work. He had no right to ask her to choose between him and New York, but he was going to do it anyway.

He stood at the edge of the escarpment, watching the setting sun warm the horizon with its crimson red and corn-yellow sky. It was hard to walk away from its intense beauty, but the thoughts it was conjuring were not ones he wanted.

Jace got into his truck, started the engine, and headed back to the Farr Reaches Ranch. It was where he belonged. He'd never even been to New York. He wasn't even sure he knew how to act or who to be in a big city. He'd learned to navigate life by living in the country. Pure and real. Texas gave a man room to think. Mia, however, would fit in wherever she went. She had an indomitable strength that was hard to shake. But him? In New York, he'd be a fish out of water, and when he couldn't be there with her, she would have Ethan to teach her how to swim.

He needed to talk to her—before the wedding. It was the right thing to do.

In the driveway of the main home was a TXUS Seeds pickup truck. His cousin, Jack—the best man—had arrived. The minute Jace opened his truck door and stepped out, Cowboy came bounding around the house in a full-out run. Jace braced himself against the truck and waited. Cowboy bounced against him and then went into twirls and spins, barking, which brought Hannah, Ameree, Travis, Jack, and his five-year-old daughter, Juli, out onto the front porch. When the Aussie settled down, Jace walked with him to the house.

"Sorry I'm late tonight, Ameree," Jace said, kissing his grandmother's cheek. Then, "Good to see you, Jack." He bear-hugged his cousin.

At her father's knee, five-year-old Juli, blonde with a thin gap between her front teeth, grinned up at Jace. "Thank you for letting me be a flower girl!" She bounced on tiptoes.

Jace picked her up and held her almost nose-to-nose with him. "Did you bring your prettiest dress?"

"Um-hum." She giggled. "Daddy bought me a new dress from the store."

"What color is it?" Jace asked her.

"It's pink." Juli smiled, her arms around Jace's neck and her legs around his waist.

"Actually," Jack corrected, "It's a dusty rose."

Juli clamped her hands to Jace's face, then whispered to him, "But it's not really dusty. It's clean."

"Boy, I'm glad to hear that." Jace laughed with the others, setting Juli down again.

After dinner, with Hannah in bed and Juli asleep in the guest room, Jace went out onto the front porch with Jack, and the two sat side by side in the rocking chairs. Clouds blocked most of the stars on the half-moon night, but a few shined through, giving Jace a point of focus for his thoughts.

"I remember when you married Kaitlin," Jace said. "She was so excited about turning that big house into a bed and breakfast. I don't think the thought ever occurred to her that she could do bigger or better things. As long as you two were together, she was perfectly happy."

"Yeah," Jack said, looking down at his boots rather than at Jace. Just the mention of his wife's name seemed to send him back in time. "She loved that house."

"She loved you."

"Yeah, she did." After a moment, Jack gave his cousin's knee an affectionate squeeze, pulling his thoughts back to present day. "You'll find out for yourself how good that feels about noon tomorrow."

"Maybe," Jace said, his focus steadied on the brightest point of light in the night sky.

"Maybe? What does that mean?"

"In about a month, Mia's moving to New York."

"Still?" Jack asked. He leaned forward in the rocking chair, his attention on Jace.

"The thing is, I told her it was okay to go when I asked her to marry me. At the time, it was okay. I was so focused on wanting her to say yes that I didn't care what else she said."

Jace pushed himself forward in his chair with his hands clasped between his knees.

"And now you don't want her to go."

"No." Jace shook his head. "I don't. I feel like our life is just getting started, and she'd rather be somewhere else." He glanced at Jack. "Am I wrong to feel this way?"

"Maybe," Jack said. "How would you feel if she asked you to give up the ranch and move to New York with her?"

"You know I can't do that," Jace told him. "I have Grandma. And this ranch is my responsibility."

"That's not what I'm saying." Jack stood, maintaining his focus on Jace. "I just want you to flip the script, buddy. Put yourself in her shoes. Nobody should have to choose between the person they love and the dream they've dreamt their whole life."

"I know," Jace said, not looking at Jack. "I just can't stand the thought of being without her, and I wish she'd change her mind."

"Have you talked to her about it?"

"No. I looked everywhere for her today, but I couldn't find her." Jace stood. "I sure hate to lay all this on her tomorrow."

Jack nodded, then pulled Jace into a brotherly hug. Afterward, he said, "All you're really doing is telling her how much you love her. That's not a bad thing."

MIA WAS UP AT DAWN, PACKING. THEY HADN'T planned a honeymoon—too many responsibilities—but they'd agreed to have their wedding at the rustic cabin she loved, which would also be their honeymoon suite. Every dream she'd ever had was coming true with the man she'd loved her whole life.

She wheeled her biggest piece of luggage out into the living room and then went back for her duffel. When she came out of her room again, her mother was there waiting.

"Why do you need to take so much? It's not like you're going anywhere afterward. And I hope that cabin is nice." Josie stopped and gave her a glare. "Is the cabin nice?"

Josie was already dressed in her new rose-colored three-piece, wide-leg chiffon pantsuit. It was more formal than Mia had planned, but the outfit was the kind that flowed easily over the big black boot her mother had to wear.

"The cabin is wonderful. It's my safe place. It's where I go when I need to remember who I am."

"Well, I can tell you who you are. You don't need a cabin for that." She put her hand on Mia's cheek and softly said, "You're my daughter. And it's your wedding day."

It was rare, but Josie was able to show love at just the right moment sometimes.

From outside the front door, Diana yelled, "Knock, knock!"

Mia hurried to open the door. "You found one! I was worried about renting one on such short notice."

Diana pushed a wheelchair into the house.

"Is that for me?" Josie asked.

"Yes," Mia said. "Believe me, you'll be glad you've got this when we get to the cabin." She motioned to Josie's leg. "Crutches and that boot are going to be more of a hindrance than a help. There's no sidewalks or cleared walkways up there. It is just bare ground embedded with rocks. I don't want you falling."

"Jace promised he had somebody to drive me up there. I think you're crazy to ride horses. Why don't you just go with me?"

Mia stopped, her interest piqued. "When did you talk to Jace?"

"Did I forget to tell you?" Josie asked. "He came looking for you yesterday. He said he needed to talk to you."

"Yeah," Diana said. "He came by the store while I was out shopping." She pulled up her pant leg to show off a boot. "He asked Oma if you'd gone to San Antonio with me."

Mia ran back to her bedroom and grabbed her phone out of her purse. She glanced at it, saying, "Oh, my gosh…" She looked at Diana. "I missed six calls from him yesterday!"

"It'll just make him miss you all the more." Diana laughed.

"I need to call him." Mia pressed the return call button, but instead of reaching him, his voicemail answered. "Hi, Jace," she said after the beep. "I'm so sorry I missed your calls. Call me when you can. I love you."

"So, are we ready?" Diana asked, then counting off her list of items to bring, she said, "I have the full-length mirror, my solar MP3 player with your music…" She glanced at Mia. "And tell me again why this place doesn't have Wi-Fi or electricity?"

"Or indoor plumbing," Mia added.

Diana's jaw dropped open. "You've got to be kidding me."

Mia laughed. "Outhouse only."

Shaking her head, Josie shouted, "Well, then, I'm not staying long!"

Mia kissed her mother's cheek. "We're counting on it." Then to Diana, she said, "I just need to grab my dress."

CHAPTER 31

It was ten after ten when Diana turned off the farm-to-market road onto the long unpaved drive leading to the main house of the Farr Reaches Ranch. The wedding was scheduled for noon. They still had plenty of time. She pulled up and parked beside the truck with a TXUS SEEDS symbol on its door.

Even before the truck stopped, Mia saw Jace. He was standing with Travis, the four ranch hands, and his cousin, Jack, who was holding the hand of a little blonde girl. As soon as Diana parked, Jace started toward them.

"Do I need to get out?" Josie asked Diana. "Or are you driving me up to the cabin?"

"My truck won't make that drive, Josie. They say the road is too primitive. Besides, I'm going with Mia. It's been a long time since I've been riding out here, and I'm looking forward to it."

Mia got out of the truck, meeting Jace halfway. She threw her arms around him, kissing him. "I'm so sorry I missed your calls," she said. "I called you back this morning but got your voicemail."

Jace reached for the phone in his back pocket and glanced at it. "Sorry. We just got back from the cabin."

"How does it look?" She couldn't stop smiling.

"Good," Jace said. "We've got the BBQ pit trailer up there already, the drink coolers…"

"The champagne?" Mia asked.

Jace nodded. "The champagne, the garden trellis you wanted, and ten folding chairs."

"Ten? We need fourteen unless someone isn't coming."

"Well, ten is all we had, but we've got those two wooden dining chairs inside the cabin, and we can use that wrought iron chair on the porch." When Mia failed to approve immediately, his hands went to his hips. "Hell, Mia," he threw a nod to the four ranch hands, "the boys can sit on the tailgate of the dually if you don't want to use those other chairs. They don't care!"

The intensity of his stress stopped Mia. She stood and stared at him. Silent.

"I'm sorry," Jace said, softer now. "I didn't mean to snap at you like that." He pulled her to him, holding her close, her head against his chest.

Mia tensed at the thumping of his heart. "Jace, what's wrong?" Fearing his answer, she'd had to force herself to ask the question. When he didn't speak, she backed up a step and looked hard into his eyes. "Tell me."

"Jace," Travis shouted to him. When Jace turned, he pointed to the car coming down the long driveway. "The reverend is here. We need to load up."

"Okay," Jace told him. He turned back to Mia. "We

need to grab your stuff from Diana's truck and put it in the dually. Travis and Ameree are driving Grandma and Josie to the cabin with Reverend Wald." He softly brushed a strand of loose hair away from her eyes. "The horses are saddled if you're ready."

Was she ready? For a moment, time stood still. She heard silence and saw nothing other than Jace. The man she loved with her whole heart. How long she'd loved him, she didn't know anymore because there had never been a minute of her life that he hadn't occupied the center of her soul.

"C'mon," he said to her, taking hold of her hand. "They're waiting for us."

Travis loaded the rest of the wedding necessities into the Ford F-450, including Hannah, Josie and her wheelchair, and the Reverend Wald. He pulled out and headed for the cabin, even before the remaining guests mounted their horses.

"Diana," Mia called to her maid of honor from horseback. "Did you remember to give the salad to Travis?"

Diana shook her head. "Nope. I thought you gave it to him."

Mia turned to Jace. "We forgot the salad. It's in the cooler on the front seat floorboard of Diana's truck."

"Too late, baby," he said, reining Ghost northward. "But if it makes you feel any better, people don't go to a country wedding and cook out to eat a salad. We'll be fine without it."

The thirty-minute ride to the cabin had Nash and Ray both vying for Diana's attention, while Jack, riding double with his daughter Juli, purposely rode alongside Cade and Kid Crisp in conversation, giving Jace a chance to talk privately to Mia.

The October morning still held the scent of summer, but the overnight clouds had left a nip of moisture in the air.

"Is that jacket warm enough for you?" Jace asked Mia.

For the ride, she'd worn new stonewashed jeans, a gray, long-sleeved waffle-knit shirt, and her old denim jacket. She'd expected love to keep her warm on the way to her wedding, but there was a chill in more than the air.

"I'm all right." She rode Hardtack alongside Jace and Ghost. "Are you going to tell me what's going on?"

Jace quieted, riding in silence for a minute before glancing at Mia. "I love you."

"I hope so," she said. "Because we're less than a mile away from our wedding."

Jace pulled up on Ghost, so Mia stopped, too. The others rode on, not noticing.

"There's something I need to tell you before we get married."

Her heart was pounding. "Okay, so tell me."

He took a breath, slowly exhaling. "I'm sorry, Mia, but I'm not okay with you going to New York."

She waited. "You're not *okay* with me going to New York?" she repeated. "That's what this is about?"

"Mia, I want to marry you." Jace gestured to the land and the sky before reaching for her hand and taking hold. "*This* is what I've wanted my whole life. You, here with me. On this land. Us having babies and raising a family together. You and me, Mia. You had your dream, but this is mine. It's been my dream for as long as I can remember, and now that it's so close to coming true, I'm afraid you're going to run off again and live your life somewhere else without me." He looked up ahead at the riders moving through the scrub brush. "I'm sorry, but I don't think I can change the man I am."

"Jace Farr." The hard tone of an executive chef in charge came out as naturally as she'd ever heard herself. When Hardtack took a step, lowering his head to graze, she adjusted herself in the saddle. "I'm never going to try to change the man you are because you are the perfect man for me, but I need you to love me truly enough to let me go. My dreams should be as important to you as yours are to me." She glanced upward, gauging time by the sun overhead, and then she looked back at Jace. "I'd rather not walk down that aisle if you can't be there heart and soul for me. If you can do that, I'll meet you at the altar. If you can't, don't lie to me. You've got less than an hour to figure it out."

Mia raised slightly in the saddle and sent Hardtack into a gallop after the others. She never looked back to see if Jace was following.

THE CABIN WAS ALIVE WITH ACTIVITY WHEN MIA arrived, with everyone going about their duties as if she weren't even there. Diana hung the full-length mirror off the high footboard of the bunkbed and then hooked the two dress hangers on the top bed frame, unzipping the garment bags.

Jack dressed Juli in a long-sleeved twirl dress and buff-colored western boots with pink glitter inlays, and he had her blonde hair tied back with a dusty pink bow that matched her dress.

Mia went to Juli and knelt. "You look so beautiful,"

she told the five-year-old. "Thank you for being our flower girl today." Mia glanced around the cabin, then looked up at Jack. "Are her flowers here?"

"Right here," Diana said, picking up a small wicker basket filled with yellow sunflowers. She handed it to Juli.

Mia looked up at Jack before she stood. "They're perfect. Did you bring these from your wildflower farm?"

"Yes." Jack laid his hand affectionately atop Juli's head. "We picked them from our best field. Jace said you love seasonal flowers, especially ones with daisy-like petals, so we chose the closest ones to daisies we could for you this time of year. Have you seen your bridal bouquet yet?"

"No." Mia turned to Diana, who smiled and held up a "just wait" finger as she went to the ice chest, opening it. She pulled out a bouquet of ruby grass with lavender mistflower, purple fall aster, and yellow tickseed tied together with thin, white satin ribbons.

Mia was drawn to the bouquet. She hadn't meant to cry, but she had so many unspoken emotions that she couldn't stop the tears.

Holding the bouquet, Diana took Mia in her arms. "Honey, what's wrong?"

Jack held his daughter's hand. "Juli and I should go. You two probably need to talk or get dressed or something," he said, fumbling with the words. "Mia, do you want me to ask your mom to come in?"

"No!" both Mia and Diana answered in unison.

After wiping her eyes, Mia turned to him. "I'm sorry," she said, taking the bouquet from Diana. "These are so beautiful. That's the reason for the tears." To

Juli, she said, "Your basket of sunflowers is almost as pretty as you are today, Juli. Thank you for bringing them."

"You're welcome." Juli giggled, then looked up at her father. "Can I stay here with Miss Mia and Miss Diana?"

"No, sweet pea," Jack said, straightening the basket handle over her arm. "We need to go out and practice your walk down the aisle, remember?"

After the father and daughter left, closing the door behind them, Mia turned to Diana. "Can you please look and see if Jace is out there?"

Diana laughed, pulling her rose-colored maid of honor dress out of the garment bag. "Where else would he be?"

"Could you just look for me?" Mia quietly asked again.

Diana gave her a curious glance, saying, "Okay." She went to the front window and peeked through the wood shutters. "I don't see him, but I can't see Travis or Nash either." She turned. "Hey, I know Nash is pretty new to the ranch, but have you met him yet? What do you think of him?"

Jace wasn't there. "Nash?" Mia asked, distracted by her thoughts.

"The new ranch hand Jace hired from Oklahoma. Have you met him? I think he's going to ask me out on a date."

"No," Mia said, trying to focus. "I haven't really met him. So, you didn't see Jace?"

"No, but stop worrying. He's probably having a beer with the boys." Diana went to Mia's garment bag and removed her dress, holding it up for her. "You should get dressed. Hannah and Josie are seated. I love simple country weddings. If I ever have one of my own, I want it to be by a river at sunset."

Quietly, Mia dressed, putting on fresh makeup and brushing her hair, her thoughts on Jace. He loved her. She knew he did, but he needed to love her *enough.* Like she loved him.

Mia slipped into her white crackle leather cowboy boots and put on her pinch-front straw Stetson. She stood staring at herself in the mirror.

"My Lord, Mia." Diana came and stared into the mirror with her. "You are beautiful, my friend."

Her casual lace-up jacquard dress was pearl gray, so subtle in color that the light of day, streaming through the half-closed louvers, cast it as white.

"Okay," Diana said after a glance at the time. "The moment has come. Nash has my MP3 and it is all set. I told him that he needed to start the player as soon as I open the door." At Mia's silence, she turned her around so that they faced each other. "Are you listening?"

"Can you check for Jace again?" Mia asked.

"What is wrong with you? You can tell me, you know?"

Startled by a knock, Diana opened the door just a crack, listened, and then closed the door again, turning to Mia.

"Jace wants to talk to you."

The scent of pecan and oak wood smoke from the BBQ pit drifted inside.

Mia stood and stared at the closed door. So many thoughts, so much love, so many tears, so much heart-break had passed between them through the years. Every emotion she'd ever felt had been caused or cured by the man who waited on the other side of the door.

She took a deep breath. *She loved him.* Her faith in

him was strong. She needed to trust him. Believe in him.

"Can you give us a minute?" she asked Diana.

"Sure," Diana quietly said to her. "I'll be right outside the door, okay?"

When Mia nodded, Diana opened the door wide enough to slide through but closed it behind her.

Mia heard Diana and Jace, but she couldn't make out what they were saying. When they quieted, Jace spoke through the door.

"Mia, is it okay if I come in?"

The hardest thing she'd ever had to do was say "yes," but she said it.

At the opened door, when Jace saw her, his hand went to his heart. "I swear, you're the most beautiful woman I've ever seen."

Jace wore his boots and hat, black jeans, a smoky-gray shirt with a black leather bolo with an arrowhead slide, his silver rodeo belt buckle, and a dark suit jacket.

"You're dressed," she said.

"A little." He gave a soft laugh. Jace closed the door and walked the old wood plank floor until he stood in front of Mia, who hadn't moved an inch from where she stood. "I need to say something to you before you walk out there."

"Okay." She steeled herself.

"I had this picture in my head of what I thought our life together would look like, and when I realized that you might not have the same picture in your head, I got scared, but it don't matter, Mia. I'm never going to tell you how to live your life or kill the dreams you have. I'm just going to hope there's always room for me. You're the only one I want. You're the only one I've ever wanted, and I want to marry you today."

Mia softly touched his cheek. "Just looking at you takes my breath away." She drew her fingertips across his lips, letting them trail down his neck, stopping over his heart. "Making sense out of us was always easy until it wasn't," she said to him. "I promise, what's meant to be will always find a way."

Softly, Jace kissed her. "Will you marry me today?"

"Yes. I'll marry you today."

Jace glanced at the door, then looked back at Mia. "What do you say we walk out together?"

"I say, let's do it."

When Jace opened the door, Diana was there, her focus falling on their arm-in-arm hold.

"Should I go? Should we start the music?" She was clearly flustered.

"Yes." Mia laughed.

Diana turned to Nash, calling out, "Hit play!"

Mia stood with Jace on the porch while Juli slowly walked to the arbor trellis draped with ribbons, dropping sunflowers on the ground along the way. Diana followed, stopping where Jack stood as best man, and then turned back to Mia and Jace.

Together, they walked the cleared path to where Reverend Wald waited beneath the arch.

After their vows, Jace kissed Mia, whispering, "I love you. I always have. And I always will."

When everyone stood, Hannah went to her grandson and took hold of his hand, giving it a squeeze. "Now you'll understand the reason for it all." She looked at Mia and smiled. "The man you just married might be the best Farr out of the whole bunch."

Smoke from the pit BBQ roiled up in the breezeless day with Travis and Ray working the grill, pulling several ribeyes from a cooler filled with steaks from

Farr Reaches Quality Beef. They also had corn on the cob grilling, and a hummingbird cake waited on the table inside the cabin.

When Jace opened the champagne, pouring two flutes, one for Mia and one for himself, he shouted for all to hear, "I love this woman so much I can't even see straight!"

But to Mia, he whispered, "We're going to make love every day 'til you get on that plane to New York."

Mia kissed him. "You'll have to do better than that." She took his hand and led him into the cabin, closing the door behind them.

"Should I shut the blinds?" he asked his bride.

Instead of answering, Mia pulled a document from her purse and handed it to him.

"What's this?" he asked, unfolding the paper.

"It's a legal agreement."

Jace read the first part, then switched his focus to Mia. Hard, he asked, "Is this what I think it is?"

"I think so." She smiled. "I'm the new owner of Boomer's Bar and Grill, soon to be called the Tastefully Texas Steakhouse."

A stuttered breath came from Jace. "You own the diner? Does this mean you're staying?"

"Steve still owns half, but it's mine to run and manage. He left for Ohio yesterday."

Jace dropped the document, a glisten in his eyes. "Why didn't you tell me?"

"If I'd told you, I would have always wondered if you'd just married me because I agreed to stay. I needed to know that you believed in me and my dreams as much as I believe in you and yours."

"I believe, Mia. When I look into my future, all I can see is you."

Mia took his face in her hands and gently kissed him. "Look harder, baby. I think you'll see a couple of kids, too."

AUTHOR'S NOTE
OFFICIAL STATE DISH OF TEXAS: CHILI

Chili became the official dish of Texas via House Concurrent Resolution No. 18 (HCR 18) on May 11, 1977, but the tradition began in San Antonio more than 150 years ago. Local women, known as the Chili Queens, would arrive at twilight at the plazas with makeshift tables and pots to cook chili—meat thoroughly saturated in chili pulp—over open fires for soldiers, cattlemen, and others. To this day, Texans claim their recipes for this dish are the best and most authentic "Bowl of Red" served anywhere.

∾

TASTEFULLY TEXAS CHILI
Total Cook Time: 3 Hours
Makes 4 – 8 oz servings

In a 4-6 quart pot, brown 2 pounds coarse chili-grind ground beef. As you are browning, leave the meat in chunks in your pot. After browning, drain off the grease and set meat aside, wiping your pot clean of residual grease. Return the meat to the pot and add the following:

- 24-ounces beef broth
- 1 8-ounce can tomato sauce
- Float 1 jalapeño pepper – poke several holes in the jalapeño

Bring to a boil, then turn the burner down to low for about 30 minutes, covered with a vented lid, then turn off the heat and let rest for 30 minutes.

Bring pot back to a boil, and then add 1st Spice Mix (shown below), gently mixing. Push the meat around with a spoon instead of stirring, being careful not to mash the meat. Lower to a simmer (again) with a vented lid for 30 minutes, then turn off the heat and let it stand 1 hour.

Bring the pot back to a boil and add the 2nd Spice Mix (shown below), gently mixing. Turn the heat down to a simmer again. Using kitchen scissors, snip meat into fingertip-size bites, larger if preferred. (At this point, if a thicker sauce is desired, mix one tablespoon Masa Harina into ¼ cup of the hot chili liquid until smooth, and then return the masa mix to the pot.) Simmer another 30 minutes. The chili should rest for another 15-30 minutes minimum before serving.

Before serving, be sure to taste for salt and heat and adjust as desired. For more heat, squeeze the juice from the jalapeño floater into the pot, then discard the pepper.

1st Spice Mix:

- 2 teaspoons onion granules or powder
- 1 ½ teaspoons garlic granules or powder
- 2 teaspoons beef granules
- 1 tablespoon chicken granules
- 2 tablespoons San Antonio Original chili powder
- 2 teaspoons Dixon Medium Hot chili powder
- 1/8 teaspoon ground white pepper
- 1/8 teaspoon sweet smoked paprika
- 1/8 teaspoon salt

2nd Spice Mix:

- 1 tablespoon ground cumin
- 1/2 teaspoon garlic granules
- 1/2 tablespoon San Antonio Original chili powder
- 1 tablespoon Cowtown Gold chili powder
- 1 tablespoon Cowtown Light chili powder
- 1 packet Sazón Goya
- 1/4 teaspoon brown sugar

A LOOK AT BOOK TWO:
ONCE IN A BLUEBONNET MOON

For airline pilot Addy Piper, the sky became a refuge from her past. Stripped of a family during her teenage years, loneliness settled where love belonged. Now, with an industry-wide furlough, she's lost her plane, her friends, and life as she knows it—again.

In need of a place to stay while interviewing as a private pilot for a billionaire businessman, Addy chooses a Bed and Breakfast—the house nearly a replica of her childhood home—from an outdated brochure kept hidden away in her "special places" box.

Jack Brown, the owner of the Texas Hill Country B & B, admits he should have closed it four years ago when his wife died, but every time he looks at his six-year-old daughter, he sees her mother and just can't let go of the dream. Estranged from his family after his brother crashed the car that killed his wife, Jack has banished every blood relative, isolating himself and his daughter.

When forced to confront painful memories, the bruised and broken pieces of their hearts will open, or close completely, to a future no one, especially them, believes can exist.

AVAILABLE IN 2023

About the Author

Karen (K.S.) Jones comes to us from the beautiful Texas Hill Country where she writes Historical Fiction and Contemporary Western Romance. In 2014, *Southern Writers* magazine awarded Karen their grand prize for "Best Short Fiction" of the year, and soon after, her first two novels, *Shadow of the Hawk*, Historical Fiction, and *Black Lightning*, a middle-grade sci-fi/fantasy, saw publication. Her work has garnered numerous literary awards, including the coveted WILLA Award from Women Writing the West in 2016, as well as the 2015 and 2017 Literary Classics International Book Award, the 2015 Chaucer Award, and the 2016 RONE Award. Her newest novel, CHANGE OF FORTUNE, was released this past February and within hours it rose to #30 on Amazon's list of top 100 in American Historical Romances. The novel is already in its third printing.

Printed in Great Britain
by Amazon

44822300R10179